Folkloric Lure

Book Two of the Folkloric Series

Karenza Grant

A L'OURS BOOKS ebook

Ebook first published in 2024 by L'Ours Books

Copyright © Karenza Grant

Cover: Deranged Doctor Design

Copyediting: Toby Selwyn

ISBN (ebook) 978-1-915737-06-9

ISBN (paperback) 978-1-915737-07-6

www.karenzagrant.com

To Minerva

FOLKLORIC
LURE

BOOK TWO OF THE FOLKLORIC SERIES

Written in British English.

The Folkloric series is best read in order.

www.karenzagrant.com

CHAPTER 1

Today was important to me.

On a one-to-ten scale of importance, it had started at a nine, then shot way past a hundred, to the point where my stomach swam and my hands would actually be shaking if I wasn't forcing myself still. And all of it because a team from the University of Toulouse's folklore department was coming to town for their summer research project. Today. In a matter of hours.

They needed someone to help out—an assistant to run errands and organise everything. That person was me, and it would mean I'd be working with Professor Margot Joly, one of the most renowned folklorists in France, if not the world. I'd be in a position to run my paper, *Recent Experiences of Ancient Folkloric Phenomena*, by her, and I'd be in the company of fourteen folklore enthusiasts, from degree students to industry experts, who I could geek out with the whole week long.

With the folklore department arriving imminently, one might wonder, then, why I was hiking toward the rounded summit of Les Calbières at dawn, dressed in semi-medieval leathers, a sword strapped to my back. One might also wonder why I was following up said hill the perfectly proportioned, ridiculously intriguing and stunningly sculpted frame of a drac—a fae that Margot Joly would insist emphatically was a folkloric concoction of the area's collective psyche, and was definitely, absolutely and completely not real.

I'd needed to get out of my loft, to get away from the project preparations spooling through my mind. They'd kept me awake for most of the night. When Lucas's text had come in at five a.m. asking if I wanted to join him on a hike to investigate the recent spate of acid attacks on cattle, I'd agreed. Either that or my head would explode.

Now I came to think of it, though, there was a chance Alice hadn't ordered extra strawberries for the brioche goûter we were serving the team at midmorning. The café's famous dish of light brioche wrapped around sticks of homemade dark chocolate, served with crème fraîche, wouldn't be the same without strawberries. Saturday was busy, so Alice might have forgotten. I'd have to check as soon as I got back. If the worse came to the worst, someone could pop out to Super U and pick up a few cartons. They might not be the best quality but—

"So, is it working?" Lucas asked over his shoulder, the bronze rays of dawn delineating his jaw, his sword swaying a little in its back scabbard as he walked.

"What?" I snapped. How was I supposed to remember anything with him interrupting?

"The distraction. Are you managing to take your mind off today?" His lips clamped tight then quirked.

Damn it. I'd gone right back to obsessing over the arrangements again. "Nope. It's not working. But being up here is definitely better than being stuck in my loft." Exercise and the outdoors always reduced my stress levels. I drew in a deep breath and absorbed the sunlight that trickled over the distant peaks. The glow brightened from bronze to gold that suffused the rocky, cattle-cropped grassland, the scattering of trees and the flock of sheep in the distance loitering around the Pons farm.

"You've been avoiding me," Lucas said as he took a bend in the path, the sun silhouetting the angles of his face.

Yes, I'd avoided him. I'd been too busy to make his morning noisette at the café, and I'd purposely not entered fae Tarascon, even though I was burning to explore—not that I would've had the time with all the preparations for the project. "What makes you think that?" I said nonchalantly.

"We haven't spoken for the last two weeks, since the whole hantaumo thing wrapped up. It's careless."

"What?" It wasn't the fact we hadn't spoken—that was true enough—but the careless part...

He gripped the chest strap of his scabbard with one hand and glanced at me with that shrewd gaze. "You know exactly what. You're spending all your time on the project preparations, but your Keeper training must come first. There's so much out there that's a threat. It's beyond careless—it's downright dangerous."

Irritation prickled through me, making the too-hot air hotter still. Mornings were usually cool in the mountains, even in the summer months. It wouldn't be midsummer for a few days, and yet it was sweltering. I stomped ahead and turned to Lucas, stopping him mid-stride. For once, due to the rising ground, I stood almost level with him. "I'm not a Keeper," I said into his face. "So I don't need to train." Becoming a Keeper of the Bounds between the fae and human realms was a big deal, and I wasn't sure it was for me.

"Come on, Camille, you can't resist the lure of Fae, the mystery, the adventure." His eyes sparkled with something that looked a lot like mischief. "And you saw the hantaumo. Having access to Fae necessitates learning about it. Or are you going to be one of those humans who wander across the bounds never to be seen again?"

I jabbed my finger at him. "This!"

"What?" He narrowed his eyes.

"This crap that you've started on. This 'You must learn everything about fae right now, and you must become a Keeper for your own good because I want you to.'" I mimicked his voice pitifully, shaking my finger some more. It was one of the reasons I'd been avoiding him. But we'd been through so much together with the hantaumo, my avoidance felt petty, and I'd hoped I'd heard the last of it. Some stupid hope.

He caught my wrist. My angry pulse throbbed under his grip. I couldn't help but shiver as his thumb ran over my skin.

"You can't hide from it," he said.

But truth be told, my irritation originated from more than his presumption that I'd become a Keeper. The attack on Tarascon—on all of us—was a lot to take on board. Not only had the queen of a bunch of lethal witchy wraiths been hell-bent on taking my life, but since the breakneck few days when we'd faced the hantaumo, I'd had to come to terms with the actual existence of fae. In a weird, counterintuitive way, spending time with one of them didn't help. It just left me reeling, and I needed time to process this new reality.

There was something else, too. Now Grampi was better, the possibility of attending university had come up again. We could probably just about manage the farm's bills if I kept working, and assisting with the summer project would help me decide if it was what I really wanted. Plus, I'd have the chance to make a good first impression on my potential tutors. But going to university would also mean I wouldn't have as much opportunity to learn about fae, and I'd have to turn down the role of Keeper. But those options were pretty overwhelming right now. It was easier not to think of them.

I yanked my wrist back. "I'm not hiding. And I'll investigate, train, learn, whatever, when I'm good and ready, and not a moment before."

His lips curved into an ungodly grin, his pupils glinting. "Made you forget about today, though, didn't I?"

It took me a second to catch up. He'd been doing it on purpose. "You sod. You absolute git."

He laughed, the ring deep and beguiling.

I pulled myself from the sound and strode toward the

summit, working my annoyance into my pace, the low sun bright in my eyes. He was such a... such a what, exactly? He'd behaved so far out of line, giving me verity without my knowledge to reveal the hidden world, and sleeping with me when he'd known what lay ahead of us, and yet he'd saved my life multiple times. He'd believed in me when I hadn't a hope left, and he'd been willing to sacrifice himself for the town, for Grampi, for me. But the threat was over, and I needed to get used to the fact that this man, the town's new doctor, wasn't human. He was other, an enigma, something I'd never had to deal with before.

And now, in his infuriating way, he'd managed to distract me. I wasn't going to admit it, but I felt a little better. Squinting against the glare, I sidestepped around a rock. Lucas darted forward and shoved his palm into my ribs, thrusting me off the path.

I stumbled, then gained my footing. "What the hell did you do that for?"

He angled himself to block the blaze of the sun and nodded to the ground. Something glinted in the path where I would've stepped. My vision adjusted. Thick bright green liquid pooled on the dry earth.

"The acid?" Everyone was talking about the attacks of the past few days. Some sicko was spraying animals with an extremely corrosive chemical, causing them slow and agonising deaths.

"Looks like it." Lucas crouched down and sniffed the substance, then took a coin from his pocket and dropped it in the gunk. It sizzled and dissolved in seconds, the acid bubbling.

Definitely not something I needed to step in.

He rummaged in his pouch, put on gloves, drew out a glass vial and plastic lab spatula, then took a sample. To our side, more acid pooled amidst the rocks.

"Spraying acid is one thing, but why would some idiot leave the stuff around like this? The sheep would probably just avoid it, anyway."

"My thoughts exactly." Lucas tucked the sample into his pouch then placed the spatula into another vial and stashed it with his gloves.

"We have to be close to the bounds." We were roughly on the other side of the mountain to Lucas's house, where I'd entered Fae for the first time. "So is it fae related?"

"Possibly..." He rose and headed off the path. I followed, and we passed another patch of acid... and another. "Look." He indicated a heap on the brow of the summit that, in the awkward light, I'd taken for a rock. We walked over, circum-navigating more gunk on the way.

The heap was a very dead Black-Face Manech ewe, one of the dairy breeds of the region with black legs and face, a white body and curly white horns. Its skin, muscle and bone had been deeply corroded across its chest, shoulder and abdomen. The sheep's intestines were visible, patches of acid pooling around them, eating away at the creature. A little vapour rose, the smell acrid. My stomach turned. It wasn't so much the goriness—after defeating the hantaumo queen, I was coping a lot better with that sort of thing. I'd say my reactions were pretty normal, rather than the complete freeze and overwhelm they had been. But what got me was the pain the animal must have gone through.

Lucas bent down and placed his hand on the ewe's acid-free throat. He stilled, his eyes locked on the creature. "It's still warm. This happened recently." His voice was rough, his features darkening, twisting, his skin shrivelling tight against bone. Lethal, saw-like teeth flashed as his lips retracted.

My heart rate spiked. I wanted to step away, but my feet were rooted to the spot. Apart from his initial introduction, Lucas had kept his other form well hidden. I shuddered at his warped features—his true self. He was an abomination from hell, so completely other to his suave and too-hot-for-his-own-good everyday self. He drew a sharp breath, and the man returned.

"Beautiful," I said, barely hiding my revulsion.

He glanced from the corner of his eye and grinned. "It's the flesh. I've not eaten fresh kill since that goat."

"How could I forget?" Not my most cherished memory.

"Though it's probably best I don't indulge. The acid would give me indigestion."

I snorted. A similar heap lay a little way off beside a gorse bush. On the lookout for more gunk, I walked over. Acid had worked into this ewe's gut and reproductive organs. Its body quivered and its eyelids flickered, its eyes dull with pain. The poor thing. "This one's still alive," I called.

Lucas strode over and scowled as he took in the mess, then he met my gaze. "Nothing can replace that amount of tissue loss. With the weapons we have, the most humane end will be stunning the sheep by cutting the nerves behind the eye, followed by decapitation." He drew his blade with a slick scrape.

I nodded and faced the other way. There was scuffling, then a thunk and a thwack. I turned back. The ewe's head lay on the ground. I breathed through the sight. He wiped his blade on the grass and sheathed it.

"The attacks are absolutely hideous," I said. "Who could be doing—"

A holler came from the direction of the farm, and a shot blasted out.

We spun toward the source.

Blood drained from my face. Even from here I could make out the lumbering gait of Monsieur Pons, but the shotgun took most of my attention. That and Ripper, his giant bear-eating Pyrenean Mountain Dog, charging toward us, his shaggy white coat and meaty chops flopping as he ran.

CHAPTER 2

ANOTHER BLAST ECHOED BEHIND US AS WE SPRINTED over the brow of the summit.

"Faster, Camille," Lucas growled at my side.

I ran a fair bit. I ran to get rid of stress. I ran to escape, and it wasn't rare for me to cover 10K of mountain terrain, my earbuds and my feet pounding out every last worry. So, by human standards, with a farmer aiming a shotgun at my ass, I was doing pretty well, possibly even up to Olympic-sprint calibre. But that was nothing compared to Lucas's drac rapidity. He was holding himself back on my account.

"Only capable of mortal running speeds," I yelled, my heart hammering wildly.

A bullet ricocheted off a rock a few feet away. We careened down the far slope of the mountain, the going precipitous. Ripper barked behind us and another blast rang out. I risked a glance over my shoulder. Both our pursuers were out of sight and range thanks to our descent. But still, it would help to put a little distance between us. We hurried onward.

We'd purposely parked away from the farm in the hope that we wouldn't be seen snooping about, but we'd been pretty exposed up there. Even so, I hadn't expected the gun. Just a casual "Get off my land" might have been nice. Although Monsieur Pons was probably on high alert with the attacks.

The slope became a scree drop, and we slid along, my Keeper leathers protecting me from the worst of the scraping. The ground levelled and we stumbled into a thicket by an outcrop of rocks. Lucas caught my arm and dragged me into a cave entrance.

"We'll be cornered in here," I said. Guy and I had used the place as a den when we were little. It was about the size of a house, and there were no other exits.

"There's a tunnel system. I checked out the map at the Keepers' post. The whole place was glamoured after three children wandered into Fae here in the early fourteenth century. They came out in the fifteenth without having aged a day."

I followed him inside, peering into the half-light. The walls and the boulders on the cave floor undulated as though alive. My eyes adjusted to the dimness. Monkeyish creatures with evil goblin faces clung to the rock, their scrawny bodies covered in metallic tufts. They bobbed on clawed limbs, their heads snapping this way and that, listening and waiting.

Lucas paused and drew his sword slowly. "Charognards," he whispered, possibly so Ripper wouldn't hear, but more likely not to disturb these critters. "They'll kill you and feed off your still-warm body."

Just great. I drew my blade, my throat tightening. "So we can't set up humane traps?"

"Not if you want to live to see your research project."

I still wasn't used to the tooth-and-claw tendencies of fae. All that aside, the charognards were blocking our advance. Monsieur Pons and Ripper would be here any second, even if they took the easy path down.

Lucas inched toward the back of the cave between two charognard-covered boulders and beckoned for me to do the same. We shifted forward, each step almost imperceptibly slow. The charognards cocked their heads, watching us with gleaming black eyes. As I lowered my foot, it crunched against grit. The charognards stilled in unison, then an almighty screeching filled the air. One sprang off the ceiling and threw itself at me, claws extended, mouth open, pointy teeth of all sizes ready to bite—my first opponent since the hantaumo queen.

Even now, I paused before striking, the thought of the gory pit I'd been trapped in as a child forcing my limbs still, making me as passive as a lamb. But that was stupid. I'd killed the queen. My fear was gone, and the charognard was about to do serious damage. I swung my blade, slicing it in two. Guts and dark blood spattered me, the charognard falling lifeless to the ground in a cloud of bronze, copper and silver particles. And... I felt okay. I could do this.

The rest of the charognards flung themselves at us, shrieking and jabbering. Lucas was at my back, my sides, my front, thrusting and cutting them down as they dove at us, glitter filling the air. He was taking the slack again, but there was no need. I'd had all the catch-up time I required.

A charognard pounced from the wall closest to me. I slashed through its neck, its head and body dropping to the ground. Spinning, I took out two more with the same cut, then I leapt to the side and speared one in the chest before Lucas could get to it.

My swordsmanship had so far been limited to one-on-one combat and reenactments, but the skill set could be adapted. I made assessments, noting the positioning, timing and distance of our small spiky foe as I would with any new opponent. The main difference was their size and the angle of attack.

On I went, taking down one after the other with calculated movements. I lacked Lucas's speed and fluency, but I was doing it. Even so, there were hundreds of the critters, and Lucas was still managing the bulk of the work.

The bombardment lulled, the charognards scampering back to the walls. Perhaps they were thinking of retreating, although there were still plenty of them. My breath heaved as we waited, the two of us back to back, my blade raised, flecks of glitter wafting around. The blood on my sword hand was beginning to sparkle. It cracked and broke to shiny particles. So that was where the glitter was coming from. But more importantly, why hadn't Ripper caught up with us? We needed to get further into the cave, but despite our efforts, we'd barely made it a few yards.

A charognard shifted on the wall to my side, then

launched itself at me, the rest of them following. I made to sweep my blade, but my phone rang. I lost more than a second, shocked by Alice's ringtone voice blaring out, "Hot doctor at nine o'clock. Hot doctor at nine o'clock. Hot doctor at nine o'clock." Alice had revenge-recorded it because I'd not been open with her about Lucas, and I hadn't removed it because my phone was usually on silent. But not today as I'd been overly paranoid that I might miss a call about the project.

Lucas was at my side, taking the slack again, and by the spluttering coming from his direction, he was attempting not to laugh as he took down critter after critter. "I can't think of a better way to tell that rabid furball that we're here."

I waved my sword ineffectually in the best defence I could muster whilst I pulled out my phone and tried to click the side button with a sweaty hand, but the damned thing was upside down. Alice's voice repeated over and over. I wouldn't hear the end of this.

"Being shot at, chased by a rabid dog and attacked by glitter monsters weren't in my plans today," I snapped. "I thought I'd have a stress-relieving walk up Les Calbières, then start the day relaxed and rejuvenated. So will you forgive me if I didn't put my phone on silent?" I should have known not to come out with Lucas. I'd not had one normal experience with him. Why did I think today was going to be different?

The ringtone continued, riling the charognards into a frenzy. My phone unlocked, having managed to recognise my blood-and-glitter-covered face. I tried yet again to reject the call. With Lucas otherwise disposed with four charognards, a critter dove at me. I swung at it but only managed to knock it from its trajectory. Its claws sliced down my arm, the pain agonising. My fingers slipped across the screen. With another lancing jab of claws, the phone flew from my hand and hit the rocky ground near the wall. Lucas slammed his fist into the charognard.

A voice rang out on speakerphone. "Hello, Camille... Is that you?"

Shit. My mother. I must have accepted the call on speaker. I skewered another charognard.

"Camille, sweetie?" Maman's voice blared. "There's a terrible din on your end of the line." Lucas's laugh was clearly audible now, joining with the commotion.

"It's probably just interference." This time it was my father's lower, clipped tone. The charognards' clamour grew.

"I'm sure it's not," Maman replied. "There... I heard screaming. Camille might be in trouble."

If I didn't sort this out, they'd think I was being murdered. The police turning up while I got the team settled would not be a good start to the project—if I ever got back there. No, I *had* to get back there.

"Hello, Maman," I shouted as I continued my onslaught. So much for being quiet. "This really isn't a good time. I'll ring you later."

"Oh, I only want a second." She never respected when I was busy. I'd end the call if I could get to the phone. I tried to edge over, but the charognards were launching themselves off the wall right by it.

"Your father and I are coming back from Portugal a week early," she continued, "and we thought we'd check in on your grandfather. We can hardly believe he's better after all these years. We'd like to see it for ourselves."

Yeah, fae curse lifted, Grampi was no longer under a compulsion to only speak about goats. Any other daughter would've been overjoyed and come straight to see him when it had happened. Not my mother. The most important things slid over her. But she had to visit and see what was going on sooner or later, and they would be driving past, so she had no excuse.

Best get this call done with as quickly as possible. "When are you arriving?" I yelled above the din. The charognards just kept on coming, Lucas and I rallying on and on.

"But, Camille, what is that racket? It sounds like wild creatures being slaughtered."

She had that right. "It's a terrible line."

"Well, we'll be there for lunch. We'll stop for a few days. Your father has business in the area, anyway."

No. No. No. Not today. Please not today. I slammed through a particularly nasty charognard, and then one more before growling out, "Today isn't good. I've got the folklore summer project starting. I'm not going to be able to see you."

"Great to hear you're thinking of academia," Papa said. "You're finally finding some direction in life. A university-organised research project sounds perfect."

"And I'm sure you'll have time to have lunch with us," Maman added.

I couldn't believe it. This was the week to end all weeks—a week of folklore with the inimitable Margot Joly—and I'd told Maman how important it was to me. Did I have the time? I didn't know yet without Joly setting out the final schedule for the week. Did I want to spend any of it with my parents, or even thinking about my parents? No, I did not. Rock-hard no.

"Have to go now," she said before I could reply. "Just approaching a pit stop. We'll see you at lunch. Bye, sweetheart."

"Shit!" I yelled. Rage surged through my blood, constricting every part of me. Before I'd had time to move, spikes drove into my shoulder blade, and a heavy lump with needle claws gripped my shoulders. Lucas kicked off the charognard and ended it. But it had been the last straw. The pain just made me wilder.

In a blind fury, I swung at charognard after charognard, allowing muscle memory to replace calculations, my instincts ruling as thought seeped away. Glitter fogged the cave as one critter fell after another. I channelled my anger into each sweep of my sword, each jab, each cut. I fought with complete abandon until I spun around, searching for my next assailant. But the cave lay still. I lowered my blade, my chest heaving, sweat dripping from my brow.

Lucas was leaning against the cave wall, his skin and Keeper gear covered in copper and bronze flecks. "I thought for a moment I might have to call in the Men, but I was mistaken. Note taken to never interrupt your plans."

I sheathed my blade, feeling better than I had for a long

time. I'd never had the chance to fight with abandon, and boy
was it something else. I felt free... different.

I picked up my phone and clicked it onto silent as footsteps thudded outside the cave. Two burly farmers flanked
Monsieur Pons and Ripper. Monsieur Pons had been so long
because he'd gone for reinforcements.

"Don't move a muscle or I'll blow you to smithereens," he
roared as he raised his shotgun. But he wouldn't be able to
see us in the dimness of the cave. Ripper, however, had smell-
o-vision. He launched forward.

"Let's go," Lucas whispered. We ran to the back and
squeezed into a crevice that had been a dead end. And yet
now, a passageway led into the mountain.

"We're through the wards," he said.

We were past the charognards, and we'd escaped
Monsieur Pons and Ripper. But now I had to deal with my
parents. They were so insensitive, coming when the project
was starting. They were only concerned about their own
lives, and everyone else had to fit in. But not today. If I had
time to see them, I would. Otherwise, they could kiss my ass.

We clicked on our phone lights, and Lucas stepped
closer, which wasn't far in the confined tunnel. His skin was
torn on his chest and arm, though not badly. He shone his
torch at my lacerated, glittering arm and back.

"How does it feel?" He palpated the skin.

I winced. "It's nothing. A scratch." Though that was
probably adrenaline speaking.

"I don't think it's deep."

But on to more important matters. I glanced at my phone.

"Three hours until the professor is due to arrive. If we were strolling about on Les Calbières I wouldn't be concerned, but seeing as we're trapped underground by an irate farmer and a dog known for tearing hikers to pieces, I have to say, I'm a little anxious."

He inclined his head. "There's a side exit we can take."

We stepped along the passage and the air glimmered as we crossed the bounds into Fae. This part of the cave was covered with prehistoric art, handprints abounding in red ochre alongside paintings of spiky things, maybe charognards, accompanied by aurochs and bears. Lucas placed his palm against one of the prints. "Andos," he said. I had no idea what we were acknowledging this time—possibly the spirit of the place—but after my experience with the tesson, I wasn't taking any risks. I followed suit.

"Where did the charognards come from?" I asked as we continued on.

"They're scavengers. They feed on small pieces of debris that other metal-eating creatures leave behind. Their presence suggests that a number of other fae might be around, but..." He gazed along the passage, and his torch shone off a puddle of green gunk.

"More acid?"

"Yep. Charognards plus acid are indicative of one particular creature."

Something caught my light. Further down the tunnel, the biggest snake I'd ever seen slithered toward us. My stomach turned to water. "We can't go back out there with Ripper and Monsieur Pons. We're trapped."

CHAPTER 3

I DREW MY BLADE AND THE SNAKE PAUSED.

The thing was massive, its girth bigger than Max the taxi driver's belly. And it wasn't exactly a snake. It had pointed ears, small clawed feet, a large swelling under its chin and a ridge of spines over deep green scales striated with copper, bronze, gold and silver. It was a serpent. Its tongue came out, testing the air, no doubt ready for its next meal.

Folklore streamed through my head, riding on a wave of panic—August 1892, an investigation was carried out into serpent sightings with the gendarmerie of Arles. A priest had seen an enormous lizard at the foot of a rock. Not counting its tail, it was as long as an ox with a bulge at its throat. In Agos, a mountain dweller saw a serpent curled around the branch of an oak tree. In Biros, a huge snake frightened passers-by. Would I please focus? It was as if recalling folklore would make this crazy situation normal. There was more where that came from. I ignored it. "We should get out of here," I whispered.

But Lucas just stood there, assessing the creature. "It's fine. It's not going to hurt us."

The serpent's jaws opened, revealing a toothless mouth, then it bent up in the middle and retched, its whole body shaking.

Lucas's eyes grew wide. "I take that back. Get against the wall. Now!"

We hurled ourselves into crevices on opposite sides of the tunnel. The serpent heaved again, like a cat bringing up a furball. This time, a mass of green goo spurted from its mouth and pooled in the passageway between us. It splashed, narrowly missing Lucas's boot. A little of the acid caught the end of my blade that I'd not tucked far enough in. I waited in dismay for it to sizzle, but nothing happened.

"Wayland's weapons," Lucas whispered. "They can withstand most things."

The serpent's body relaxed and it slid into a low side tunnel I'd not noticed.

"*That* caused the acid attacks?" I couldn't believe it—the thing was a giant spitting cobra.

"Looks like it. And it explains the charognards' presence too. They sometimes feed off ore serpent droppings. But ore serpents don't often rise up into cave systems, and they're unknown above ground. They're usually found deep down in Fae, where they live off minerals." Lucas eased around the acid and headed along the tunnel.

I followed. "Until now. They've been up on Les Calbières."

"Not to mention they normally use their acid selectively for ingestion. They don't discharge it randomly, and I've not heard of them attacking animals or people. We need to find out what's going on." He bent down and examined the tunnel the serpent had taken. "We can get through here. That thing wasn't moving fast." He dropped onto all fours and scrambled forward.

"Uh... just one moment. You do realise I have Margot Joly arriving at the café soon. There's no way I'm going to be late." I had no idea how long it would take to get out of here, never mind the hike to the car. "You'll have to come back for the serpent."

Lucas reversed out of the hole and turned to me, his chin raised. "You saw those sheep. Are you going to risk all that carrying on?"

Damn him. Those poor ewes. I couldn't say no. "I can't believe you actually have the moral high ground," I muttered under my breath.

He scrambled forward into the squeeze. "I'll have you know I'm a very conscientious person."

"A complete all round conscientious creature from hell." I crouched down.

He chuckled infuriatingly as he crawled ahead.

The smooth, cool limestone closed in around us until we were forced to scramble on our bellies, pushing our blades before us. Thinking of all that mountain above would've freaked out some people, but I felt at home, the chalky air comforting, the taste of it on my tongue familiar. I'd grown up exploring the abundance of caves in the area, and underground, I felt as though the Earth held me, as though I was part of everything.

But it was getting tight. "How did that fat serpent get through here?" I hauled myself on, stones digging into my arms.

"When they enter a small space, they morph. They can even become gelatinous to access cracks."

"Well, there you go. I'm learning." In the narrow confines, Lucas's scent—sweat mixed with a hint of rosemary and something earthy—filled the space. I tried to ignore it and his horizontal rear view.

We hauled ourselves out into a round chamber. The serpent slithered into a large tunnel on the other side, its body thin and maybe five times longer than before. It turned its head, noting our presence, then slid onward. We sprinted after it, but where the tunnel curved, it stopped and bunched up again, arching and rocking to and fro.

"Grab its tail," Lucas called as we ran. "I'll go for the head."

"And do what?" Serpent-wrestling wasn't exactly something I did every day.

"Just pin it down."

We pelted toward it. The serpent clocked our approach amidst retching, its eyes bulging. Lucas took a running jump and landed on the beast just behind its ears. My weight pinned its tail flat. The serpent squelched down, becoming nothing more than metallic goo beneath the both of us. Then it bunched up once again, reforming its original shape and heaving violently. A blast of acid shot out and hit the far wall, then the serpent slumped down lifeless.

"Is it dead?" I asked.

"I'm not dead."

I gasped. The soft voice had just sort of slid into my head.

"It's how they speak," Lucas said. So presumably he'd heard it too. Right, something else to get used to.

Lucas drew his blade and held it to the back of the creature's neck. "Move and I'll slice you in two."

"I'm not going anywhere." The serpent's dull words slipped into my consciousness. Apart from its flickering tongue, all the fight had drained out of the creature. Lucas clambered off, brandishing his blade. I released its slimy tail.

"What's going on?" Lucas demanded. "Why are you above ground damaging livestock and leaving acid everywhere?"

The creature lifted its head as if making an effort to look alert, then it slumped back down, narrowing its eyes against Lucas's light. Lucas turned it off. I angled mine away. I wasn't going to plunge us into total darkness.

"I have no idea," the serpent communicated. "It started a few weeks ago. We felt an urge to rise from the depths as though we were being drawn upward." The creature quivered, its stunning skin shimmering. It was afraid. "Then we produced more acid. A little at first, then masses of it. So much more than we need to digest ore." The iridescent spines on its back trembled then lay flat.

"We're attempting to drain it into magma streams to burn

it off," it continued, "but we're making too much—we can't get rid of it fast enough. The young ones are crazed, unable to control themselves. They feel the urge to ascend to the surface and discharge there. We're trying to stop them, but it's like they're possessed." As it talked, the swelling in its neck grew. "We're all exhausted by it. Several serpents have passed over to the Great Ouroboros. More are on the verge of passing."

"Someone has to help them," I said to Lucas.

He rubbed his chin. "Yes, though I don't know how."

Lucas lowered his blade and met the creature's gaze. "Whatever you do, keep your kind off the surface."

"We will try." And with that, it slithered away down the tunnel, the sound of retching echoing back.

"Looks like we have our answer," I said. "But the poor creature. It was exhausted."

"We have one answer," Lucas replied. "But what's drawing the ore serpents to the surface and causing them to produce excess acid? I've not heard of anything like that happening before."

I glanced at my phone. "I hate to hurry you. Actually, scrap that. I don't hate to hurry you at all. And I'm sure the serpent problem can't be sorted out right here, right now, so I'd like to get out of here. I have some folklorists to attend to." We were cutting it fine. The thought of being late for Professor Joly was so much worse than giant serpents and deadly metal-scavengers.

Lucas studied me. Glitter mingling with sweat sparkled on his cheekbones, jaw and neck. He looked like something from a myth. "I wouldn't want to prevent you leaving actual Fae so you can go discuss theoretical ideas about it in a classroom," he said dryly.

Yes, there was a massive contradiction there, and I truly was fascinated with Fae, but I'd not known of its existence until very recently, and I was a folklorist. I had been for years. It was a community I'd yearned to be a part of. I couldn't let it all go, just like that. I wasn't even sure I wanted to.

"Which way out?" I said with a glare. But then, he'd studied a map of the cave. He had to have known we were coming here. Heat rose to my face, and my jaw grew so rigid I had to make an effort to speak. "You planned this morning, didn't you. You knew about the charognards and the ore serpents, too. This is your idea of training, isn't it?"

He tipped his chin up, met my gaze and laughed. He actually had the audacity to laugh. "I'm surprised it took you this long to catch on. I'd heard there was a gang of charognards in the cave. Perfect opportunity. Though I certainly didn't arrange the farmer and his dog, and I only suspected the ore serpent's presence. All in all, it turned into quite a nice exercise."

"No way. No fucking way." I couldn't believe it. "How could you do this to me hours before the project's start?"

His mouth straightened and his gaze grew intense, making him look even more unworldly. "You've been invited to be a Keeper. You're vulnerable. More vulnerable than you know." Then his lips curved upward. "I did try asking nicely. Anyway, I was always going to have you back on time."

I glowered at him "You absolute—" But no. I had to focus. Right now, I had much more important things to deal with. I closed my eyes and drew in a breath through my nose. "Get me the hell out of here," I growled. "Right now."

He tittered as he turned on his torch and shone it at a vertical squeeze. "This should take us to the original tunnel and then the surface."

Attempting to think only of the project, I pushed myself into the gap and eased along, Lucas behind. The squeeze opened out into a passage that was passible at a stoop, then a series of narrow bends led us back into the main tunnel.

After a little more walking and a fair bit of climbing through a boulder-strewn chamber, light appeared in the distance, and the tunnel broadened. I picked up my pace, then paused. A black chasm yawned ahead, blocking our path. It had to be about six feet across. It wasn't the usual type of drop that it was so crucial to look out for when exploring underground, it was black—utterly black. A nothing. An absence of life itself.

One thing was for sure, going out with Lucas had been an absolutely stupid idea.

CHAPTER 4

THE CHASM NOT ONLY DIVIDED THE ROCK AT OUR FEET, but it extended all around, along the walls and across the roof. Dark cracks radiated out like the whole thing was growing. Caves in the area were a constant fifty-five degrees all year round, but the air was glacial. It wasn't just the cold that chilled me, though. I felt nauseous looking at the crevasse. It unnerved me. I tried to peer down to see how deep it was, but my vision blurred as if my brain couldn't process what I was seeing.

Lucas drew up by my shoulder. "Bounds cracks."

I didn't want to talk to him ever again, but we had to get out of here, and I wanted to know what was going on. "Like up at the dolmen of Sem." When the hantaumo were up to their tricks, we'd helped Roux secure the bounds between the fae and human realms, and there had been a smaller patch there. "But this is massive."

"The cracks have grown... all of them." All humour gone,

Lucas dragged a hand through his hair, casting glitter into the void. "And I don't know why. But if they keep expanding like this... My best guess is that the realms will be torn apart."

The fae and human realms formed the whole that made up the world. They balanced and complemented each other. Humans needed the intuition, emotion and inspiration of fae, and fae needed the logic, structure and materiality of the human realm. One couldn't survive without the other. "And if that happens...?"

He fixed me with a steady gaze. "Best guess, mass insanity, physical sickness, death. The Earth couldn't survive, so massive environmental upheaval, not that we'd be around to see it."

Wonderful. "And Roux's been securing the bounds?"

"He's on a roll, doing it every day. This is something different."

I tried to push the anxiety away. It was one emotion too many right at this moment. "One thing is for sure. We need to get across. Unless you know another alternative?"

"It's this way or risk whether Ripper is still in the other exit."

We didn't have time to go back through the cave system. "And when you say 'this way', you mean...?"

"Jump."

Yep. What I'd thought. I crouched down and reached out a finger to touch a small crack, needing to know what we were up against. Lucas grasped my hand and stilled it, his skin warm against the chill. "Best not. We don't want you dissolving into nothing, what with Professor Joly arriving soon."

"But it's okay to jump through?"

"As long as we don't touch any of it."

The roof wasn't high. We'd have to leap long and flat. I swallowed. This morning "hike" was supposed to be chilling me out. Okay, the charognards had definitely helped. Not the rest of it, though. But the chasm wasn't that wide. It was the fear of putting a foot wrong that was getting to me. Before I could fret anymore, I took a few steps back, then turned, sprinted toward the abyss and sprang across. Icy cold seeped into my scalp as I came too close to the roof, then my feet touched rock. I stumbled, but I was clear. Lucas jumped over easily, despite his height, making it look like a walk in the park.

I shrugged off the chill. The entrance and the outside world shone before us, the morning bright and beckoning. The scent of ferns, ivy and life wafted in, and further along the valley my preparations for the project waited.

———

Lucas turned his SUV into the café car park. I'd left my truck here earlier when I'd agreed to meet him, and I had my study bag and a change of clothes inside. Recent events had encouraged me to keep spares handy at all times. My Keeper gear was glamoured, but I'd be more comfortable in something normal.

During the mile hike from the cave, I'd barely spoken to

Lucas. I'd been seething. Today was just too important. I couldn't believe he'd set me up. We'd passed a spring and freshened up as much as possible, washing off glitter, sweat and blood. At the car, Lucas had given me a healing potion for the charognard bite and scratches. Not wanting anything from him, I'd only taken it because I'd been an absolute mess, and I hadn't wanted to turn up at the project like that. At some point during the drive back, my fury had morphed into nerves, which were now building to a crescendo.

The SUV pulled to a halt. Grabbing my blade, I jumped out. I opened my truck and hooked my bag onto my good shoulder, then picked up *Recent Experiences of Ancient Folkloric Phenomena*, which I'd printed out on nice paper— people were more likely to read a hard copy. It was the sum total of the research I'd done in the past two years. Joly was arriving just before the others, and this was my chance to mention it to her.

The café was always a welcome sight, the broad, shuttered chalet inviting, the timber-framed buildings of fae Tarascon rising up to the side. It had been my idea to host the project here. The attendees were staying at the Hôtel Teranostra in the centre of town, but its conference room had been damaged last week due to a leaking pipe. The events room at the back of the café made a great alternative, plus the patisserie was sure to make a good impression. But, the irony of it. The folklore department of Toulouse University would be based in a café filled with fae, situated right behind the fae part of town.

I headed through the propped-open door. A stunning

sun thistle hung from the frame, the plant a symbol of midsummer and Abellion, the Pyrenean sun god. The old traditions lived on, even in the human realm.

The place looked amazing with midsummer wreaths of mugwort and St John's wort strung from the gabled ceiling, and vases of chamomile on the tables. Inès had done a super job with the decorations. She'd taken a step back from baking with Blanche around. Relaxing wasn't something she managed easily, but she was getting there, and it was still early days.

I scanned the clientele, but there was no sign of project early arrivals. The D&D geeks sat in their nook, a Saturday campaign in full swing, although on second glance, Gabe was absent. Félix and the others had been joined by two guys I didn't recognise. And alone in the far corner, staring out of the window, sat Nora. After her close encounter with hantaumo-possessed Gabe, she'd abandoned her posse, and she'd been understandably quiet, taking her time to accept the side of the world that had been revealed to her. She gazed at a goblin sitting nearby with barely disguised curiosity.

There were more fae in the café now, glamoured as usual. Fae–human integration helped bind the realms, and a number of fae had taken up our invite. Max the troll sat in his customary place. He'd been a little less bigoted lately. In addition, there were two elves deep in conversation in the comfy armchairs, and a group of goblins at a table. Of course, there were plenty of regular human clientele too, everyone dressed for the stifling weather.

I crossed the room, taking a breath and exhaling slowly in

an attempt to shed my nerves. Snippets of conversation discussing the animal acid attacks drifted over. It was the topic du jour. Behind the counter, I wove between the part-time waiting staff and almost collided with Alice.

"Please tell me no one has interfered with my preparations in the events room?" I said. I had the crockery all sorted for the first lot of refreshments, I'd arranged the tables into what I hoped was a useful horseshoe shape, and I'd cleaned the place to a sparkle. Guy had helped me hang a whiteboard I'd borrowed from the town hall at the front, and all in all, the room looked professional.

She grinned, her choppy shoulder-length hair swaying as she shook her head. "Nothing has been touched. Although, I have to say, I expected you here at the crack of dawn, fussing around."

I studied her attractive, earthy features. Somehow, she was always a comfort. "I went for a walk to calm my nerves." It was the truth by admission. I couldn't tell her about Fae, and it twisted me up.

She peered at my hairline, her eyes narrowing. Then she drew up her hand and ruffled my head. Copper and gold sprinkled out. "Some walk," she said stiffly. Looked like my glamour didn't extend to glitter in my hair. The wash in spring water hadn't done much good either. Noted for next time I collided with a load of charognards.

But how was I going to explain this? Alice wasn't stupid —she was one of the most intelligent people I knew—and she was aware of the half-truths I'd fed her since I'd had the verity. There had never been anything in the way of our relationship, but now we kept pinging between Alice's suspicion and my defence. A chasm was opening and I didn't know how to bridge it. She looked away. I guessed she hated it as much as I did.

"What about the brioche and the strawberries?" I asked, not knowing what else to say.

"All ready as instructed." Her tone softened. "Guy and Blanche have taken extra care over the brioche, especially for you. And the strawberries arrived this morning."

I breathed out. Everything was on track. Thankfully, the team was due to arrange their own lunches in town.

"And you're not working this week," she added. "Not officially, anyway. So let us deal with all that, and you go enjoy yourself."

"I'll try." If I could let go of my nerves.

She peered over my shoulder at Lucas, who was heading in. A flare of anger rose within me once more. I still couldn't believe what he'd put me through this morning.

"Were you out walking together?" Alice asked. "I saw you arrive with him."

Damn it. This would only add fuel to her conviction that there was something going on. There was, but nothing intimate. Just the whole Keeper thing.

The other staff occupied, Alice stepped over to the till. "Lucas. What can I get you?" His blue-collar glamour hid his Keeper gear, and he appeared reasonably tidy. I busied myself, straightening the patisserie display.

"The usual," he said, "and make it a double. It's been one hell of a morning." He raised his brow at me. Alice glanced between us before turning to the machine to make his coffee.

"Don't say anything," I mouthed at him, my eyes flashing.

Alice turned back with Lucas's order just as he swept his hair to the side. A shower of sparkles rained down on the counter. Alice stared at the glitter, then placed the cup and saucer down on top, smirking and scowling at the same time. "You and Camille have clearly been enjoying yourselves."

"You could say that," he replied, his face set in his best serious-doctor expression. "Camille managed to pin down my large snake."

Alice's jaw dropped.

"Bastard," I mouthed, glowering at him.

He grinned and made his way to a table with his noisette.

"He's winding you up," I said. "In no way have I spent the morning wrangling any part of him." But there was no explaining what we'd been doing together to get covered in glitter.

She shook her head and walked away.

Shit. Desperation roiled in my chest. I had to do something before our friendship fell apart. But right now, I couldn't. I had to clean myself up and be ready for Joly and the team.

I went out back, stowed my blade in a corner of the office and put *Recent Experiences* on top of the filing cabinet—the safest place I could find—then headed to the staff washroom.

It took me a while to get as much of the glitter out of my hair as possible, then I tied it into a ponytail and changed into jeans and a lightweight blouse that would cover the worst of the charognard damage, which by now had healed to red welts. I looked okay. There was bound to be remaining glitter, but it wasn't visible.

As I stuffed my Keeper gear into my bag, my phone vibrated. I pulled it from my pocket. A message from Grampi —he would make lunch for my parents. My heart sank. What with our underground incarceration and everything else, I'd forgotten about that.

Chapter 5

I tapped out a message to Grampi, explaining I'd only return for lunch if there was time. Otherwise, they'd have to manage without me. A scared-face emoji came back, and then a thumbs up. He was looking forward to my parents' visit as much as me.

But I didn't want to think about them at the moment. I needed to double-check the refreshments were ready. I stashed my Keeper gear in the office and headed to the kitchen.

"Camille!" Dame Blanche called brightly as I entered. "All organised for the big day?"

I paused for a second, unable to answer. Blanche always took my breath away. I supposed her being a personification of the mother goddess did that to people. Her white hair was swirled into its customary bun, her blue eyes sparkling in her homely round face, her smile somehow nurturing. She jostled a ball of dough in her hands, her ankle-length skirts shifting under her apron.

But, come on, was I going to fall to my knees in reverence every time I saw her? We'd never get anything done, plus Alice would think I was even more unhinged than I'd appeared of late. And that aside, Blanche was lovely. I pushed my insecurities away and met her unfathomable gaze. "All okay, I hope. Just checking the baked goods are ready for morning coffee."

"Oh, hey, Camille," Guy boomed as he came in from the café, his mop of blond hair in his eyes as usual. He was like one of the Mérens mountain horses with masses of mane. I couldn't figure out how he saw anything, but he managed just fine. His baking session finished, he'd been clearing tables due to the rush. "I hope your morning's been as good as ours. We stomped it. The brioche rose like a dream. The crumb's like pow pow."

"You do realise it's almost midsummer?" I smiled back at the plump-lipped grin in his tanned face. "It kind of feels too hot for snowboarding analogies."

He paused. "Uh, yeah, but what else am I supposed to compare it to?" He stood completely still as he thought about it, then he bounced back to attention. "Anyway, the folk-lorists are going to love it. This batch is gnarly." He flipped his hair out of his eyes and frowned. "Having said that, there's a guy at one of the back tables weeping to himself. He's left most of his brioche on his plate. And there was a woman who ran out of the place in hysterics a couple of minutes ago. She left hers, too."

"What?" Not waiting for an answer, I strode out to the counter and peered across the café. Lucas sat at his usual table nearby, his gaze fixed on me. I ignored him. There truly was a middle-aged guy with a full beard and shaggy hair weeping over his brioche. And there was a couple on the settee also crying quietly, pieces of brioche goûter abandoned on their plates.

Alice brushed past. "Look." She inclined her head toward Lucas. "He looks like he wants to devour you. You can't tell me there's nothing going on." Her words went over my head. Pyrenee's brioche was the best in the South of France, and the folklore department was due to have it on arrival with coffee, madeleines and some viennoiserie—the yeast-baked pastries. I stormed back to the kitchen. "Three customers are in tears over the brioche."

"Oh, man, it's food poisoning!" Guy cried as he wiped the preparation counters.

"Would you keep your voice down?" I said. "Since when did food poisoning cause people to weep pitifully?"

Blanche stared out of the window as though fae Tarascon was suddenly the most interesting thing around—which it probably was. But suspicious much? "Blanche?"

She turned her head and shrugged, looking like the fragile old lady she most definitely wasn't. "Well, dear, I just baked a little damnation into the brioche."

"What?" I spluttered. I couldn't have heard her correctly.

Her eyebrows rose. "Yes, a little damnation and judgement. Never does folk harm. Lends a degree of introspection to the day. Although I have to say, it only affects those who deserve it."

Guy clapped her on the back. "Gotta love this woman. She's such a laugh."

Of course, he thought it was all a joke. He had no idea what she was. But damnation? No way. Absolutely no way. There had been an incident last week when a food critic had requested to meet the chef to pass on his compliments at the most delectable brioche he'd ever tasted. After he'd met Blanche's gaze, the man dropped to the ground and curled into a ball. We'd had to call an ambulance to get him out of the café. I'd dismissed it as, I don't know... a foible... one of those strange things that happen. But now this.

"Part of that batch will be going to the events room for the folklorists, right?" I asked.

She glanced at me as if butter wouldn't melt. But I knew differently. I knew snow would fall at her command and winter would end when she was good and ready.

"Folklorists don't need introspection," I growled. "They need good brioche that tastes amazing, and nothing else."

"Are you in a position to know that, dear?" she replied.

"Of course I'm not." I didn't have her omniscience. "But I know one thing for sure. The folklorists are not going to be fed brioche with damnation. Not. On. My. Watch."

"Camille," Guy said, drawing out the word. "Don't get your knickers in a twist. There's another batch. Plenty to go around."

"A batch without judgement?" I asked. "Nothing but average, everyday ingredients?"

Blanche nodded. "Yes, there is. And if you insist, we'll plate it up." She still looked so sweet and completely unperturbed. "Just give us a few minutes. We have time, don't we, dear?"

I glanced at my phone. We had half an hour before the professor was due. The rest of the project would arrive shortly after that, and then we'd serve coffee. "Yes, there's time."

"But mark my word"—she turned her dough over and pressed in the heel of her palm—"you can't stop the tide of fate. If damnation is due, it's due."

What the fuck did that mean? "I'm choosing not to use this moment to philosophically dissect whatever the hell you just said."

"Damnation Brioche," Guy pronounced, picking up an armful of washing-up. "Sounds like the name of a band. I like it. And anyway, we'll carry on selling it in the café. It won't go to waste."

"No," I said firmly. "No damnation brioche to anyone. You'll have to chuck it."

Alice chose that second to come in. She strode to the fridge and opened the door. "Something up with the brioche?"

I looked at Blanche, who shrugged.

"One batch isn't quite right," I said. "We'll give the best lot to the folklorists, so we might be a little short today."

"Oh, no problem." She exited with a gateau.

I stared at her back, then at Dame Blanche. I was straddling two worlds, and it was eating away at my soul.

"Right, Guy," Blanche said in her sprightly old-women-can-do-anything voice. Let's get plating up. The folklorists will get their just desserts one way or the other." She tittered, and Guy roared with laughter.

An all-knowing deity making bad jokes about the fate of mortals was more than I could take. I slunk out. The irony wasn't lost, though, that a snow goddess and someone who worshipped the slopes had become besties. That aside, what with my parents and the brioche, those swimming nerves were doing a good impression of a tidal wave in my gut. I couldn't just stand there waiting for the professor. There was a long queue at the till. The part-time staff were barely keeping up, and Alice was busy at the espresso machine. I began taking orders even though I wasn't officially supposed to be working.

"Gotcha!" Félix cried from the D&D nook as I slid a raspberry millefeuille onto a plate, then, "Take that, you foul fiend!"

Gabe walked in, dressed in his usual cloak. The silicone ear tips he wore over his glamoured elven ears ensured that everyone saw him as the elf he was. He'd recovered quickly from his ordeal with the hantaumo, and his bronze skin glowed. He'd even managed to have a reasonably successful shave. "Hot chocolate, please, High Warrior," he said.

From the other side of the café, Nora locked eyes on him and froze, then she rushed out with an expression I couldn't interpret—possibly fury or terror. Definitely not a good sign. I really needed to ask how she was doing. Gabe stared a little too hard at the counter, then he cast a side-eye at the D&D

nook, but the gang was purposely ignoring him. There were problems in that department, too.

"Not working on the campaign today?" I asked as I made up his order, my gaze flicking to an old Ford truck drawing up outside. I also couldn't help notice that Lucas's eyes were fixed on me once again. The utter wanker. There was no way I'd forgive him for this morning. He took a sip of coffee without shifting his gaze, then he looked away and tapped something into his phone.

"Nah," Gabe said, yanking my attention back. "Got other stuff on." I placed his hot chocolate on the counter and processed his payment.

Roux bustled in and made a beeline for Gabe. Several of the clientele stared at the bounds mage. Was it his shabby cloak, or his staff that for some reason now had a singed end, or was it the oak leaf caught in his beard? His recent transition from drunk and sleeping in doorways to spritely and dressed pretty much like Gandalf minus the hat had been something of a surprise to many of the townsfolk. That aside, I didn't have a clue how he managed to wear wizard-style robes in this weather—Gabe too, for that matter. Did they have anything on underneath? But no, I wasn't going there.

"All set?" Roux asked Gabe, then turned to me. "How goes it, Camille?"

There wasn't a simple answer. I opted for, "Almost ready for the big week."

"Oh yes," he muttered. "Good, good. Well, Gabe and I are off to do a little potion work. The lad's a natural and we must encourage his talent."

Gabe beamed. The two of them had clicked. It had something to do with Roux finding Gabe at the helm of an evil-looking pentagram in the town hall basement, having recently been possessed by a hantaumo he'd evoked. I had the impression there was some shared history, and there was definitely a mutual penchant for dabbling in magic.

"Let's make a move," Roux said to Gabe. "I've a decoction on the brew in the Keepers' post, and it won't wait."

I stepped back from the till, allowing a part-timer to take over as I weighed up whether I should check on the events room. I'd peeked in before I'd met up with Lucas earlier, and it had been fine. No one had been in there since, so I could relax. I glanced at the time again. Joly would be here any minute now. The traffic from Toulouse should be light on a Saturday morning.

Someone's mobile rang, abandoned under the counter. "Guy," Alice yelled. "It's yours."

Guy sped in and dove for it. "What's up?" he answered much too loudly, then he paced around, agreeing repeatedly with the person on the other end before hanging up. "I can't believe it," he pronounced to pretty much the whole café, but particularly to Alice and me. "Papa's had five more acid attacks this morning. And this time he spotted the sleazeballs —a man and a woman, the man dressed in work clothes."

Shit. Monsieur Pons couldn't have identified us. I mean, I'd not had a decent conversation with the man in years. But I really didn't need this right now. I glanced over at Lucas, who was tittering to himself.

"He chased them down the other side of Les Calbières,"

Guy continued, his usually carefree face lined with distress. "Freaks from the city, probably. And not only did they maim the ewes, but they sliced the head off our best milker. And... and the weird thing was, they stunned her first. Whatever they were up to, those creeps knew what they were doing..." His jaw grated. "That's the scariest thing of all."

Lucas downed the last of his noisette then sauntered toward the door, shaking his head. "I can't imagine what kind of a twisted person would do something like that." He stared fixedly at me as he passed.

"Sick. Absolutely sick," Alice agreed. "I hope the police catch them soon."

Lucas raised an eyebrow and pushed outside.

"Not to mention Papa can't afford to lose any more ewes," Guy added. "The farm is utterly broke. Those psychos are killing us."

I rubbed my temples, visions of mutilated sheep, charognards and ore snakes filling my head. Would the professor please hurry up or I was going to explode. From everything I'd read about, I imagined Joly was the sort of person who would be ultra efficient, probably early. But I was obsessing again. The woman was only human, and she'd be here when she was here.

"What are you standing there for, hon?" Alice asked. "I'm sure you have better things to do than help us out right now."

"Just waiting for the prof. She's due any second."

She narrowed her brow. "But I sent you a text not long before you arrived. She's here already, in the events room.

She asked not to be disturbed, though she wants to meet with you as soon as possible. I thought you'd been in there." My stomach dropped away as I fumbled with my mobile. There was Alice's text, sure enough. Somehow, amidst everything, I'd missed it.

I closed my eyes, clutched my phone to my chest and muttered, "She's in there. Margot Joly is in there."

CHAPTER 6

THE ENTRANCE TO THE EVENTS ROOM LAY AT THE FAR end of the café, past the D&D nook and the cosy armchairs. I strode over, *Recent Experiences of Ancient Folkloric Phenomena* clutched to my chest.

Making a good first impression was really important to me. I'd wanted to be here early, and now this. But I wasn't late. Professor Margot Joly was due right about now—only she'd been here for the past hour. But no matter. I could still be professional.

I pushed the door open. There she was, stationed at the helm—the desk at the head of the horseshoe—her head lowered over the folders and papers scattered around her. She looked up.

Taking a deep breath, I drew my shoulders back and raised my chin. I wasn't going to get anywhere acting like a wet blanket. Everything was in order. I was on time. I strode around the side of the horseshoe and held out my hand. "Professor Joly, I'm Camille Amiel. It's amazing to finally meet you."

The perfect arch of an eyebrow rose, and she studied me with an astute gaze, her make-up immaculate on flawless skin, her wavy black hair swept back and tucked in at the nape of her neck. At first glance, her white utility shirt had the air of an academic on a field trip, but it was made of silk. All in all, she gave the impression of confidence, success and the kind of chic that only money could buy.

"The assistant the mayor arranged, am I right?" She held out a fine, manicured hand, her nails coated with clear polish, a far cry from my own, scuffed and broken as they were, with half a cave wedged beneath the tips. We shook, and a small cloud of glitter rained down between us. Shit.

Glitter aside, I couldn't believe I was talking to *the* Margot Joly, one of the most important members of the Société du Folklore Français. She was a board member of both England's Folklore Society and the American Folklore Society—the only person to hold a role on both at the same time—and her speciality was fairy encounters, particularly in the Pyrenees. She'd published innumerable papers on the subject plus a number of academic tomes and lay books that had introduced folklore to a wider population. She'd won plenty of awards for her contributions, too, over her thirty-year career. This woman *was* folklore.

She was staring at me impatiently, waiting for an answer. I pulled myself together. "Yes, that's me. I hope you'll find the room satisfactory and everything in order."

"It was a shame about the hotel," she replied. "There would've been much more space, but this room will do. And I had thought you might be here earlier so we could run through a few things."

"I'd hoped so too, but..." But I'd sound unprofessional if I said I'd been waiting outside due to a misunderstanding. "Uh... should we get on with it now?" Although the rest of the project would arrive soon, and I desperately wanted to mention *Recent Experiences* before we got busy.

I briefly scanned the room, checking that everything else was okay. Joly had opened the French doors and some of the windows to allow in the scant breeze. The room faced west, so we wouldn't get much direct sunlight. A positive in this heat. It also faced the fae town, the old roofs visible above the café's back wall, the place reminding me of Lucas's words in the cave—we'd be discussing theoretical ideas about fae when the real thing lay out there. I pushed the thought away.

"We certainly should," she replied. "I'll announce the details of the research itself once everyone has arrived. We'll be dividing into groups of two or three for the interviews in the field, and I need you to ensure there's transport for all. The details are here." She handed me a piece of paper, then gestured to some boxes on the floor at her side. "The recording equipment is there. Check it and distribute it to the groups. Most importantly, ensure there are plenty of refreshments at all times."

I nodded. "I'm on that already."

"You'll be the intermediary for any problems that come up." Her subtly rouged lips pursed.

"Absolutely."

"And I'll need you with me at interviews to operate the recording equipment and generally assist. There's not much else to it."

That was pretty much what I'd expected, and the best thing about it was that as Joly's PA, I'd be by her side, observing her research methods. Which reminded me of my own paper clutched in my clammy hand. "You... uh... might remember from my introductory email that Pyrenean folklore is a passion of mine too. I've read every paper on the subject, and I've been conducting my own research for the past two years on modern-day experiences of ancient folklore."

She gazed steadily at me, the corners of her mouth tightening.

"Uh... I've collated the findings in a paper," I continued. "I wondered if you'd be willing to have a look." I passed her *Recent Experiences*. There. I'd done it.

She stared at me for a moment, then took the paper and gave it a cursory glance. "Hmmm. We're very appreciative of the host of lay researchers who tirelessly record elements of folklore around the globe. I know I'll be very busy during the project—"

The door burst open and a large-framed man wearing cream chinos and a pink shirt paced in. He beamed from amidst a cropped beard that was only a little darker than his skin, his bright eyes sparkling. "Margot," he cried. "You arrived before me." The guy had to be Professor Stephan

Sissoko, Joly's partner in heading the summer project. He was also on the board of the Société du Folklore Français and was noted for his work on the use of memes as a modern form of folklore, although now he was focusing on witchcraft in this region.

"Stephan!" Joly rose and placed my paper on her desk, her jaw relaxing as she walked over, her face filled with life, revealing the person beneath the professionalism. I couldn't help but note Joly's trail-style shorts, similar to the shirt in that they yelled couture, and her flat, strappy sandals that attempted to look like they might possibly be worn on a mountain, but only if that mountain was made by Gucci. But hey, as far as I was aware, we weren't hiking anywhere. The difference was city style compared to this area's country practicality.

Sissoko clasped Joly on the shoulders as they exchanged kisses, then drew her into a bear hug, releasing her quickly. "Good to see you, Margot."

"How was the trip to Yale?" Joly asked, beaming.

"Fine, fine. Picked up a great new contact in the field of Native American study. I'll give you the details later."

A few students, loaded with boxes of equipment, pushed through the door.

"But who do we have here," Stephan said, glancing at me with warm curiosity as he stepped over.

Joly's face closed in. "This is Camille Amiel. Our local assistant."

He grasped me and kissed both cheeks.

"Nice to meet you, Professor Sissoko," I said.

"Call me Stephan. We're so grateful for all you've done in setting everything up for us. And I hear you'll be joining us for the interviews."

I was rather taken aback by his warmth after Joly's cooler welcome, and I couldn't help smiling in return. "I'm looking forward to it. And if there's anything I can help you with, just let me know." More students pushed in through the door, greeting each other, unpacking equipment and settling at the horseshoe. Margot stepped away to meet them.

"Camille, that's very kind of you," he replied. "I don't know what we would have done without your assistance, especially after the hotel's leak. And this room is perfect. Let's get in and settled, shall we? Then we can get the project rolling." With that, he broke off to greet students with loud cries of "So glad you could make it" and "Looks like this year is going to be great". What a lovely guy.

I headed over to Joly's boxes, wondering if I should print out a copy of my paper for Sissoko. He seemed more receptive. I scanned the equipment. Laptops, tripods and padded camcorder cases. It looked pretty standard.

I carried everything to the far corner, where there was a little space. As I went through the boxes, Alice wheeled in a trolley of drinks, closely followed by Blanche with the baked goods. I eyed her and the brioche goûter suspiciously. But I knew in my bones that Blanche was a woman of her word. More than that, if her word failed, mountains would crumble. But I needed to focus, not think about fae.

Alice shot me an encouraging grin as she laid out the refreshments on the table. I sent a smile back, catching something grey and scrawny in the corner of my eye. A goblin was bouncing at the window.

CHAPTER 7

I SCANNED THE ROOM, WONDERING IF ANYONE HAD noticed the critter. It didn't have a glamour—I was developing the knack of seeing projections when I needed to. Even so, the others wouldn't see the creature as a goblin. They'd see what they wanted to see. But everyone was too busy chatting to notice. When I turned back to the window, the goblin had gone. Hopefully, it had been a freak occurrence, perhaps just a curious fae.

Returning to the equipment, I took out three Canon camcorders—expensive pieces of kit. One had low battery and would need a charge before we went out for interviews. Camcorder in one hand, I rummaged through a box, searching for a charger.

A pair of brown brogues stepped into my periphery. "What are you doing?" A guy with stylish clothes gazed down through round-rimmed glasses. He flipped his amber hair to one side and squared his shoulders, pulling his close-fitting fashionista shirt tight across his chest. "You have to be careful with the equipment. It cost the department a fortune." He snatched the camcorder from my hand and tapped the screen.

What was his problem? I rose to his level. "They're normal camcorders, right? Or is there something I need to be aware of?" I cast a glance at the window. Still no sign of the goblin, thank heavens.

The guy's wiggly lips tightened. "Of course they're normal camcorders."

"Well, what's wrong?" Impatience gnawed at me. I wanted to get everything sorted, but perhaps I'd messed with something I shouldn't have.

He huffed, as though the question was ridiculous. "You were *fumbling* with them. They're expensive and need handling with care. I saw you jostling them around." He continued tapping the screen.

What was wrong with this guy? "I can assure you I wasn't jostling anything."

"I saw you right there. Honestly. You're the assistant, aren't you?" He didn't wait for a reply. "I have no idea why they didn't choose one of the students for the job, rather than relying on someone who hasn't a clue what they're doing."

The answer was obvious. They'd wanted someone with local knowledge for the bookings and travel arrangements. But this guy was off his head. "It's not rocket science." My voice rose, my fingers clenching. "I'm perfectly capable—"

"Simon!" A well-built guy came over. His blond, close-cropped hair was bright against his tan. "Making yourself useful as usual, I see."

My equipment-capabilities assessor glowered. "What do you want?"

"Joly was asking after you for some reason," he replied nonchalantly.

A girl with sumptuous curves and an open face joined his side. "Yeah. Something about needing your assistance." She tucked her night-black hair behind her ear.

Simon glanced over to the professor, his chest swelling as he straightened his glasses. He handed the camera back. "Be careful. We can't be held responsible if you damage anything." With a contemptuous glare, he strutted away.

I realised my mouth was open.

"Sorry about that," the guy said. "I'm Pascale. And you must be Camille, right?"

"Oh, Pascale. It's good to meet you." He'd been my main contact during the preparations—a PhD student organising the project at their end of things. When we'd emailed, I certainly hadn't imagined his square jaw and heavy brow above that come-to-bed gaze, or the fit physique attempting to hide under his T-shirt. But I was more interested in his work on the connection between saints, springs and ancient deities. Damn, I wanted to ask this guy so many questions.

"And this is Meera, my research partner," he added.

Meera bobbed forward and squeezed my arm. Her dark brown doe eyes lit with enthusiasm. "I've heard all about you from Pascale. You've done research on recently experienced ancient phenomena, haven't you?"

I nodded, speechless for a moment that my research was being referred to. I pulled myself together. "Yeah, that's me."

"I can't wait to read your paper," she said. "The subject intrigues me."

"Me too." Pascale smiled. "Send us over copies, will you?"

'Sure.' Things were looking up. Actually some interest in *Recent Experiences*. I'd email it to them pronto.

"And ignore Simon," Meera added. "He's an absolute knobwangle who can't help interfering. He's just finished his master's and has done quite well, apparently, but he seems to think of everything as a competition, and he hates that we're above him in the hierarchy. In fact, he hates anyone who's not in charge."

"Got the impression he wanted to PA for Joly this week," Pascale said.

Meera laughed. "Except Joly has him sussed. She avoids him like the plague. And anyway, she's going to be pretty busy, what with a little research, and a lot of Stephan Sissoko." She glanced slyly out of the corner of her eye to where Sissoko was laughing heartily with a couple of students. He cast a quick smile to Joly, who stood at the refreshments table, scowling at whatever Simon was saying.

"What? Her and Sissoko?" This was grounding my sky-high notions of Joly.

"Everyone knows the summer research project is their favourite getaway," Pascale added. "The relaxed schedule gives them plenty of time to—"

Meera slapped his arm. "With a husband like Joly's, I'd

cheat too. Actually, I think they have an arrangement. I don't know why she attempts to keep it secret, because it's so clearly not."

"And on a completely different note," Pascale said, "let's get coffees before everything's cold.

"Yes, let's," Meera added. "Camille, you must need one as much as us." After a sleepless night followed by mutilated sheep, being shot at and attacked, then narrowly averting disaster with the brioche, I'd risk a guess that I needed a coffee even more than Pascale and Meera. But hey, I had no idea what kind of a morning they'd had. I followed them to the refreshments, poured a coffee with cream and decided against the brioche. Instead, I took a madeleine.

Meera glanced to the front of the room. "Looks like she's ready to start."

Joly stood before her desk, jostling through papers. She pushed *Recent Experiences* aside to gather up a printout then took a sip of coffee. "Right, people, let's begin."

Everyone shuffled to the horseshoe. Pascale sat down at one of the back desks. He drew a chair out for me. "Makes sense if we sit together."

I obliged.

"I never get that kind of attention," Meera said with a smirk as she sat down on his other side.

"Welcome to this year's summer research project," Joly announced as the last of the stragglers settled. Sissoko sat on her right. Simon, at the closest desk on her left, scowled at me.

"It's such a pleasure to be able to get out in the field once in a while," she continued, "and together we form a dedicated and enthusiastic team. For those of you who've not had firsthand experience of research, this week will be invaluable."

"Definitely," Sissoko muttered.

I leant back in my chair and sipped my coffee as I listened. For the first time in days, the tension began to ease from my shoulders. Joly was clearly human, if a little stiff, and everyone else, apart from Simon, seemed really nice. I guess I'd not known what to expect, and that had been a big part of my nerves. Now I could enjoy my week-long indulgence in academic folklore.

"I'm sure you're all aware," Joly went on, "that our original topic of study was going to be the folkloric echoes of the sun god Abellion in the Ariège valley." There were nods from most of the group, accompanied by a squeaking from the window. The goblin was back.

No. Please, no.

It pressed itself up to the glass, its features and one of its large ears squished like a rather unpleasant leech, its jerkin and breeches flattened against the pane. All my nervous energy returned, my skin buzzing. But what the hell was the goblin doing right here, right now? I glared at it. I thought it cringed, but it could have been the light playing on the glass. The creature seemed familiar. There was a chance I might have seen it in fae Tarascon.

Joly explained about Abellion, the ruler of the Pyrenean pantheon, akin to Apollo in Greek mythology, but I could only focus on the goblin bouncing up and down, goggling at us. Joly glanced at it, a furrow at her brow, then she raised her chin and carried on.

My phone vibrated. I pulled it from my pocket and checked the screen surreptitiously under the desk. It was Lucas. *Hope your day's going well?* Of all the nerve—texting after this morning.

I have a goblin joggling at the window, I sent back.

He replied, *Well, you have a room full of experts on the subject. Shouldn't be a problem.* He was such an asshole. Then, *Do you want me to sort it out?*

Like I'd want him anywhere near me. *You have to be joking?* I didn't even want to think of him or what he'd put me through.

I focussed on Joly, ignoring the creature now running its tongue down the glass. I wanted to get up and sort it out, but if Joly wasn't bothered, I wasn't going to cause a disturbance.

"However," she continued, "the research Pascale and Meera have gathered lately has brought to light the abundance of material on golden-horned sheep in this area in particular. The primary source appears to be the tales surrounding the cyclops Bécut, known in some areas as Lou Gigant, and noted in the 1853 almanac as being a hideous colossus that lies in wait in the mountains." This was interesting. There were definitely plenty of Bécut and golden-horned sheep stories around here. The goblin began knocking on the window. Joly paused and chewed her cheek. "Camille, please remove that cat from the windowsill."

"Sure." My pleasure. It was a shame I didn't have my

blade, but I could think of other ways to prevent the critter coming back.

Joly carried on as I made my way out of the French doors and onto the path that used to be one of Roux's favourite haunts, but the goblin was gone. Clenching my jaw, I checked around the corner and scanned as much of fae Tarascon as I could see, but no sign of it. I returned to the events room and eased into my chair, attempting to breathe away the tightness in my shoulders as I picked up Joly's thread.

"Our general itinerary will be interviewing sources in the mornings," she said, "then lunch and siesta before reconvening in the afternoon for review and discussion." Damn, it would mean I'd have no excuse not to have lunch with my parents. "We'll head out for our first interviews imminently. See Camille for your groups, equipment and any transport problems. All it leaves me to say is I hope you enjoy the week. And let's get to it."

"Hear, hear," Sissoko added.

"More like let's get done with the interviews so she and Sissoko can get back to the hotel," Pascale whispered as we rose.

Attempting to restrain a laugh, I returned to the equipment where I'd left Joly's groups list. As Joly sat down, one of the students bustling past bumped into her back. Her coffee slopped. She caught the drips in her hand then placed the cup down on *Recent Experiences* to mop up the rest. A large brown ring expanded into my life's work.

CHAPTER 8

THE TINY FLORAL LIVING ROOM WAS A SAUNA. NOT THAT Madame Mazet noticed, hunched over in her armchair, a cardigan drawn around her shoulders. Joly, sitting on the sofa opposite, was perspiring elegantly as she interviewed the old woman.

Simon, next to her, wasn't coping with such finesse, his hair slick with sweat, his shirt blooming with moisture at the armpits. Why he was scribbling notes was beyond me as the interviews would be transcribed. He shifted his legs, bumping the coffee table set with the abandoned tea things. There wasn't enough room for the furniture in here, all of it crammed amidst stacked bookshelves and two standard lamps.

As there wasn't anywhere else to sit, I stood behind the camcorder by the open window, but even the breeze was hot. I hoped that by standing here, keeping an eye on the recording, I'd be a picture of attentive professionalism. Making a good impression on Joly would help if I did apply to university.

Madame Mazet peered at the camcorder suspiciously as she continued. "My mother was up on Guinguilles when she saw the sheep, its golden horns glimmering in the distance." She'd repeated this line four times, her voice shaking, her short silver hair crowding a face that was lined by ninety-eight years. She was a living piece of history.

It felt good to be finally getting into the project, to actually be out on the first interview. Pascale and I had assigned groups of two or three, each with a senior academic, then we'd checked the transport arrangements, and the lot of us had headed out.

I had to give it to Joly, she had enough class to saddle herself with Simon, rather than lumber another poor victim with him. It just meant that, as Joly's PA, I was also saddled with the guy. He was currently wiping his sweaty hands down his shirt.

"And that's what I call new technology," Madame Mazet croaked in my general direction, inclining her head to the camcorder. I smiled reassuringly. Simon scowled at me. I'd explained to the old lady what the camcorder was, and that we were videoing her account for prosperity, but I don't think it had sunk in, which made me wonder how ethical it was to record her. That and having three researchers crammed in her living room didn't exactly make it the most natural environment for recounting old tales. It was entirely possible that the story would've come out very differently told to friends.

"It's very impressive, new technology," she added. "You can do all sorts of things these days. Of course, my Jules never had the chance to see much of it. He died in Bosnia. Twenty-seventh May, 1995. They say he died bravely." We'd already heard how her son had passed away. A large photo of the handsome peacekeeper in a silver frame sat on the sideboard. It had been his last gift to his mother.

"And was your mother with anyone else when she saw the sheep?" Joly asked. She really was doing her best to keep Madame Mazet on track.

"Come now, everyone," the old lady replied, leaning forward. "Pass your cups over and I'll top you up. There's nothing like a thé au citron in the warm weather."

Simon took another croustillant à la violette, leaving a few crystallised violet petals on the plate.

The corner of Joly's mouth tightened. "No—thank you, Madame. The tea was very refreshing, but we must focus on the sheep."

Madame Mazet peered at Joly through slit eyes, her wrinkles deepening. "Ah, yes, the sheep."

"You mentioned you had three accounts to tell us," Joly said patiently. "We've had two already, and we're very grateful for them, but you have one more?"

"The third story is mine. I saw one of the creatures myself, with my own eyes. Jules would love to hear this. Sometimes I feel he's in the room with me, laughing at my yarns."

Madame Mazet continued on about her son's antics when he was little. Joly's mouth tightened a bit more, which didn't do much for her striking looks. As I attempted to ignore Simon rolling his eyes, I caught a movement in the shadows behind the old lady's armchair. Probably a mouse. I sure hoped it wasn't a rat. I'd had enough rats for a lifetime.

As Joly redirected Madame Mazet once again, whatever it was shifted to the side, and spindly legs, a narrow face and a long nose slunk into the light. She wasn't a mouse or a rat, she was an osencame, a much smaller goblin than the one at the window this morning. The type that delighted in making mischief around the home.

"Oh, yes. When I saw the golden sheep... yes... that was from my own back garden. I've a lovely view of the mountainside from here." I half listened, but I was more curious about the goblin. Was she a permanent resident of the house, just as Mushum lurked around the café in the hope of gleaning the odd choquette? And how many places had one?

She pulled her doublet down over her banded trousers and scratched her leathery head, messing her tufty hair. Then she pootled over to the camcorder tripod and inspected the legs. I stood stock still, not daring to move as she wheezed and snuffled under me. She didn't know I could see her, and this was my chance to observe an osencame in its natural environment.

She ambled around the tripod into the kitchen doorway, stroking her chin as she gazed thoughtfully at the nonslip mat that lay in the entrance—a precaution for Madame Mazet on the terracotta tiles. With a wiggle of her fingers, she folded over the end so it stuck up. The little blighter. Madame

Mazet would be sure to trip. A broad smirk grew on her face and her shoulders shook with glee.

"And the sheep just rambled across the mountainside..." I vaguely registered Madame Mazet talking as I watched the creature study Joly and Simon from the side. Then she hopped up onto the back of the sofa and grimaced at Simon's sweaty mop, before padding over to Joly and staring in fascination at her shining locks.

This was my opportunity. I eased very slowly across to the kitchen doorway and nudged the mat with my foot, flattening it back down. The goblin's head shot around and our eyes met. So much for remaining inconspicuous.

"And Odette next door saw the sheep too," Madame Mazet continued as the critter and I sized each other up. Her mouth curved into an ugly, sharp-toothed grin, then she grabbed one of Joly's shiny ebony hairs, wrapped it around her finger and pulled.

"Ouch!" Joly cried, glaring back. Fortunately, I was just a little too far away to be implicated. I raised my brow in faux curiosity, as if to say, "Is there a problem and can this extremely efficient and very helpful assistant be of any use?" She frowned, rubbed her head, then returned to the old lady. The goblin jumped down and danced a jig before me, her belly shaking, her spluttery laugh a little too loud. The swine. She knew I couldn't react.

Simon twisted around. I had no idea how the goblin's laughter sounded to him and the others, but it was coming from my direction. I faked a coughing fit, causing a stern glance from Joly and a sneer from Simon.

"Are you alright, my dear?" Madame Mazet said.

"All good. Please don't let me interrupt."

"You just did," Simon whispered, then sighed dramatically, his meaning clear. The old lady was off track *again*, this time thanks to me.

The goblin's grin became wicked as she turned her attention to the other side of the room.

"So when exactly was your sighting of the golden sheep, Madame Mazet?" Joly asked.

"Let me see..." She tapped her fingers together, counting away the years in her head.

The goblin hopped onto the sideboard and continued her jig in and out of Madame Mazet's ornaments, skirting a vase, narrowly missing a china dog, circumnavigating a candlestick. Then she paused right behind handsome Jules in his photo frame, and her grin expanded almost beyond the confines of her face. With a waggle of her brow, she grasped the frame and raised it above her head. My heart raced. Not the frame. Not Madame Mazet's last keepsake of her beloved son. It would surely smash on the tiles.

"I'm trying to remember exactly when I saw that sheep," Madame Mazet said, still tapping her fingers.

The goblin struggled with the frame, teetering about. I tried to think how I could stop the creature without making a bad impression, but nothing came.

"I think it was ten a.m.," she continued. "I recall now because I was hanging the washing out."

Simon raised an eyebrow.

"I'm capable of doing the chores, young lad," she replied.

"I may be ninety-eight, but I'm still going strong, and I was hanging out the washing before Bernard came over for morning tea. He always arrives at ten, but he was five minutes late. Very unlike him."

"Ten o'clock in the morning," Joly said. "But which day... which year?"

"Oh, just yesterday. Silly me, I got all in a muddle for a moment. I couldn't decide if I'd seen it before or after lunch. But it was definitely yesterday, before Bernard popped in."

The goblin managed to balance the frame. She drew it back, then launched it into the air. My heart thrashing, I half jumped, half sprinted the two steps along the length of the sofa. My fingers wrapped around the cool metal just before it hit the ground, my foot catching on a standard lamp. As I regained my footing, the lamp toppled toward the table. I tried to grab it, but I was too late. The shade crashed into the tea things, tea slopping everywhere.

Joly rose, her legs splattered. "Camille, what on earth do you think you're doing?"

"I'm so sorry," I spluttered as I cradled Jules in my hands. "The frame was about to fall off the sideboard. I... uh... caught it."

"It was right at the back," Simon added helpfully. "There was no way it was going anywhere."

Joly stared at me with a mixture of disbelief and irritation. I had to sort this out. I placed the frame on the side, grabbed the standard lamp and righted it, revealing a smashed tea set.

Madame Mazet reached over and took my hand. "Not to

worry, my dear, I've plenty more crockery. You accumulate too much junk through the years." She beamed up at me, truly appearing not to be bothered. "Thank you for catching the frame. That was the important thing. I'll clear up." She made to rise.

"No, please, Madame Mazet, let me," I said. "It's the least I can do. You focus on the interview."

"Well, I think that would make the other two happy," she muttered with a chuckle.

"Actually, we're finished," Joly snapped.

CHAPTER 9

Yes, I could've said I was busy with the project, or made up some other excuse so I wouldn't have to return to the farm for lunch, but seeing Maman and Papa now meant getting it over and done with. And what with this morning's disastrous interview, I could get all the crap sorted in one go then conveniently disappear for the majority of my parents' visit, having done my minimum daughterly duty.

I wasn't exactly rushing to the farmhouse. Despite knowing my parents were waiting, and Grampi was probably wanting to serve an already late lunch, I couldn't garner the enthusiasm. Taking my time in my loft apartment above the barn, I had a cool shower and made sure the last of the glitter was gone, all the while trying not to see the look on Joly's face at Madame Mazet's. But it was curious that the old lady had seen a golden-horned sheep yesterday. I might have concluded it was her age-addled memory mixing things up if my own life hadn't been one massive fae reveal of late.

I donned a lightweight cotton cardi—too hot for the weather, but I didn't want my parents asking about the now faint scratches down my arm. Heat hit me as I headed across the yard to the farmhouse, the scent of dry straw tickling my nose. Most of the goats were lying in the shade under the trees, but Delphine approached. I scratched her chin in her favourite spot, then Rose came over and nuzzled me. I smoothed her ears. They were looking very well after their hantaumo ordeal. I had a sneaky suspicion that whatever Aherbelste had done to them had something to do with it.

The kitchen door was already open, a sun thistle hanging in the centre. The aroma of baking salmon and fennel greeted me as I climbed the steps and made my way inside.

"Camiiiiiille." My mother's voice soared through the room. She teetered across the flagstones on low kitten heels, her smile overly broad, her eyes curved in exaggerated happiness. What with her shoulder-length highlights and her smart slacks and blouse, she was out of place in the rugged, old-world kitchen. "So good to see you," she murmured as she hauled me into a hug that I had absolutely no say in whatsoever.

"Hey, Maman," I said from amidst her hair, her curves warm, her palmarosa scent melting me. "It's good to see you too." Despite all my niggles, I couldn't deny the motherly comfort.

The hug threatening to last forever, I pulled back. "Talk about a surprise visit." My voice was stiff. "I know you were intending to come at some point, but I hadn't expected you right at this moment during the project."

She cocked an eyebrow at my tone then doffed my shoulder. "Oh, it made perfect sense, especially with us cutting our holiday short, and what with your grandfather—"

"Chouchou," Papa boomed from the hallway. He strode in, his long legs eating the distance, his neatly combed salt-and-pepper hair tidy, his gaze holding that familiar hardness as if he was set in stone. One thing was for sure, I got my features from my mother and my grandfather. "As beautiful as ever." He wrapped me in a brief hug, then shook me by the arms, just like he'd always done. "How is my little one?" I was pretty sure I was still ten in his eyes.

"All good," I said, because mentioning Blanche's damnation brioche and the goblin hell bent on ruining my life wasn't on the cards. My parents were definitely not open in that way.

Grampi's clattering came from the scullery off the side of the kitchen.

"Sweetie, your grandfather is doing so well." Maman glanced toward the noise. "We've had time to catch up. I can't actually believe he's better..."

She did seem to be at a loss for words—unusual for her. His recovery from only ever being able to speak about goats had astonished us all.

"An almost miraculous turn of events." Papa scraped his hand over his chin. "I have to say, I'm stunned. And out of the blue like that, too. Well, PTSD can do that to a person."

PTSD resolving itself had been the doctor's conclusion. It made more sense than a fae curse, that was for sure. Of course, it helped that his doctor was Lucas.

There was a crash from the kitchen. "Sacrebleu!" It wasn't like Grampi to be so vocal or so edgy.

Maman swung around. "I told him not to fuss with lunch —at his age! A simple salad and some bread would've done."

I squeezed her shoulder. "I'll go see what's up."

She shrugged. The goat-speak thing had caused a seventeen-year rift between them, their attempted communications strained at best.

Peering around the scullery door, I blanched at the three Men of Bédeilhac scrubbing the washing-up, the sleeves of their prehistoric leather tunics rolled up, bubbles covering their arms and beards. They eyed Grampi cautiously as he stooped to retrieve the baking tray from the floor, muttering under his breath. I'd expected the Men gone. It didn't seem sensible to have them helping out with my parents about, but Grampi had been a Keeper—he had to know how much of a fae presence my parents could take before they noticed something was up.

He rose and shot me a steely glare, his bright eyes flashing amidst his crown of white hair and full snowy beard. It was so unlike his usual warmth.

I stepped in and closed the door. "You didn't have to cook for Maman and Papa." He clearly found it difficult to accept that he was an octogenarian that had spent years plagued by a fae curse.

"The food's no trouble." He cast the baking tray into the washing-up, sending a tidal wave of suds over the Men, the wooden worktop and terracotta wall tiles.

I stared at it for a second then studied him—the tension

in his shoulders under his lumberjack shirt, the way he seized the rocket and tore it to tiny shreds as he prepared the salad. "Then what's up?"

His face softened and his shoulders sagged. There was the Grampi I knew, the kindness in his eyes returning. "Camille." He sighed, placed the rocket down, and draped his arm around my shoulder, drawing me to him. I felt his bones, his slight tremble, but this was Grampi, and he was home. "You know I love you very much?" He'd not been able to tell me that all the while he'd been cursed, although I'd seen it in his eyes. He'd used the days since his recovery to tell me repeatedly. And we'd laughed—a lot—about the goat-speak that had plagued him, about our weird way of communicating during that time and how spot on it had been, about so many things we'd been up against with the farm. But it was humour with a hard edge—the years of being incommunicado *had* been difficult. And now they were over, we were in a new space—a good space—even though we hadn't yet got to discussing fae or anything related to being a Keeper. It was as if we were apprehensive about exploring that side of each other.

"I know," I replied, "and I love you too. But...?" There was definitely a "but" on the tip of his tongue.

He squeezed me again, then drew a long breath and returned to pulverising brassicas. "But... this morning..." He was trying to keep his voice soft, but an edge had crept in. "Where were you?"

This was curious. Even when I'd been younger, he'd never outwardly worried about me. Though communication was tricky, I had the sense he trusted me entirely. It was the basis of our relationship.

"I couldn't sleep," I replied. "Nerves about the project. We went up to Les Calbières. Lucas had an idea that the acid attacks might be fae related."

He turned to me, his hand resting on the worktop. "I thought you weren't sure about being a Keeper."

My brow narrowed as his eyes hardened again. What on earth was up with him? "Yes. You know that. But I needed the distraction." Crockery clattered out in the kitchen as my parents set the table. I grabbed the tomatoes and a knife and started slicing. "Do you have a problem with that?"

He began flaking the parmesan. "It's dangerous," he said gently.

"I have no doubt about that." Apart from still coming to terms with the actual existence of fae, the sheer level of bloodshed, gore and death recently had left a deep scar. Although I had to admit, letting go and pulverising charognards this morning had felt so darned good. I added the tomato to the salad and rubbed the shoulder of my sword arm.

Grampi finished with the parmesan and wiped his hands on a tea towel, his face lined with solemnity. Drawn by the weight of his expression, I couldn't look away. He reached out and tugged at my hand as though he were reining me in. "I... I don't know what I expected to happen with your invitation to be a Keeper, but I've been thinking about it all. Camille, it's too dangerous. I don't want you to do it."

My lips parted. "What...? Why?"

"You can trust me," he said. "I know what's involved."

That was undeniable. I didn't know when he'd taken the role himself or when he'd dropped it, if he ever had. He definitely went for strolls into fae almost daily, and since he could communicate again, he'd been spending time at the Keepers' post, catching up with Roux. One way or another, he'd been on the job for years.

"I know the danger you'll be subject to," he added. "The role isn't appropriate—the assembly made a mistake."

"Not appropriate... for me. Why? It seems like I'm more applicable than most." Or at least that's what I'd been told by Lucas, Blanche and Wayland—that my knowledge of folklore and skill with a blade were perfect for the role. Yeah, I had to admit, I had serious doubts, especially with my understanding of fae only skimming the surface, and with my thoughts about university. But *not appropriate*...

I stiffened with indignation. I was Grampi's star pupil with the medieval sword, and I'd surpassed his skill years ago, although some of that had to do with his age and probably the fae curse too. Even so, he'd always been encouraging in swordplay and life. His supreme confidence in me was my rock.

"It's too hazardous," he said flatly. "The risks are much too high."

Warmth rose from my chest, creeping up my neck. "So I can trust you not to trust me?" The edge to my voice was razor sharp.

He shook his head. "It's not like that. Being a Keeper just isn't suitable."

"And you were right for the task, yet I've not got what it takes?"

"Camille, even with military training, I can't tell you how many times my life has been on the line."

Yes, he was ex-military. Yes, he'd had combat training, and from what I'd experienced so far, everything to do with Fae *was* ridiculously dangerous. Still, his doubt left me weak in the middle. Grampi walked out with the salad.

My phone vibrated, and I drew it out.

Lucas. *We need to talk. Where are you?* After this morning, he could go jump.

I tucked away my mobile and stacked dirties, glaring at Grampi as he came back in. He took a roll of his homemade goat's cheese from the dairy fridge. I eyed it with suspicion. He'd only just started making it again, wanting to ensure the hantaumo were well and truly out of the goats' systems.

"And it's not only that..." he said.

"What? There's more?" I snapped. "Oh, joy."

"It's that drac." He plated up the cheese. "I don't trust him. One thing I'm certain of, you should keep away."

This I couldn't believe. Alright, there was a lot not to trust about Lucas, especially after our dodgy start. But despite how completely pissed off I was with him at this precise moment, the truth was plain to see. "We wouldn't be here right now if it wasn't for him." I plonked the dirties in the sink. The Men had produced oilskins from somewhere, the rudimentary garments made of... skin and oil.

"Dracs can't be trusted." He threw the cheese wrapper in the bin.

Really? Was he really saying this? "Your partner was a hantaumo," I snapped. "I can't believe you of all people would come out with something like that. And what about the Men?" The little guys shrank back. "They're in Lucas's service, yet you let them fix up the farm and you're keeping them on to help around the place."

He huffed. "The Men do exactly what they want, and that's not the point. The point is"—he drew himself up and stiffened his jaw—"Lucas Rouseau is bad news, especially with a family like that. Keep well away."

CHAPTER 10

"You always did wonders with saumon à l'oseille, Papa," Maman said to Grampi. "But I don't know what you've done to your goat's cheese. It has a wonderful edge to it." The salmon finished, they'd started on the cheese with Pyrenee's fougasse and Grenache grapes, but I could only see resurrected Daisy munching rotten hantaumo flesh.

I listened to Maman, Papa and Grampi making small talk as I sipped wine and nibbled on bread. My phone vibrated twice more, Lucas again. What with everything, I just wanted him to leave me alone.

Grampi had managed to push his annoyance away for my parents' sake, and was managing to sound reasonably convivial. Most likely, he wanted to put on a good front so Maman wouldn't worry. Although she was trying to be subtle, she was obviously assessing him for soundness of mind after his recovery. Papa had made a number of comments about how the farm was looking in remarkable repair. Mostly due to the Men's efforts, of course.

I made light conversation, but my mind was on Grampi's words. They'd come out of the blue, the timing spot on after my delightful morning. Although thinking back, when Lucas had done his post-hantaumo assessment of Grampi, Grampi had been rather brusque.

Ugh. I really didn't need this. What I wanted was to return to the project and make sure everything went smoothly. But first I needed to suss out my parents' plans so I could give them a wide berth.

"Anyway," I said, "how come you two are staying for a few days?" There was always an ulterior motive. I loosened my cardi. It was too hot, even with the windows open. The range that burned all year round didn't help.

"Come on, Camille," Maman scorned as she adjusted her napkin. "We told you, we're here for Papa. It's so wonderful he's better."

Grampi grunted through a mouthful of bread. He wasn't fooled.

Maman took some grapes from the cheese board and glanced at me from the corner of her eye. "But as you mention it, I've got a list of people I must see." Here it came. "Yvonne is having a luncheon tomorrow, and then there's Colette from the hotel. I must catch up with her. Oh, and I've a spa day arranged with Denise and dinner after."

This was more like Maman—and Papa too, for that matter. They were peas in a pod, but where Maman's contacts were openly social, Papa's hid behind the guise of work. In a strange way, their separate circles of friends and contacts connected them. They understood each other. They did their circuits, only pausing to converge for practical matters, then off they went again.

Maman had worked at a string of top-notch hotels, socialising her way to the top of the managerial chain. She was still at it in Menton, where they lived now. And her connections were the reason she was here. It bugged me that she used Grampi as a pretence. She certainly wasn't going to be spending much time with him.

"And your father has a meeting in Toulouse," Maman added. "Something about an award he's organising for young and talented chemists."

Papa's face lit up. I couldn't help comparing it to the disappointment in his eyes when I'd informed him I wasn't going to university a few years ago.

A crash sounded from the scullery. The Men.

"Just my new dishwashers," Grampi said nonchalantly. I grimaced. Maman would be in there later looking for the appliances. Mind you, she'd brush it off as senility.

"We're so excited about the award," Papa said. "We want it to be available to those who've flown academically and have shown the most potential but need a financial leg up. We're finalising the details tomorrow." Well, it wasn't as if I'd expected Papa to stick around either. He and Grampi had never gotten on. Papa had travelled a lot for work during the years my parents had lived at the farm and later nearby. He and Grampi had managed to keep the peace by avoidance, mainly.

"So, Camille," Papa said, the ridges between his brows tweaking as he assessed me, "I want to hear more about this research project. I have to say, I'm over the moon you took the position. Even though folklore studies is one of the softer fields, it's a step in the right direction." For Papa, a chemist who'd taken consultancies around the country before turning to lecturing at Aix-Marseille University, academia was all that was good and right in the world.

It was ridiculous, but my stomach lightened at his interest as though I was a child. His implication wasn't even that positive. A step in the right direction meant a step away from the choices I'd made—staying at the farm to look after Grampi and working at the café. But my reaction was instinctual.

"Sounds super," Maman added, although that was probably as far as her interest went.

Grampi made eye contact. "Definitely a good use of her time."

I glared back.

"It would be wonderful if you made it to university now things are sorted," Papa said.

It was what I'd always wanted, at least before the events of the last few weeks had made me question everything. Although, after all the self-study I'd done over the past years, I wondered if the folklore-degree syllabus would be a bit light. It certainly looked like it from what I'd read. "It would be good," I replied noncommittally. "We'll see how this week goes."

"I'm actually familiar with Stephan Sissoko," he said.

"Oh?" That was a surprise. Papa had tons of academic contacts, but I wasn't aware of many in social sciences.

"We did chemistry together in my first year in Paris—until he abandoned us to ethnography. I couldn't understand it, but he's a good man. We've stayed in touch over the years. In fact, when I mentioned you'd be working with the project, he was very enthusiastic. Invited me out for lunch tomorrow."

"I'm glad you didn't include me in that," Maman added. "I can't stand all that back-in-the-day."

But I'd come to a halt on Papa's disclosure, the warmth of the room suffocating. "You're meeting with Stephan Sissoko tomorrow?" My words dripped with indignation. My parents' visit hadn't been an inconsiderate inconvenience coinciding with the project—my father was muscling in. And folklore wasn't even something he was interested in.

"Absolutely." Papa bunched up his napkin and dropped it on the table. "It will be super to see him."

"But... this is *my* thing..." I seethed. "What are you going to do, put in a good word with Sissoko to get me a place at university?"

"Well..." He shook his head as though my annoyance was a silly trifle. Yep. That was exactly his plan.

"So first of all," I growled, "you think I need a leg up—that I'm not able to get there alone—"

He sighed. "I think you're perfectly capable. The fact that you've delayed your career by working at a café..."

"And secondly—and this really takes the biscuit—you're muscling in on my project, something that's special to me."

The small lines at the side of his mouth tensed as they always did when he tried to justify himself. "Don't be so preposterous. It's not your project. In fact, it was organised long before your involvement. And preparing the refreshments and booking accommodation hardly qualifies you to lay claim over it. As a waitress, you have absolutely no academic grounding, and not much else to show for yourself."

And there it was, his true opinion. Outrage filled me. Working at the café and spending my life at the farm were worth so much. Papa was a conceited asshole who couldn't see further than his pedantic, academic nose. It was like the time I'd gotten onto the gym team, then he'd arranged for me to have extra lessons so I'd be top notch, or that time I'd won a prize for a history paper at school, then he'd ripped apart everything I'd written to "help me improve in the future", or that time I'd gotten a placement in the museum at the Château de Foix. I'd found out it was because Papa had known the curator.

I glowered at him, my blood boiling, years of me not knowing how to cope with this rubbish muddling my head.

Papa munched a piece of bread and shrugged.

Chapter 11

Maman rubbed my arm. Her customary gesture when she was stuck between Papa and I. "Sweetie, you know what your father is like. He only wants the best for you."

"It appears that everyone wants the best for me today." I glared at Papa and Grampi.

She took my hand and squeezed it before fixing my gaze. "We're only here for a few days, and what with your project and our arrangements, it doesn't look as though we'll see much of each other, so..."

Her implication was clear. We'd had this conversation countless times. Papa wasn't going to change, and it was better for everyone if I kept quiet. Better for her, more like. She hated arguments. Her life was all about connection, bringing people together.

I gritted my teeth. I certainly didn't want to drop it. Just for once, I wanted Papa to see the implications of his thick-headed actions. I tore off a chunk of bread and chewed it, then attempted to swallow. It scraped down my throat.

She squeezed my hand again and mouthed, "Thank you—"

A rap sounded at the doorway and Lucas's angular face peered in. "Taxi service."

"What the...?" I muttered, glaring at him. How did he even know I was here? But it wouldn't take much to guess.

"Thought you might need a lift back to the café," he said.

Maman's mouth had fallen open. For the second time today, she was speechless. Lucas's appearance did that to people. Even Papa seemed curious.

Grampi had noted my death stare at the new arrival and was rising to kick him out. But as much as I loved Grampi, I wasn't going to let him dictate my company. Plus, this was the ideal escape.

I raised a hand. "Don't get up. It's just my ride."

If looks could kill, Grampi's would've speared Lucas through the middle then mangled his insides. Lucas didn't notice, so Grampi shot me a "what the hell is that drac doing here?" raised brow. I sent him back an "it's none of your goddamned business" glower. We'd had years of practice at nonverbal communication.

Maman gathered herself. "Camille, please do introduce us." She got up from the table and walked to the door.

I rose and joined them. "This is Lucas Rouseau. Grampi's doctor. He's the one who completed Grampi's most recent medical report."

Lucas smiled with perfect charm. "Pleased to meet you, Madame...?"

Didn't look like I was going to get away without the niceties. "This is my mother, Olivia, and my father, Julien," I said, not looking at Papa.

Maman tucked her hair behind her ear. "Thank you so much for doing the report, and for looking after Papa so well, Doctor Rouseau. If you'll just give Camille a second..."

She drew me aside as Lucas and Papa exchanged platitudes. "Camille, you didn't say anything," she murmured. "How long have you been seeing him? He's utterly gorgeous."

I snorted. "I'm not seeing him. He's giving me a lift."

"Oh, come on. The way he's looking at you..."

"What? Not you too?" It was bad enough with Alice going on about it. I glanced at Lucas. He did indeed have his eyes on me once again before they flicked back to Papa, who'd asked him where he'd trained. Lucas spieled off a list of first-class universities. I caught the Sorbonne, the University of Munich and Yale. The look of smug satisfaction on Papa's face as he conversed with an accomplished equal was too much to bear.

"That training is all well and good," Grampi muttered, "until he eats one of his patients."

Lucas glanced at him in curiosity. My parents paused, then my father shook his head in the most condescending way possible.

"Papa, don't be so silly," Maman said.

Colour flamed in Grampi's cheeks. Instant dismissal as an old fool. But he must have expected it, saying something like that.

Definitely time to get out of here. "Look, I have to go," I said to Maman. "Have a good time with Colette and Yvonne."

She hugged me. "It's so lovely to see you, sweetie."

"You too." I squeezed her back.

Calling goodbyes, Lucas and I headed out. I considered taking my truck, so I wouldn't have to deal with Lucas. But finding out what he wanted so I could get him off my back was an even better idea. And the walk home later would help me relax.

We jumped in Lucas's SUV. As he pulled away, I slumped in my seat. I'd made it out of there. Papa had been way out of line—even for him. Had I expected any different? But it irked that he'd swooped in from the margins of my life to throw his weight around. For heaven's sake, I was a grown woman. It was years since he'd been a fixture in my life. And Grampi's remarks about Lucas... They just felt controlling. Less like opinion and more like a tirade.

I ran my hands over my face. "Agh. My family."

Lucas chuckled. "I wouldn't say you have much to worry about. My folks, on the other hand..."

I shot him a side glance. "I warn you, I'm still extremely pissed off about earlier. Anyway, what's so important that you have to turn up at the farm uninvited?" Although since lunch, he'd actually moved down the list of people I least wanted to see. He'd been at pole position, and now he was at number three. No, counting Simon, that would be four. I never would've thought it possible.

He ignored my question, staring at the road. "Izac... I think he wants to protect you. It's natural—I'm a predator. In fact, I still have a little chamois in my teeth." He picked at a canine. "You'll be glad to know I've fed."

Was Grampi right? Did I really have something to be afraid of? Yes, my instincts told me a dangerous killer lay under Lucas's perfect exterior. And truly, I knew nothing about him or his family. But I'd witnessed him sacrifice everything for the town, for me, and that was a lot more than I could say for my family right now. But the fact that dracs were incubi was playing on my mind. Even now, with me infuriated with Lucas, he was just sort of beguiling. Was he doing something to me? That aside, I couldn't let go of this morning...

"Do you realise that when you pull a stunt like the charognards, not only does it make me never want to see you again, but it erodes everything we've built? How can I trust you when I think we're going for a hike and all that happens?"

He grinned. "You're going to have to get used to the way fae work. There's generally a fair amount of trickery involved in most things."

"And you use that trickery at work, do you?" His reputation would be destroyed in a second if he did.

"Of course not. But especially for you, I'm holding true to my nature."

He was utterly incomprehensible. "Just how much danger am I in with you?"

He frowned. "Never mind me. I'd say you're in very real danger from various types of fae, if you don't take your training seriously."

He'd avoided the question. I scraped my teeth together. "I can't believe you're on at me about this again. Why can't you give me this week? And considering you've had the chance to attend pretty much every university on the planet. Do you think I could just have a few days to..."

His fingers whitened around the wheel, ridges of sinew striating his neck. "To what, Camille?" His words were slow and deadly. "You're thinking about going to university, aren't you?"

I stiffened with indignation. "That's none of your concern. You seem to have a very strange notion that you have a say in the course of my life. You may have drugged me with verity, but you have absolutely no say in... in... *me.*" I slapped my chest. "And anyway, why shouldn't I have my chance?" Although it would be gone if things went on like this morning. I needed to rectify that pronto. That damned goblin.

He chewed at his lip, wrenching the gears as we entered town, his chest rising and falling slowly as if he was restraining what lay within. Then he pulled himself together. "The reason I want to talk to you is that there have been a load more acid-attack reports this morning, mainly up on higher ground."

"Snakes with problems aren't my problem."

"Plus, there have been two sightings of golden-horned sheep in those unaware of fae."

I couldn't help my curiosity. "Where?"

"In the Vicdessos valley."

"Not far from the Pons farm, then. Golden-horned sheep are the focus of the research project, and our interviewee, Madame Mazet in Saurat said she saw one yesterday." I cringed as I recalled the lamp crashing into the old lady's china. Joly's anger... I pushed the images away. "But why would folk who aren't aware of fae be able to see golden-horned sheep?"

We drove over the bridge, the Ariège rushing beneath us. "That's the question. In the past, people were more open to the hidden world. Sometimes folk would catch the odd glimpse of fae, especially at certain times of year. But with the development of logical thinking, that faded. Now, it's extremely rare."

He braked for a corner, dropping a gear. "Oh, and there are a number of fae in Tarascon who have reported their gold stolen."

"A lot of curious shit happening, I'll give you that. But as I'm not a Keeper, and I'm only considering the role, which isn't massively appealing right now, given how dangerous everything to do with fae seems to be..." Grampi's words came back. He would be agreeing with the sentiment, and that completely addled me. Argh, everything was so messed up. "And considering I'm doing other things today—important things—why the hell do I need to know?"

He scowled, his dark eyes boring into the tarmac as he

swung into the café car park. "Because, what with all that and the ore serpents, not to mention the bounds cracks expanding, it can't be coincidental. Something is kicking off."

Chapter 12

Velvet hot chocolate wrapped me in its reassuring embrace, the sensation fortified by the comforting hum of the café. I'd snuck out this morning before my parents or Grampi could catch me because I needed this moment to centre myself prior to the project reconvening.

The project discussion yesterday afternoon had gone well, and today would follow suit. In a little while, the teams would collect their equipment and head straight out to morning interviews. But not yet.

I took another sip, and Papa's, Grampi's and Lucas's interference, plus the disastrous interview, drifted away. Lucas's insistence that something was kicking off still niggled. But he had no leads, and anyway, that was his problem.

Alice wasn't here, today being her day off, and that was helping me relax. As much as I wanted to see her, I couldn't bear the gulf that lay between us. It was one thing too much at the moment.

I dipped my croissant into the hot chocolate and bit into it. It melted in my mouth. It was more of Blanche's viennoiserie, and I'd hesitated after the damnation brioche, but I hadn't been able to resist. As I ate, I noticed Gabe chatting with Roux at one of the small tables. The D&D gang, tucked into their nook, glanced at them and sniggered.

My phone vibrated, ringing silently. Papa. Tension crept up my spine. Couldn't I have a second to relax? No doubt Maman had asked him to smooth things over. But I knew him. There was no way he'd cancel lunch with Sissoko, so what was the point?

The phone stopped ringing. I'd almost managed to forget about it when a text came in.

Your mother wanted me to sort things out with you. I have no idea why you would have a problem with me having a drink with an old friend. Honestly, it's preposterous. But Maman doesn't want us to argue. For her sake, let's be civil.

In my head, I screamed—a deafening, blood-curdling scream. Why had he even bothered?

And another buzz, this time from Maman. *Hope you've sorted everything out with your father. Have a super day. Xxx*

I slumped back. Why couldn't they see how lightweight it was to only smooth things over?

Closing my eyes, I caught Guy's projectile voice. "And he had four more attacks last night. There've been reports from a load of other farms, too." A distraction. Great. Well, not great—it was awful for the ore serpents and Guy's family, not to mention the sheep.

"Papa's losing money left, right and centre," Guy continued. "The government might compensate partially, but by the time they've processed his claims it's gonna be way too late. That's why I'm doing the extra shift. But all that's about to change... Hey, Camille, come and look at this."

No rest for the wicked.

I opened my eyes. Guy was waving a bunch of leaves around. The customers at the counter were gazing at it with curiosity. If I was going to get out of this chair, it had better be interesting. Although I could grab another croissant at the same time.

I hauled myself up, slipped behind the counter and took a croissant from the basket. Guy thrust his bundle before me. Broad, deep green leaves sprouted from a plump root. Fat rhizomes that looked just like chubby arms and legs extended out, the top of it like a pudgy head—a head that scrunched a little. Two beady eyes appeared, then a twisted mouth that grizzled.

"A mandragore," Guy said, beaming.

"Uh, it sure is." It scrunched up its face some more. So, it was true that mandrake plants were fae. It wasn't happy at having been pulled from its earthy home, though.

"Find a mandragore at midsummer and... get totally rich. That's how the old saying goes—or something like that." Guy waved the root around for the customers to see, his smile broadening. "Looks like Papa has nothing to worry about. Our fortunes are changing."

In this day and age, Guy couldn't really believe that. I guess he was hanging on to whatever hope he could. He found an empty jar on the shelf behind the espresso machine, shoved the mandragore in and screwed on the lid. The poor creature looked stunned.

"Ummm, you better make some air holes in that lid," I said.

Guy cocked an eyebrow.

"Just so it doesn't go musty... then the magic might not work." The mandragore was going to get worse than musty if it got left in there, but Guy would think I was mad if I... what? Potted it out back? Plus, I didn't want to dash his hopes of riches. I'd have to think of something, though.

"Good point, Camille. Thanks." Guy dug several holes into the top with the gateau knife, narrowly missing the poor creature. He shoved the jar back on the shelf to take an order from a customer. I noticed a flash of yellow in the jar and peered closer. The mandragore, clearly distressed, had produced a golden nugget from somewhere. I hated to think of where. Maybe Guy was right—he *was* going to get rich. The thing wriggled, nudging the nugget behind it. The creature was fascinating, but I couldn't stare at it all day.

Nora was being served by one of the part-time staff. Her perfect brow creased as she glared at Gabe. He noticed and cringed. But at least she hadn't run out this time. One small step for womankind.

"We really need to talk," I said to her. "Join me?"

She looked me over. I couldn't figure out if she was considering the idea or about to tell me where I could stick my invite, but her shoulders sank. She followed me to my table, sat opposite and placed her cup down.

"How are you doing?" I asked, settling in my chair and placing my pilfered croissant on my plate. We'd not spoken since the attack, although she'd had a few sessions with Lucas, discussing it all.

"As well as could be expected for someone who was abducted by a boy possessed by the personification of evil." Her tone was dry, her powder-blue irises icy amidst expertly done kohl. She flicked her jet-black hair back, the ends curling under her stiff jaw. In fact, every part of her was stiff.

"You're actually in the same room as him today." I dunked my croissant.

"You noticed my reactions?"

"I think everyone's noticed."

She sat back, her gaze flicking to Gabe.

"But it's completely understandable," I added. "You went through a lot, and now you're having to come to terms with Fae."

"Weirdly, Fae is the least of it. It just makes sense of so many strange things that I could never quite work out, like all the creepy folklore, or why Max is such a troll, or why my gran had her washing stolen repeatedly."

I raised an eyebrow.

"Osencame." She took a sip of her espresso then placed it back on the table. "Caught it red-handed the other day. Looked the thing up in *Old Lore of the Pyrenees*."

"Good one." Perhaps there *were* quite a few of them around.

She glanced at Gabe again, her fingers tangling together. "But I just can't get over him... his face back in the basement... the feeling that came off him. It was..." She stared at the garland on the wall. "Terrifying."

"Freak," someone muttered from the D&D nook, the word just loud enough for Gabe to hear. He caved in, his shoulders rounding so his cloak fell forward, his drink becoming more fascinating than Roux, who was talking with animated gestures. It was unlike the gang to target anyone, let alone Gabe, one of their founding members. They'd always been inseparable, and none of them knew Gabe's actual involvement in the hantaumo attack.

I shot daggers at the gang, who tried their best not to shrink from my gaze. Félix blushing, the colour clashing with his caramel curls. There was the culprit.

"You know it wasn't Gabe," I said, turning my attention back to Nora. "He was possessed, and I truly don't think he would have done anything like that to you... to the town... otherwise. The hantaumo are pretty horrible creatures. I'm not sure having one take over your mind is that pleasant either."

She scrunched up her lips, pushing them one way then the other.

"Having said that," I continued, "what you went through must have been tremendously difficult, and if you never came to terms with it... with Gabe... I'd completely respect that. Despite what happened to him, he's going to have to accept the consequences."

"Yeah, well, thanks for saying that, Camille. Right now, I

don't know what I feel about him. One thing's for certain, I'm not ready to buy him a coffee." She downed the rest of her espresso and rose. "Got places to be. See you later." She strode to the door.

"Later," I called. Had that gone well? At least we'd made contact. I should've spoken to her sooner.

I finished my croissant, pausing mid-chew as Alice headed through the doors, pulling Raphaël after her. Damn it. What was she doing here today?

She walked over, leaving Raphaël standing by the entrance. I glared at the faker, peering through his dishy glamour—all wavy hair and long eyelashes—to see the ugly goblin he truly was. He turned away, pretending not to notice, but he knew I knew. The charlatan.

"Popped in for my purse," Alice said as we hugged. "Left it in the office. But Camille, we had such a good time last night." Her eyes sparkled. The white petals of her rose tattoo that peeked out of her top reminded me of the time she'd had it done. Of how we used to do so much together. Of how we used to discuss everything. "Dinner and clubs," she added, "then we spent the rest of the night... Well, I've told you before, he's vigorous. So keen. I don't know how many times I—"

"Uh... great," I managed, attempting not to see my best friend doing anything with that massive, pot-bellied, scrawny-limbed, wrinkled, bug-eyed thing. And she was falling for him—I could tell. The whole of her glowed with it. The worst of it was, I couldn't say a damned word. The quickest way to alienate my best friend would be explaining that her boyfriend was a fae monster.

She didn't notice my lack of enthusiasm, she just looked dreamy. "He's so considerate and sensitive. It's early days, but I... I don't know... I truly think he might be the one."

CHAPTER 13

I PLACED THE EQUIPMENT BOX ON THE BUILT-IN PICNIC table that stood beneath the acacias at the side of Chalet de Larcat. Due to the hot weather, we were going to do the interview outside in the shade.

Martin and Ariane Lahoud's holiday rental was all red shutters and equally red geraniums with a backdrop of acacias. They'd wanted to meet us here as they were cleaning between bookings. The front of the chalet was supported by pillars, the land dropping away steeply. A precautionary fence ringed the chalet itself, but by the picnic table, a steep, grassy slope descended to meadows below.

The view was superb. Larcat village and the Ariège valley lay below, soaking up the heat and glowing with early-summer green. I loved vistas like this. Not too low to feel pinned down between the foothills, yet not too high to lose sight of civilisation. Our farm was at a similar altitude.

Joly and Simon were explaining the interview process to

the Lahouds on the veranda of the chalet. Martin was a stocky guy made almost entirely of stubble, his buzz cut hiding his receding hairline. Ariane had a friendly face and a mane of cappuccino locks that she swept back from the newborn baby cradled to her chest in a sling. She had a story her great-grandfather had recounted about a golden-horned sheep up on Trois Seigneurs.

Simon was going to conduct the interview, and the notes he clutched were considerable. Wondering how many questions he could possibly ask, I secured the tripod legs, then placed it a little way from the picnic table. As I clipped the camcorder on top, a car rolled up the drive and parked. Pascale's Citroën.

He jumped out and strode over, his physique noticeable under the shirt he'd donned for interviewing. "Camille, what are you doing here?" Joly was clearly thinking the same about him as she frowned in our direction.

"Um, we were scheduled here," I replied.

He drew out his phone and tapped. "Shit. My mistake. I assigned both groups to the same place."

"Hey, these things happen. Where's your partner?" Pascale had been put with one of the degree students.

"Migraine. She's taking a break."

Joly headed over, an eyebrow arched. Simon followed.

"I've scheduled both groups to the same location," Pascale said to Joly, wincing a little. "My complete stupid-ass mix-up. All the other interviews are allocated. The guy at Bédeilhac postponed until tomorrow."

She frowned. "Camille, I thought I asked you to check

the arrangements."

"I checked them yesterday, but—"

"No buts. You should have double-checked today."

My lips parted. There was no logical reason to repeat the process. Everything had been confirmed and Pascale had slipped up, that was all.

"My mistake, Professor," he said. "I changed things at the last minute."

Joly just shook her head, her attention focussed solely on me. Great, just great.

Pascale's brow knitted. "You really can't blame Cami—"

"It's time we began." Joly turned to the couple, who'd stepped over. "We're ready if you are?"

They nodded.

"Pascale," she continued. "Presuming you've prepared for the interview, you may as well do this one. Simon, you can do the next."

Simon lasered me with his gaze, raising his interview notes. "Thanks a lot, Camille."

I glowered back. Of course he'd blame me for this.

Pascale grimaced another apology before taking a seat at one side of the picnic table with Joly. Martin, Ariane and the baby sat opposite. Stationed behind the camcorder, I started the recording. Simon hovered nearby, his eyes on the interview.

"Ariane, Martin, if I could start by confirming your names and contact details," Pascale said.

The Lahouds obliged, then Ariane added, "It's so strange you're here, asking about my grandfather's story now, when our friends said they thought they saw a golden-horned sheep up near Miglos yesterday." She laughed lightly.

Martin frowned. "Must have been a trick of the light. But they were completely convinced." I dragged my teeth over my lip. More sightings. Perhaps something really was kicking off.

"Yeah," Ariane agreed, joggling the baby, who was fretting softly. "I can't imagine why they'd think they saw something like that. I guess it was a superstition in my grandfather's day, but now—"

Shrill clucking came from the acacias, and a large flock of hens emerged from the undergrowth. We glanced at one another as they scurried to the picnic table and swarmed around us, flapping in consternation, some jumping on top.

"So sorry." Ariane swept away a hen that was trying to flutter onto her lap. "It's the neighbours' flock. They sometimes come over here. Although I have no idea what's gotten them spooked."

Martin rose. "I'll sort them out. You carry on with the interview. It's not my story, anyway." He clapped his hands at the hens, endeavouring to shoo them from the table. Joly made a half-hearted attempt to do the same. She really wasn't country material. Pascale got up and waved his notepad about.

The hens continued their commotion, flapping and dashing in all directions. Simon danced about, jumping from one leg to the other, doing his best not to come into contact with any of them. "My allergies," he cried. "I'll go into anaphylactic shock with this many feathers."

I held on to the tripod as a couple of hens brushed past, wobbling it. Martin's shooing had worked, though. As one, they scurried down the slope. But when they'd gotten halfway down, they paused and ran back again. A white hen with a red comb tried to fly onto Ariane's head. She flailed with one hand, the other protecting the baby, who broke into an awe-inspiring howl, the din accompanying the squawks and clucks.

Some of the hens jolted as if stung. I caught a movement lower down the slope. There must be a fox or something riling them. But no, just below us, not quite camouflaged amidst the rocks at the side of the slope, were two goblins throwing stones.

All I could do was stare, my heart thumping. Like an avalanche, everything fell into place. One of the goblins was taller and gangly. It had been at the window yesterday. The other was tiny, the osencame with a long nose that had been at Madame Mazet's, which meant none of the fae interference was coincidental. For some unknown reason, fae were targeting the project... or me. Anger flashed hot through my middle. That was damned well it. I didn't have to look further than that conniving, mischievous, devious drac. He didn't want me to do this, he wanted me to train, so he'd set me up. What the hell was wrong with him?

One of the hens attempted to run from the goblins' bombardment, angling across the slope. A stone stung its neck, then another—not from the goblins but from a short troll-like thing crouched by the bushes on the other side. Then a mighty screeching arose from the irate flock as the osencame darted for us. The critter ran into the midst of the avian throng and dove toward the tripod. She slid underneath, grasped the legs and toppled it.

No way.

Before it could fall, I grabbed the camera in one hand and the tripod in the other and tried to wrestle it from the goblin. The critter was strong, shaking it like a dog with a rat, but I wasn't going to let the Canon camera, worth who knew how much, smash on the ground.

Joly stopped hen-shushing and gaped at me. I sent her a reassuring smile that I was sure came out like a demented grimace. If she couldn't see the goblin, then I looked as though I was shaking the thing. Crap.

Simon bumped into my back as he narrowly avoided an irate speckled hen that had taken an interest in his worm-like shoelaces. "Camille, do something," he muttered desperately. "If it touches me, I'm dead."

He was asking me for help? But the shaking had stopped. I glanced down. The goblin had reached through my legs and was tying Simon's shoelaces together. It sprang off and hurled a stone at the speckled hen, sending it fluttering in Simon's direction.

"Just stand still, Simon," I yelled. But he lurched away from his feathery assailant. Unable to take a stride, he teetered to the side in tiny, laced-up footsteps that carried him much too close to the slope. I dove for him, but he toppled out of my reach and pitched over the edge. Down he rolled, over and over, until he slumped into a heap at the bottom.

CHAPTER 14

THE EVENTS ROOM BUZZED AS PEOPLE ORGANISED equipment, typed on laptops, uploaded files, made transcripts and chatted non-stop about recent sightings of golden-horned sheep. The aroma of late-morning coffee and freshly baked brioche competed with the odour of sweaty folklorists. Thankfully the refreshments were winning.

I sat at the back, checking tomorrow's schedule and interview allocations for the hundredth time. Yes, it hadn't been my mistake earlier, but it sure as hell wasn't going to happen again. The goblins were another matter. They'd blitzed the interview. Although on the good side, at least Joly couldn't blame me for the hen attack. But Lucas, on the other hand... I was furious with him. He'd set the whole thing up.

Simon sat in the centre of the horseshoe in front of my desk, his leg raised on a chair, a madeleine in his fingers and a coffee resting in his lap. He was rather grubby, covered in dust and grass.

I had to admire his impression of being seriously injured —his body slumped with exhaustion, his expression pained. He'd been fine in the car on the way back. He'd definitely hurt his ankle in the tumble, though, and cut his leg.

Lucas had been called. I would have it out with him, but this wasn't the best place. As soon as we were finished here, he was in serious trouble.

Pascale sat down next to me, his hair mussed, his face grave. "I'm so sorry about earlier. I have no idea why Joly thought it was your mistake.

"Hey, no problem." I had no idea either—not the slightest hint of one.

"Everyone," Joly pronounced from behind her desk. Her face was uncustomarily flushed, and she actually looked a little excited or possibly stressed. Whatever it was, her usual composure had slipped. With a small smile at her, Sissoko tapped a spoon on his cup. The room hushed.

"We realise," Joly began, "that you're all curious about the recent sightings of golden-horned sheep. Pascale has collated ten additional reports in the past three days."

Pascale nodded.

"It appears that what we have here," she continued, "is a community-wide psychogenic delusion provoked by folkloric memory. It doesn't need stating that these things do not occur frequently, and it would be remiss of the department to let the opportunity of studying such a thing pass by."

I shifted in my seat. The sheep shouldn't be visible to the population at large, and having the project nose directly into fae business made me queasy.

"Therefore," she added, "we will give priority to recent sightings over old, and we have a new schedule for the rest of the week." She inclined her head to me.

My jaw stiffened. She could have given me warning. I'd worked so hard on the other one.

"For now," Sissoko said, "collate the information you have, enjoy the delicious viennoiserie"—he raised his pain au chocolat in the air—"and we'll reconvene to discuss the sociological implications this afternoon."

The room filled with chat and bustle once again.

"Camille," Joly called.

And here came the new schedule.

I headed over. Joly had sat back down next to Sissoko, and both wore grave expressions. They'd arranged a chair opposite. My stomach sank. I had no idea what was going on, but this was more than the handing over of a new agenda.

I couldn't help but notice *Recent Experiences of Ancient Folkloric Phenomena*, identifiable by the coffee stain, almost covered by a pile of papers and a couple of books. A copy lay on Sissoko's desk, too. I'd given him a printout this morning. He'd looked at it with curiosity, but now it was also abandoned.

"Have a seat, Camille." Sissoko indicated the chair.

I sat down.

"Obviously we didn't have the most successful morning," Joly said, her mouth set. "The situation with the hens was outrageous, but I noted a couple of things amidst the furore."

"Oh?" I raised my brow.

Sissoko stroked his beard. "And just to say, we're not

accusing you of anything. We're only at the stage of considering opening an enquiry."

My stomach flipped. "What...? What is this?"

"During the poultry attack," Joly said, "firstly, rather than help rid the place of hens, I noticed you jumping up and down holding the camcorder."

"Now, we do understand," Sissoko added, "that a situation with so many chickens might be stressful for anyone, but your reaction does sound a little inappropriate."

Joly sucked in a slow breath. "Then when Simon panicked..." She fixed me in the eye. "I saw what looked like you pushing him down the slope."

"What!" My mouth went dry. "You can't possibly believe that. I saw him heading for the drop. I tried to stop him."

Studying my face, Sissoko sat back. "Of course, most of us have considered physical action against Simon at one time or another—"

Joly shot him a glare. "But Camille, if you have committed such an act, the ramifications are very serious—"

"But—"

"But there was a lot going on back there." She raised her chin. "There is a possibility that I might have been confused."

I just couldn't believe what I was hearing. "I can say with complete honesty that I would never do something like that. He stumbled and I reached out to grab him. I give you my word."

"Simon doesn't know what happened," she said. "He was in too much of a panic about the chickens, so we'll have to give you the benefit of the doubt." She sipped her coffee. "This kind of situation is very confusing. The arrangements you made for the summer project were all satisfactory, and you came with a good reference from the mayor. I'm hoping what I thought I saw was wrong."

"Not to mention she's Julien's daughter," Sissoko murmured to Joly.

Wonderful. My father was managing to interfere when he wasn't even here. High five, Papa.

Joly handed me the new schedule, a handwritten scrawl I couldn't immediately make out. "Make sure everything runs smoothly and that we have no other reason to doubt you."

I rose. "Absolutely. No need to doubt me at all. Everything will be just fine." Why was I defending myself? I wasn't guilty. But so much for making a good impression.

I headed back to my desk. Lucas had arrived and was seated by Simon, assessing him. Pascale had abandoned me for the refreshments table. As I sat down, I caught Lucas's eye and glowered as though my gaze could dissolve him into the stinking goo that made up his soul. My fingers dug into the new schedule. He'd ruined everything.

"What?" he mouthed, then shrugged.

"Camille was at the storming of the picnic table," Simon said to Lucas, his eyes almost as wide as his glasses frames. "She might be able to tell you what happened." He sneezed into his elbow.

A couple of degree students came over with coffee and brioche. "We got these for you, Doctor Rouseau," one said. They placed the refreshments on the table at his side.

"That's very kind of you." He shot them a wicked grin as he palpated Simon's ankle. They exchanged looks and giggled—they actually giggled like five-year-olds. I glanced about. Three other girls and two guys were ogling Lucas with fascination. If they only knew.

"I think you tripped," I said to Simon, wanting to explain about the goblins to Lucas with the tip of my blade running across his throat. "I tried to grab you, but missed."

Simon tutted. "Well, that's just like you, Camille, never managing to do a job properly."

Lucas frowned.

"Honestly," he continued, "the double booking you made this morning was laughable, on top of everything yesterday. Joly should have you replaced."

Lucas tweaked his brow in my direction, which clearly meant "What the hell?". His hands tensed around Simon's ankle, the sinews tight as though Lucas was struggling not to rip his foot off.

"It was so irresponsible of the Lahouds," Simon went on, "with all those... bird monsters about. I told Joly we should conduct the interview indoors. It would've been the most sensible option."

"If you could focus on the examination for a moment?" Lucas said. "Tell me if it hurts here?" He jammed his finger into Simon's leg.

"Aowwwwww!" he screamed.

"So it does," Lucas murmured.

I had to restrain a guffaw, despite myself.

"I think we've found the problem. Your ankle is sprained.

Ice it regularly, and I'll drop you in a compression bandage later." He placed Simon's foot down. "And you have a cut?"

Simon sneezed again, then rolled up his trouser leg to reveal little more than a scratch on his shin. I returned to the schedule. I needed a few moments to get my head around it in case there was anything I needed to take up with Joly.

"There's certainly no need for stitches," Lucas said. I tried to block him out, but his voice was a continuous reminder that he'd set me up again. "You say it's been washed?"

"Thoroughly," Simon replied.

"I have an antiseptic wipe." Lucas rummaged in his bag, found a sachet and ripped it open. "I'll—"

"Wait." Simon's lips parted. "Is that natural? I only use natural medicine. But I don't suppose you'd know anything about that."

The corners of Lucas's mouth turned up. "I'm experienced in traditional Chinese medicine, herbal medicine, homeopathy, ayurveda, a little-known form of blood enrichment involving vomiting leaches, oh and acupuncture. I haven't brought my needles with me, but..." He dove into his bag and pulled out a large spike. "I could stimulate healing on ST36, just below the knee, if you'd prefer? I trained with the venerable Hua Tuo for a year. He always used to remark in that sagacious way of his, if the needle isn't hurting, the needle isn't working." He drew the spike toward Simon's leg.

"Umm, no," he stammered, "the wipe will be, uh... fine."

"Good, then. You should be all set." Lucas closed his bag. As he rose and picked up his coffee, he was accosted by the five students who'd had their eyes on him. He leant on a desk a little way along the horseshoe, making small talk and sipping his drink. Good. Now I could focus on the schedule.

As Simon hobbled back to his desk, Pascale and Meera came over, coffees in hand.

"All work and no play makes Camille Joly's slave," she said, placing a cup before me. The two of them slid onto the desks either side. Pascale's shorts rode up a little. I forced myself not to eye his muscular legs. But there was no way I could focus on the schedule. Defeated, I put it down. I needed a coffee, anyway.

"Who is the delicious doctor?" Meera whispered in my ear.

Lucas smirked. Damned drac hearing.

"Joly wasn't giving you more stick just now, was she?" Pascale asked, not having heard Meera's remark.

"Yep," I said. Although I wasn't going to repeat Joly's accusation. If it got out, people would wonder about me, not her. Lucas, amidst his gaggle of attention, had his eyes on me again. He could go jump.

"I don't know what's up with Joly." Pascale's angular jaw grew rigid. "I've tried to tell her how successfully we've worked together. She won't listen."

"Actually, Camille," Meera said, "we didn't want to dis her when we'd just met, but she can be a complete bitch."

Bitch or otherwise, most of my problems had been caused by fae, though Joly was definitely falling from the pedestal I'd placed her on. "I'm beginning to think she sees what she wants to see of me," I replied.

"Oh, and I loved *Recent Experiences of Ancient Folkloric Phenomena*." Pascale's lips curved into a smile.

I stared at him. He'd read it.

"Me too," Meera said. "It's super research. I can't believe you did it all yourself."

"And pertinent to the whole golden-sheep thing," Pascale added. "Your conclusions are great. It should definitely be published. I know the guy who takes submissions for *Folklore Français*. I'll have a word with him about it."

My heart rose to my throat. "That would be beyond amazing. I don't know what to say."

"In fact, I'd like to discuss your findings further." Pascale grinned, those come-to-bed eyes glinting. "Over dinner?"

I shook myself inwardly. I hadn't expected that, but what a lovely surprise after this morning.

There was a crunch and a clatter to our side. The three of us turned to see Lucas's gaggle fussing over him. His saucer had broken, the pieces lying on the floor. "It must have been cracked," he said, glaring at me with an arrogant tilt to his chin, though I had no idea why.

Shifting her attention back, Meera sighed. "Considering I haven't been invited to Pascale's dinner, I'm going to presume this is his attempt to seduce you."

"Not seduction," he said. "I'd love to know Camille better."

Meera's brows drew together. "And the fact that you asked her out straight after offering to put in a word for her paper isn't creepy at all?" The tease was clear in her voice.

Pascale's face fell. "Shit, Camille. I didn't mean it like that."

I laughed at him—at them both. Their friendship reminded me of what I used to have with Alice. "I know you didn't."

"Well, this is where I exit stage left," Meera said. "I wouldn't want to get in the way." She waggled her eyebrows and headed off to a group of students.

I studied Pascale. There was an honesty, an openness about him that drew me, and his love of folklore was hot. But the last time I'd gotten involved with someone interested in the subject, look where it had ended. I glanced at Lucas. Now devoid of coffee, his hands clutched the edge of his desk a little too tightly. He appeared to have lost all interest in the people swamping him, his menacing stare only for me.

I focussed fully on the gorgeous guy before me, who was treating me with the respect and civility I deserved. "Pascale, I'd love to have dinner with you. How about tonight?"

Crunch.

Lucas had taken a chunk out of the desk.

CHAPTER 15

"FAULTY FURNITURE," LUCAS MUTTERED AS SPLINTERS of desk fell from his fingers. His gaggle flapped around him, asking if he was alright, but he only glowered. More drac weirdness. Well, he could keep it to himself.

Pascale frowned, confusion in his eyes. Then he turned back to me and smiled again. "Shall we see when this afternoon's meeting ends, then arrange a time for dinner?"

"Sounds perfect." It would be so good to have the company of someone seriously interested in folklore—the beliefs and customs kind of folklore that I'd loved for so long, not the kind that drugged me and put my life on the line.

"Pascale," Joly called.

"The boss wants me. See you in a bit."

As he walked away, a little warmth managed to forced through my frothing emotions. Pascale's invite was a welcome distraction from everything else.

Lucas shouldered through his admirers and stormed

over. The distraction had officially ended, and my warmth morphed into flames of anger. I rose to meet him. I didn't want to do it here, but if we could get a moment away from the others, I was going to put him well and truly straight.

"What do you think you're doing?" he growled, his gaze imperious.

I'd been going to berate him, but his tone took me back. "I have no idea what you're talking about."

He just stared at me, his jaw clenching, releasing and clenching again. A blood vessel pulsed in his ribbed neck. If he had an aneurysm, we'd be stuffed, him being the only doctor. Not that I gave a shit right now.

"I can't believe you." My eyes blazed. "I can't believe you've sabotaged the project just because you want me to be a Keeper."

My words snapped him out of whatever screwed-up place he'd been in. Confusion glimmered through the arrogance. "Sabotage. I would never—"

"As if it wasn't enough, ruining yesterday morning, but the goblins really were the icing on the cake. Looks like you've destroyed any chance I had at impressing Joly, and not to mention Simon was hurt." Okay, so if I was completely honest with myself, Simon had only sprained his ankle and a part of me had relished watching him tumble down the slope, but right this second I'd use anything I could against Lucas.

He searched my face. "Camille, I don't know what you mean."

He really did look... well, not innocent. Lucas never looked innocent. But one thing I'd learnt about him was that he enjoyed owning up to his pranks, and despite all his other faults, he was truthful. "You didn't arrange for a couple of goblins and a troll to mess up my interviews?"

"Of course not." Whatever he'd been riled about before still tightened his voice. "I know how important this is to you."

"But yesterday morning was okay?"

He fixed me in the eye, all arrogance gone. "I would've gotten you back in plenty of time, no matter what. I told you that."

"Shit." A little of my anger drained away. "If you didn't set me up, then those fae were interfering for some other reason." Which was worse, because even though I'd been furious with Lucas, I'd been certain I could put a stop to his meddling. But now, I didn't have a clue what was going on or how to sort it out.

But maybe Lucas knew the goblins. "There was an osen-came with a bit of a snout, a taller, gangly goblin three or four feet high with big ears, and a troll, short compared to Max. He sort of looked like a rock."

Lucas shook his head. "They're pretty standard descriptions. The last one could be a river troll, though. They're much smaller than the usual type, and they tend to be rather round."

River troll. That was new to me. There appeared to be many different kinds of goblin, so why not trolls?

"Your goblin problems aside"—he raised his hand, a chunk of wood still in his fingers—"there have been a load of golden-horned sheep sightings, and we need to do something. They shouldn't be visible to the population at large."

I squared my jaw. "I don't care about your Keeper motives for sorting this out, but with all the golden-horned sheep reports, the project is going to focus on recent sightings exclusively. I want everything to go normally. A load of geeks talking about traditions, beliefs and stories is just fine by me. There shouldn't be sparkly sheep on hillsides or goblins in bushes. I'm going to make sure there's no more fae interference if it's the last thing I do."

Lucas pursed his lips. "I'd hate to think the project would actually do some proper research into fae."

I glared at him.

"Slaughter," he said.

The Men of Bédeilhac's small yet fearless leader popped up and saluted, his eyes keen, his chestnut beard even bushier than before." Reporting for duty, sir!" The axe in his belt swung against his carefully sewn animal skins as he saluted. He turned to me. "Alright, ma'am?"

"Good to see you, Slaughter. How are you?" I loved having some of the Men around at the farm, but I'd missed Slaughter since the hantaumo attack. I'd wanted to catch up with him, but it seemed a liberty to call his name and compel him to appear.

"Top notch, thanks for asking," he replied. "Been quiet, though. Me and the Men got nothing to do when there's no slaying and pillaging. We did clean out the cave, but the Men didn't like that one bit. Would have thought I'd asked them to take a bath. We only do that at the turn of millennia—"

Lucas cleared his throat.

Slaughter pulled himself up to his full height of probably just under a foot. "Sorry, gov, only I've not seen Camille for a couple of weeks."

Possibly amusement but probably annoyance glimmered in Lucas's eyes. "Have your Men guard the members of the research project, no matter where they go or what they do."

"With much enjoyment and excitement, gov." He disappeared behind a folklorist's leg.

"Good idea," I said. "Do we have any leads on the golden-horned sheep?"

"They belong to the cyclops Bécut. His cave is up near Siguer, just over the bounds. It might be an idea if we pay him a visit."

A real-life cyclops. Another first. But presumably all or most of the creatures in folklore were real, and I needed to get used to it. "Sounds like a plan."

"There have been more acid attacks and gold thefts, too," he said. "Oh, and a dwarf is mining at Rancie."

"Is that unusual?" I noticed Pascale glance over from his conversation with Joly.

"Not in itself." Lucas placed his chunk of wood on the table to his side and brushed off his hands. "But Rancie is only a couple of miles from where Bécut usually keeps his sheep. According to Roux, it's normal for the occasional dwarf to go there for a mining holiday as the place still has plenty of ore, but it's enough of a coincidence for us to check it out."

"And I'm sure I've seen one of the goblins before," I said.

"The gangly one with the ears. I guess it was in fae Tarascon. If I could only remember where..."

"Until we have something to go on with the goblin, let's get the rest of it sorted."

"I have a few hours over lunch and siesta," I said. "Best we get started."

A large grin drew across Lucas's face.

"What?" I snapped.

His grin widened. "Training."

"It's not training," I replied. "It's sorting out my mess of a life."

———

We pulled into the parking area by Rancie mine, not far from Sem village and the dolmen of Sem. Mining records began here in 1294, but the place had fallen into disuse years ago. Now the plateau before the entrance consisted of sheep-cropped grassland over disturbed ground. A few houses were scattered around the edge, and there was a quietness about the area that belied its bustling past.

Heat hit me as we jumped out. Air-con was the only reason we'd taken Lucas's SUV, but I had to admit, his car, brand new after the hantaumo had pulverised the last one, was a lot more comfortable than my truck.

Two forest-clad summits rose before us, the mine situated under the left, a pass rising between the two. Beyond, distant peaks were topped with snow. I drew our blades from the footwell, handed Lucas his and sheathed my own. My scabbard and my Keeper gear were beginning to feel like a second skin.

After joining the pass at the grated-off mine entrance, we branched along an animal track that led up the mountain. There were plenty of open entrances further up. As teenagers, a gang of us, Alice and Guy included, had explored the place as a laugh.

As we wove in and out of chestnuts and beech, I tried to remember where I'd seen that blasted goblin. I also tried not to notice how Lucas's Keeper leathers flexed over his well-developed pecs and pulled tight to his abs. What I really needed was a quiet, normal session with the project this afternoon, followed by a lovely, run-of-the-mill date with Pascale, who was also blessed in the anatomy department, plus he had a whole lot else going for him.

Something flickered in the trees ahead and disappeared over the rise. "Come on," I said.

We jogged up the incline and rounded the top, which gave us a good view of the forest. A small, hunched figure with a pickaxe on his shoulder skitted between the trees and headed into a dark hole—one of the natural caves the miners had utilised.

"Hey," Lucas shouted, but the figure didn't stop.

We ran after, ducking into darkness. I'd been about to pull out my phone for the light, but flaming torches hung from the tunnel walls. A sheen of a glamour surrounded them, no doubt in case of human intrusion.

The dwarf swung around and raised his free hand.

"Whoa, there." His voice was tremulous. "You certainly gave me a surprise."

He was something to look at, his face thickened with age, his nose bulbous, his back hunched under a sort of light armour combined with bulky sheepskin. And the hair... All of it, his eyebrows and beard included, was like steel wire stuck out at all angles.

"Who are you?" Lucas demanded. "What are you doing here?"

"Ras is my name," he muttered, pinprick eyes glinting. "From the Eastern Court. Here on my holidays."

"Mind if we come in?" Lucas pushed past without waiting for an answer.

"It's not my property," the dwarf mumbled. "But might I ask who wants to know?" He scurried after Lucas. I took the rear, my feet crunching on rockfall, the smooth cave walls morphing into a hewn rock passage.

We emerged into a massive circular cavern, the sides lit with torches. Although the light didn't reach far in the immense space, it showed numerous side tunnels, a small makeshift table and a barrel of wine or ale. A slight dank smell hung about, the kind that often lingered in mine workings rather than natural caves, as if water pooled, unable to take its natural course.

"We're Keepers from Tarascon." Lucas's voice echoed.

"I don't want trouble." Ras's fingers tightened around his axe.

"Neither do we," Lucas replied. "Just a brief inspection and we'll be on our way."

"Good, good." Ras added. "It's a nice little mine. Perfect for a getaway and"—he opened his palm to reveal a small chunk of gold ore—"it's not without rewards. Still plenty of minerals left. There's seam upon seam that hasn't been worked." He curled his fingers over the nugget and placed it inside his soft armour, then readjusted his pickaxe. "I'll be here a few more days, then I'll be on my way."

Lucas nodded and headed to the far side of the cavern. I followed, leaving Ras to look on. We paused near the far wall, the air shimmering before us.

"The bounds run around the edge of this part of the cavern," he said. "But there's no sign of bounds cracks."

I peered into the gloom. "If anything, Ras has cleaned the place up." There was usually a scattering of rubbish from teenagers who brought wine and food up here, just as we had.

"Dwarves like a tidy mine. There's nothing suspicious. I think we're good to go." We returned to Ras.

"We've had reports of golden-horned sheep," I said. "Have you seen any?"

"Golden-horned...?" He scratched his cheek. "Curious, but no, I've not."

"We'll be off then," Lucas said. "If you see one, or anything else out of the ordinary, let us know."

"I most certainly will," Ras replied.

We headed out. "Enjoy your holiday," I called.

There came a small, strangulated noise from Lucas's throat. As we walked back down through the woods he said,

"Enjoy your holiday?" He looked as though he didn't know whether to laugh or scowl.

"What?"

"I mean, not 'keep your nose clean or I'll tear out your liver', or 'put a foot wrong and you'll perish painfully by my blade'? 'Enjoy your holiday' isn't exactly the Keeper aesthetic."

There was one good reason for that. "Must be because I'm not a Keeper."

He shook his head.

As we strode into the car park, something glinted amidst a sprinkling of pines to our side. A sheep similar to the Black-Face Manechs that Guy's family farmed stood between the trees. The difference was that this one was much bigger and it had massive golden horns.

"A perfect specimen," Lucas said. "Slaughter."

"Boss." The Man popped out from behind a car.

"Take that sheep back to Bécut."

"We're on it, gov," he replied. "And for your information, a battalion of Men have been posted to the project." I wondered for a moment whether the goblins might be less trouble than a bodyguard of Men, but as Slaughter constantly demonstrated, the little guys had the knack of keeping out of the way.

"Good." Lucas straightened his scabbard. "We need to get to Bécut."

Chapter 16

It took all of fifteen minutes to zoom down remote lanes and tracks as we drove as close as we could to Pic du Midi de Siguer. Then we hiked at a smart pace for twenty minutes. I pulled my mobile out to check the time, but it had died. I'd charged it fully this morning, damn it. I glanced at Lucas's old, expensive-looking watch. We still had plenty of time to make it back for the afternoon session.

We wove our way through a pass, skirting a couple of patches of ore serpent venom. Cliffs rose to our sides, and in the distance, peaks were patched with snow melting early in the warm weather. It was cooler up here, but I still sweltered. And it still niggled me that I couldn't put my finger on where I'd seen the interfering goblin. But figuring out what was going on with the golden-horned sheep had to be a step in the right direction.

We rounded a rock face and the place felt lighter, the air

shimmering. We'd crossed into Fae. To my side, a lightless incision scarred a promontory. More bounds cracks.

Not far after, on the opposite side of the pass, a massive vertical crevice split the cliff. In its midst was a spoulga—a cave fortified with crenellated rock walls. There wasn't a doorway. Presumably the exit lay in the scrub beneath. On the far side, the escarpment sloped down into small rocky meadows.

We climbed up to the bottom of the spoulga. Lucas raised his hands to his mouth. "Andos, Bécut," he hollered.

"Andos, and no need to shout," Bécut replied, his voice booming off the surrounding rock. "Who's asking?"

"Lucas Rouseau and Camille Amiel. Keepers from Tarascon. Come out and talk to us."

"No," came the flat reply.

Well, fair enough.

"Roux said he's shy," Lucas murmured.

"You'd be shy too if you were me," Bécut rumbled. Shy, but with good hearing.

"Cyclopes don't possess much ability to glamour," Lucas added without bothering to lower his voice. "They have a hard time hiding themselves, and due to their size, humans have trouble imagining them into something else. Their general response is to faint. But what cyclopes lack in glamour they make up for in other ways. There isn't a ward in existence they can't break."

"After a few hundred years of fainting," Bécut said, "it starts to be off-putting." I could imagine.

"Is he shy of fae too?" I asked Lucas.

He shrugged. "Most people, fae and human alike, get a bit fixated on the single eye. You don't realise how normal it is to stare into two until there's only one." I thought of the came-cruise that the Men had brought to my apartment. Its one eye had been weird.

"Is there anything I can do to persuade you to come out?" Lucas called.

"No."

Lucas ground his jaw.

It looked like we'd have to communicate from here. "Andos, Bécut," I called. "We need to know why your sheep are scattered everywhere and why humans are seeing them."

"Oh," the giant said. "Yes, scattered. Four days ago. I don't know why it happened, and it's news to me that humans can see them, but I want my flock back. They're my family."

"Can't you go out at night and get them?" Although I didn't know if it was a good idea to have a giant on the loose.

"No. Not going out... not going anywhere... ever. I'll stay in my cave on my land where there's no one around."

"But don't you want to save them?"

"Save them from what? They'll be fine. They'll come back eventually."

"With golden horns," Lucas called, "there's a good reason why they might not."

Soft weeping came from the spoulga, but nothing more.

A movement caught my eye down the pass, a sheep on its back with its legs in the air, zooming toward us with preternatural speed. The Men. Considering the instantaneous way they did most things, they'd taken their time.

"Sorry, boss," Slaughter said as they drew near. "The ewe gave us a bit of trouble. Those horns definitely have a use. Had to restrain her—that was after we lost three Men." The sheep's feet were tied together, and she was snorting in a rather pissed-off way.

The cyclops's weeping turned into gulps. At a wild guess, he was happy the sheep had been returned.

"Untie her in the meadows," Lucas said to the Men.

But there had to be a reason the sheep were scattered. "Bécut," I called, "did you see anything unusual around the time the flock ran off?"

"Hmmm. Let me think."

The Men took the ewe to the field and tipped her onto her side. She thrashed about as they attempted to dive in and cut her leg ties.

"Ummm," Bécut said, "yes, I did see something. Just before they disappeared, two cloaked figures came along the pass, hoods up. I don't get anyone up here. Even the shepherds have enough instinct to keep to the human realm. I thought to myself at the time that it was strange. And one of them... he didn't so much as walk as shuffle and wobble... like he was giddy or maybe drunk. But that was all I saw. Nothing else."

"Giddy... drunk... That's it," I said to Lucas. "I'm not sure who the hooded figures are, but I remember where I'd seen the goblin." About a week ago, I'd parked at the café for my shift, and there had been a kerfuffle coming from the tavern just inside fae Tarascon. The door had swung open and out teetered three goblins of various sizes, so drunk they could barely walk in a straight line. I'd been completely over-whelmed by all the fae—everything was so new—and I hadn't taken in individual characteristics, but one of them had been the scrawny goblin, I was sure of it. "It's time we visited the Peppered Parsnip."

CHAPTER 17

LUCAS AND I ENTERED FAE TARASCON FROM THE PATH alongside the café car park. The fae part of town was lined with old shops. Tree trunks and boughs were built into their timber frames. Hawthorns supported one, its leaves an awning over the windows and door. An ancient oak with sparse foliage formed the sturdy structure of another. Midsummer garlands hung everywhere, and it was difficult to tell where nature ended and architecture began.

The cobbled street bustled with goblins, elves, dwarves and a couple of trolls, which reminded me of something I'd been wanting to ask Lucas. "There are so many different types of fae. Why are there only a few types in fae Tarascon and the café?"

A group of goblins divided around us, eyeing us warily. An elegant elf paused before entering the apothecary and stared, her lips parted.

Lucas didn't seem to notice their reactions. "Some races

are more abundant than others. But most fae are happy in their lands. It's only the curious ones that want anything to do with the human realm."

"Makes sense." A couple more goblins skittered to the other side of the street. "Ummm. Aren't Keepers popular?"

"What makes you think that? From the accounts I've heard, your grandfather was very popular."

"Really? Can't you see all the fae diving for cover?" A bearded man wearing a tunic and sandals hurried to the side.

We reached the Peppered Parsnip. Its signboard above the door featured a half-rotten parsnip and a few other root vegetables. "It's not Keepers they're avoiding," Lucas said, stopping. "And it's not you, Camille. It's me."

I frowned. "Uh, why? Most humans like you fine." Certainly the folklore department of Toulouse University had no problem with him, and he was already a well-liked doctor in the town. Of course, those chiselled features and much-too-intelligent eyes helped. Not to mention the way his jaw flexed, but I didn't need to think of that.

"Most fae can sense my true nature," he said.

"And that guy over there?" I gestured to the man in the tunic who'd taken a sudden interest in a garland of St John's wort.

"He's probably heard of me or my family."

Grampi's warning swam through my head. Couldn't be worse than my father, though.

Three goblins, two clad in leather, and one with armour and a helmet, muttered as we passed. They glared at Lucas, then me. One of them inclined his head to another. "She killed the hantaumo queen."

Huh. So I had a reputation too. But I needed to focus on the task at hand. "Let's get going."

I made to step into the tavern, but Lucas's arm barred my way. "Wait."

I glanced in askance at him.

"It's not the most... civilised of places," he said. "One of the reasons for the uptake at Pyrenee's—that and the brioche, of course. I'm just warning you."

"Alright." I'd been in my share of dives.

"And in case these goblins and troll of yours are hanging out inside, I'll take the back door." He disappeared around the corner.

The crowd relaxed and went about their business without a care in the world now Lucas was out of sight. I studied the iron-studded wooden door. I didn't have a clue what I'd do if the scumbags were in there, but I could wing it. I made to grasp the hilt of my sword, then paused. A drawn blade might be too confrontational, especially if the fae in question weren't there. Leaving my sword in its scabbard, I stepped inside.

My immediate impression as the door swung closed behind me was chaos. Goblin after goblin of all shapes and sizes mixed with a few trolls. Hens sat everywhere, on tables, on trolls, some on the bare boughs of the trees from which the place was built. There were also two goats and a sarramauca —a hairy black cat-like thing that suffocated people in their sleep. It sat alone, empty seats around it.

The tavern clamoured in a cacophony of shouts, whoops, raucous laughter, slurred conversation, clanking tankards, slamming fists, catcalls, clucks and bleats. One goblin, standing on a table, played a lute badly. Another jumped up and joined him, singing. The bar stood along the back wall, stacked with barrels and jewel-coloured glass bottles. A couple of wizened goblins served beer and cusses to their customers.

Noticing me, every head, avian and caprine included, turned my way. The room hushed.

Uncomfortable, much? I fought the instinct to creep back out as I scanned the place. I had no idea how I'd find my fae in here—or even where to begin asking for information.

There was a movement in the far corner. Two creatures sprang up, plunged across the floor and barrelled out of a door by the bar. It had to be them.

Before I could move, a crash came from out back, then a smash and a tinkle, followed by groaning. Lucas strode in, a goblin in each hand, dangling by the scruffs of their tunics. The collective gaze swung from me to him.

"These yours, Camille?" he asked.

There wasn't a shadow of a doubt. The small osencame with the snout and the scrawny goblin with the big ears looked horror-struck in Lucas's grip.

Fury bubbled in my blood. "You!" I cried. "Why are you messing with my project?"

They shrank into themselves. The large one shot a glance up at Lucas and shuddered. Lucas shook them and they spluttered, half choking in their collars.

As I stepped toward them, something hit me on the back of the head and gooped down my neck. I turned around, and the room drew a breath. The river troll stood by the far wall, a leer on his face, a handful of eggs in his palm. He threw another, which splatted on my forehead and didn't exactly do much for my mood.

I scraped it off. "You little—"

With battle cries, Lucas's captors began wiggling and stamping. One threw orange dust into Lucas's eyes. He screwed them tight. The goblins scratched and tore at his wrists. I ran over to help him, but they pulled free before I could get there, and with their escape, a mighty roar rose from the clientele.

If I'd thought the room was chaotic previously, now it was a symphony of anarchy. Numerous items of food had appeared from nowhere. Eggs, potatoes, carrots and onions flew around, striking creatures left, right and centre. Their wielders hollered with varying degrees of merriment or fury. Hens fluttered and squawked. Goats butted. Goblins wrestled each other, or poured ale over their compadres' heads.

With Lucas flailing and unable to see, my fae made an attempt to run. The backdoor was blocked by a mean-looking goat, so they pelted for the front, but they couldn't get past a mass of goblins wrestling a troll. I charged through the throng and threw myself at the creeps, catching one by the belt and the other by its jerkin. My weight brought us down onto a pile of straw. Another egg landed on my butt.

Whilst I struggled with the squirming goblins, the river troll, deplete of missiles, ran at Lucas. Having regained some of his sight, Lucas dove out the way. The troll crashed into the bar, wedging himself well and truly in.

My critters wouldn't stop struggling. As I clambered on top of them, pinning down their limbs, something jumped onto my back. A hairy sensation came over me, as if my nose and mouth were filled with fluff. I gasped for breath, desperately clawing at my face. The goblins gained leverage and darted away.

Squirming and twisting and choking, I pushed myself up. Whatever was on my back sprang down, and the fluff sensation abated. The hairy sarramauca walked off with a flick of its tail, fae instinctively giving it a wide berth. I hauled in delicious mouthfuls of air, but my goblins were almost at the exit. Lucas hurled two wine bottles at them.

Clank. Clank.

The bottles struck the centre of their heads. One goblin, then the other, dropped to the ground.

And still the commotion raged. Bored with root vegetables, some fae were clouting each other with sticks. Furniture had become the weapon du jour, though, and chairs swung about. A couple of goblins were headbutting each other, and the goats were doing plenty of damage with their horns.

Lucas hauled in a deep breath. "Enough!" he bellowed.

The tavern stilled.

My goblins stirred. I jumped up, blocked the entrance door and drew my blade. "Get up."

They scrambled to their feet, the large one swaying from side to side. "Over there." I inclined my head, and they shuffled reluctantly to where Lucas was attempting to haul the giant bowling ball of a river troll from the bar.

One of the serving goblins came out with a metal pail and waved it under the nearest customer's nose. "You know the rules. You breaks, you pays, or you fixes." A hapless goblin dropped in a pouch of herbs. The room began to stir as some fae set about straightening the mess and others fished in their pockets.

Lucas pulled the troll free and drew his blade, his eyes red and swollen above a mean grimace. He indicated for the creature to stand with the others. They goggled at him. The little osencame shook, its snout trembling.

"Right," I growled. "What's going on?" Fury twisted through me. Fury and something I couldn't put my finger on... something strangely light. "Why are you ruining my research project?"

The rest of the clientele continued tidying as though they hadn't a care for what we were doing—all apart from the myriad of twitching ears.

The three critters exchanged looks. The small one shrugged, her nose trembling some more. I could see her evil face as she threw Madame Mazet's photograph off the sideboard. I had to restrain myself from skewering her.

"Memes, ain't it, Gidditch," she said to the bigger goblin.

Gidditch nodded earnestly, undulating on his scrawny legs. "Wheezle's got it right. Memes are trouble."

"Memes?" I really didn't get it. "Explain."

Gidditch inclined his head to the troll. "Eggnog got made into a meme. It's all over the socials. And offensive it is.

Nasty. They made him look meaner than he is, too. It's abuse against trolls, that's what it is."

Memes were a recent form of folklore. Even so, I didn't get it. "Someone took a photo of you? Is that possible?" I glanced at Lucas.

He shook his head. "Some complex glamours hold in photos, but I doubt this lot would have bothered. Usually fae can't be captured digitally or on film."

The sarramauca strode toward us, fae easing away as it progressed through the room. It sat down by Eggnog. One thing was for sure, I wasn't going to let it jump on me again.

"Not a photo," Eggnog said, as if we were stupid. "It was a drawing. A likeness. And it said that trolls are brainless. Really unfair stuff."

"So we had a few drinks," Wheezle added with a sniffle. "And we decided we should do something about it. Or at least stop it happening again."

"And it's not just trolls," Gidditch said. "There are all sorts of memes about goblins, elves and dwarves, too. We realised that the problem is folklore. We get a bad reputation. There are all kinds of stories about us. When we heard that a load of highfalutin folklore researchers were here from some important university—"

"We had to put a stop to it," Eggnog put in, shuffling his feet.

"You're kidding me?" Was I hearing this right? There were more glances and shrugs. "You've made a mess of every-thing, just because of a meme?" I could barely believe it. My blade hand trembled as I battled the urge to slice them in two.

Lucas's eyes were narrowed in disbelief. He stepped behind Eggnog and secured his blade against the troll's throat. Sweat poured from Eggnog's rotund brow. "Go on the internet," Lucas said, "you'll find bad memes. That's no reason to endanger humans." Blood trickled from Eggnog's neck.

"What do we do with them now?" I said. "No way are they going free to mess with my life."

"Slice their throats," Lucas said, "and that would be lenient."

The three of them searched around for another means of escape. Eggnog had no chance, and Wheezle was trapped in the middle, but Gidditch darted forward, making it about a step before I swung my blade in an arc and stilled the point at his gut. A large object fell from his tunic and clinked to the ground. A golden horn

I picked it up. It weighed a ton—it had to be worth a fortune.

The three fae gulped.

"Where did you get it?" Lucas rumbled.

It couldn't be a coincidence. The same critters that had wrecked my project had a golden horn. Plus, the scrawny one couldn't walk in a straight line, like the hooded figure Bécut had mentioned.

"We just found it," Gidditch said, wobbling even more. "Up on the other side of Cousterous. On the ground, like."

"Like on the ground, or actually on the ground?" I asked.

Gidditch cringed.

Lucas released Eggnog, stepped in front of the fae and ran his blade across Eggnog's and Gidditch's middles, slicing open their clothes, then he held the point to Wheezle's snout. "I think you might know more than you're letting on. Now really is a good time to speak, before you lose body parts."

"We don't know anything other than that," Wheezle snuffled. "Finders keepers. That gold's ours."

"Looks like I found it, then," I said.

"Slaughter," Lucas called.

The Man appeared, axe at the ready, no doubt because of the surroundings. "Can't believe you didn't call us to help with the scrap, gov." It was the first time I'd seen him look put out.

Lucas ignored the accusation. "Take these fae to Les Calbières and have them clear up all the ore serpent acid there and in the area. I've prepared a neutralising solution. It's in the Keepers' post. It should be enough to get them started. I'll give you the recipe to make more. Keep your eyes on them at all times."

The trio sagged.

"At the rate the ore serpents are going," Slaughter replied, "that will take forever."

Lucas managed a twisted smile. "Perfect. If at any moment they decide to let us know what's really going on, bring them to me."

"Sorted," I said.

A throng of Men guided the protesting fae out of the door whilst attempting to avoid the sarramauca, who followed in their wake. We sheathed our blades and walked out after them.

As we stepped into the afternoon heat, the sun baking egg into my hair, I breathed away my irritation. I still couldn't believe it—memes. But the project could proceed without interference.

That other feeling I'd felt before grew... that lightness. It rose from my middle to my throat, then tugged at my lips until a broad smile shaped my mouth. I paused on the top step, my hand on the wall. I'd felt the same after I'd fought the charognards. Despite my love for folklore research, I'd always been a physical person. I needed to move, whether it was with swordplay or running. The scuffle in the tavern had felt free—wild—as though a part of me was untangling. That part of me needed this so much. I needed this so much.

Lucas faced me, his eyes red and bloodshot. He raised an eyebrow. "What?"

"I've just been pelted with eggs and sat on by a sarra-mauca amongst everything else. I can't believe I'm going to say this, but... that was damned good fun."

Chapter 18

I left fae Tarascon and strode across the café car park, a spring in my step. The golden-horned sheep problem hadn't been sorted yet, but there would be no more goblins interfering with the project. Now I could get on with repairing the damage.

My hair was still wet from the wash I'd given it at the Keepers' post. There had only been soap verte, so I was in for frizz. Not a professional look, but at least the egg was out. I'd managed to wash the rest of me in the kitchen too, and I'd pulled on the change of clothes I kept there. Considering I'd been in a bar brawl, I'd cleaned up alright.

I had hoped to make it back much earlier to the events room to double-check my tasks were done and show commitment. According to the clock at the Keepers' post, I was still five minutes early. Everyone else would be there already, but considering I'd saved the project from disaster, it was well worth being the last one in.

The café's Sunday-afternoon chilled vibe warmed me as I entered, French gypsy playing softly on the sound system. The place was pretty busy. Max glared at me then turned away. The D&D gang sans Gabe was still in the nook and engrossed in a campaign. Had they actually moved since yesterday? The part-time staff were behind the counter, and the kitchen was quiet, although Guy had to be somewhere as he was supervising.

I headed to the events room and pushed the door open, but the equipment-filled tables were devoid of life. No Joly, no Pascale, no students. Just an eerie silence.

Where was everyone? I dropped my glamoured Keeper-gear bag and blade under my desk, my stomach swishing. There must have been a change of plan—that was all. Maybe a later meet-up. They would've let me know, but my phone had died.

Someone's charger lay in a socket behind me. I plugged my phone in and switched on the power. I'd been so sure I'd charged it fully this morning, but it would come on in a couple of minutes, and then I'd find out what was going on.

After typing the new schedule into my laptop, I returned to my phone and clicked it on. A shiny blank screen stared at me. Damn it. It couldn't have chosen a worse time to give up the ghost. I needed some other way to find out where everyone was.

I went back into the café and made my way to the till, dodging customers.

"Camille!" Guy called as he plated up a pain aux raisins. He truly never had an apathetic moment.

I leant on the counter. "Guy... the project. Where is everyone?"

"Oh, they went out maybe half an hour after you and the doc left. That woman, Joly, came in wanting filled baguettes for the lot of them right in the middle of the lunch rush."

Okay, so it had been a change of plan.

"How come you don't know about it?" Guy said.

"My phone broke."

"Bummer." He flicked his hair from his face. "But I guess they should be back any minute now. They still want afternoon coffee. I'm just about to make it."

Good. "They must be running late. I don't think there's any point in doing drinks until they return."

"Sure," he said, before taking an order.

The mandragore in its jar above the espresso machine caught my eye. I still needed to figure out what to do with the poor thing. I stepped around the counter behind Guy and surreptitiously peered up at it whilst pretending to look for something on the shelf. The creature had fallen asleep, its scrunched-up face pressed against the glass, its chest rising and falling steadily. It looked alright. I'd ask Lucas what to do with it once the meeting was over.

I headed back to the events room and sat before my laptop, gazing at *Recent Experiences of Ancient Folkloric Phenomena*, which lay forlornly on Joly's desk. There wasn't much I could do until everyone returned. I checked my socials to see if anything had been posted about where they were. That came up blank, so I went over the schedule again, struggling to ignore the swishing in my gut. There was no need to worry. They'd be back any minute.

Half an hour passed. I'd well and truly memorised the schedule and I'd finished an article in *Folklore* magazine on devil's footprints. My gut had progressed from swishing to churning. Joly was so organised, Pascale too. They would've thought to call and postpone afternoon refreshments if they'd made other plans or been delayed.

But it struck me, the Men were guarding the project, and they would've reported if something had happened—if anything *could* happen to sixteen folklorists. Anyway, I could check.

"Slaughter." I waited for him to appear from beneath the table. Nothing. I tried again without success. Slaughter had always popped up instantaneously, apart from the time we were trapped inside the hantaumo ward. This was making me nervous.

But I had everyone's details on my laptop. If I could just make contact... Email was a possibility, but text might mean a faster response. I went back to the café and pushed past the queue at the till. "Guy, can I borrow your phone for a mo?"

"Still no folklorists?" he asked.

"Nope."

He passed a receipt to a lady, then drew his mobile from his pocket, unlocked it and handed it over.

"You're a star," I said.

"An about-to-be-very-rich star," he called, inclining his head to the mandragore.

Inside the events room, I brought up Pascale's details and

texted him. *It's Camille on a different number. I'm at the café and no one's here. Did you have a change of plan?*

Waiting for a response, I continually tapped the screen so the phone wouldn't lock. But nothing. I called Pascale, and it went to voicemail. There was a chance he was out of range or his phone was out of battery. I tried Meera too, also with no reply. Five minutes of sitting there tapping Guy's phone and still nothing.

I'd better text Joly. I didn't want to—I didn't want to appear unprofessional—but I had to do it. *Hi, Camille here. I didn't get the info about the change of plans. Can you let me know the new schedule for the day?*

I sat there, tapping Guy's phone, my muscles tight. But it really wouldn't be all that unusual for them to be out of range. There were plenty of dead spots in the mountains.

Guy poked his head around the door. "I've found your crew."

"Oh?"

"Yeah. I was just on the phone to Maman. Apparently Old Len told Elsa Basket, who told Shroom-Jean, who told Madame Ballon, who told Maman that he'd seen a group of people at Rancie with video equipment. A whole load of cars were parked up by the mine, one of them partially blocking the gateway to Mean Gert's field. He was having a right rant about it because there's plenty of space to park down there. Took him ages to edge the tractor through.

"Thanks." I handed Guy his phone then paced about the empty room. Rancie plus Slaughter not answering. I had a bad feeling.

We'd seen a golden-horned sheep near the mine, so it was likely the project were there for sightings, although it was strange they'd all gone to the same place. But Slaughter not appearing... that was too suspicious.

I had to check it out. If they were fine, I could join them. Joly's Range Rover and Pascale's ancient Citroën would be easy to spot if they were heading back, so I wouldn't miss them.

I returned to my desk and tapped out an email to Lucas. *The project has gone to Rancie, probably for golden-horned sheep sightings. I'm going to meet them. Letting you know as a precaution as Slaughter isn't answering and my phone's died.*

One thing was for sure, I wasn't going to wait around here.

Chapter 19

Pascale's Citroën was parked outside the mine. I pulled in next to it. Guy's informant had been right. The project was here... somewhere. I jumped out and glanced at the scattering of houses, but there were no open doors, distant voices or anything to indicate folklorists. The group might have gone to the mine. It had a fascinating history with all kinds of associated traditions.

Something moved in the forest above the grated-off tunnel. It was too upright to be an animal. Perhaps it was Ras. I could ask him if he'd seen anyone, but... but what? Did I really think something was going on? I guess it didn't harm to be cautious, especially as the place felt creepy today. It was too quiet, although that was probably my overactive imagination. My Keeper gear was in the truck. Just in case, I shouldered my scabbard and blade.

Heading to where I'd seen the movement, I strode across the car park and through the forest. My ears buzzed in the quiet as I searched about, skirting brambles, fallen branches and the occasional patch of ore serpent venom.

I caught a flicker in the trees ahead. Instinctively, I tucked behind the nearest oak, the hairs on my arms rising and my heart pounding as footsteps thudded toward me. But I was being ridiculous. It was probably one of the project or Ras.

The steps thumped past. I risked a glance. Two massive charognards marched in the direction of the mine entrance that Lucas and I had investigated earlier. A tree trunk extended between their shoulders, and tied to it, dangling upside down by its feet, was a struggling and furious golden-horned sheep. Those monkey critters came in super-size, and I hadn't taken them as intelligent enough to be sheep rustlers.

Behind the sheep hung a basket. As the charognards turned the corner, its contents came into view—jewellery and pieces of armour, all of it made of gold. Suspicious? Definitely. But it didn't necessarily indicate involvement with the project.

The charognards disappeared over the rise. Halfway up, something lay on the mulch. A shoe. I was too far away to be certain, but it looked like one of Joly's strappy sandals. Shit.

As quietly as possible, I stepped closer, the creepiness building to a sickening unease.

"Don't you dare touch me!" The yell came from the direction of the mine. I stepped forward but my head spun wildly, my vision growing fuzzy, my heart pounding in my throat. What the hell was happening? I stumbled and caught hold of the nearest tree, but my knees buckled and the forest dimmed.

Something grabbed me and hauled me over its shoulder. "Get your hands off me!" I yelled, thrashing about, but a mirky gauze lay over everything—even my panic. My mind was a fog, my blood icy cold. The ground rushed past as whatever had me in its grip sprinted through the forest. It was speaking softly, but I couldn't make out the words. I struggled and shouted some more. The creature drew to a halt, swung me down and propped me against a tree.

The mirk eased a little. I rubbed my eyes and the woodland became clearer. Two legs stepped into my line of vision. They bent at the knees, and Lucas's pensive mouth and assessing eyes appeared. "Shhhhh," he said. "We have to be quiet. You okay now?"

The mirk sank away some more, but every cell in my body screamed that we had to get out of here.

"Camille, speak to me," he said.

"Uh, I'm fine," I managed, my vision levelling.

"We need to get away—run. Either that or I carry you. But we have to do it as quietly and quickly as we can."

"I'm fine," I murmured, getting up. And I really was. Everything had returned to normal. We pelted through the forest, passing small heaps of animal skins near the car park, some of them stirring.

"Slaughter, get up," Lucas hissed, not waiting for a response. "Get into my car," he said to me, pulling my keys from my pocket. He clearly had an idea what was going on, so I wasn't going to argue. I climbed in. Lucas pulled my bag from my truck then jumped behind the wheel of the SUV. His foot hit the accelerator and we shot toward the village.

As we took the bends through Sem down to the valley and the Tarascon road, I breathed deeply, coming fully back to myself.

"Better?" Lucas asked.

"Just about." Although my heart still thrashed. "What the hell happened?"

He swung the car around a hair-pin bend. "A black ward."

"A what?"

"It's the strongest form of defensive ward. It's so powerful it's not even possible to get near. You stepped too close."

I turned to him, taking in his angular cheekbone, his mess of hair. "If you hadn't arrived...?"

"You had about five minutes." He stared ahead. "I'm glad you sent me that email."

Me too. I slumped back. "You saved me." Again.

"Touché. It wasn't much fun having my chest ripped open by the hantaumo queen."

I'd saved him after he'd saved my butt multiple times. Yes, he was the one who'd gotten me into danger in the first place by giving me the verity, although if the hantaumo queen had come for me, and I'd not been prepared... I shuddered.

"It's what partners do." He had to add *that*. I shot him a sideways glance. He met my gaze and smiled sweetly.

"I'm still pissed about yesterday morning, though." I shook my head.

He laughed.

"And we're heading away from Rancie at high speed for a reason?" The road was rushing past much too quickly.

"Ras has to be involved with whatever's going on back there. If he can make a black ward, then he's extremely powerful. In a confrontation, we wouldn't stand a chance, but we should be far enough away by now." He slowed a little. "When did your mobile stop working?"

"When we were at the mine this morning. At the time, I thought the battery had died."

"Me too. It's my guess that Ras was projecting a massive glamour so we couldn't see what he was up to. Our phones were fried. Check the glove box."

I clicked it open. A packaged phone lay inside.

"One of my spares," he said. "Take it. I keep a few. I don't always come out of Fae with mine in one piece."

I pulled it out and set about transferring my sim. "I saw Joly's shoe in the forest. I was heading over to pick it up. I also saw two charognards hauling a golden-horned sheep and a basket of gold into the cave."

He nodded. "Even more reports are coming in of gold being stolen in Fae. Seems like Ras is behind it, though I have no idea what he's up to."

A small, bushy chestnut head appeared in the gap between our seats. Even though Slaughter clutched the leather on either side, he swayed, his eyes rolling about. He tried to rub his jaw but almost fell into the back. "Reporting in, boss," he slurred.

"What happened to the folklorists?" Lucas asked.

"They were in Sem for golden-horned sheep sightings, then they wanted to look in the mine. As they went up there, me and a battalion of Men were keeping an eye on them from the trees a little way back, and that's the last I knew of it. I'm thinking we was ambushed from behind, maybe with rocks or something blunt."

"I'm surprised whoever it was didn't kill you," Lucas said. "Which means they're so confident in their defences they can afford to be shoddy."

"I heard a shout, so they're alive," I said. Despite everything I'd done to protect the project, all of them, including *the* Margot Joly, had been kidnapped by fae. I dragged my hands over my face. Pascale and Meera... I hoped to hell they were alright.

Lucas's brow lowered. "The ward would've prevented the project from accidentally stumbling across whatever is going on in the mine, so it's likely they've been taken for a reason. Though what Ras wants them for, I have no idea."

One thing was for sure, the research project was utterly beyond redemption.

Chapter 20

The old wooden door of the Keepers' post swung open on chunky iron hinges as Lucas and I pushed inside. I'd called Roux to tell him to meet us here so we could put our heads together and figure out our next step. He was ridding a house of scraples and would come as soon as he'd finished, otherwise the house was going to fall down and crush the family, who, not being able to see the problem, refused to leave. I had no idea what scraples were, but I imagined having Roux, the town vagrant who sported only the most ragged wizard wear, telling you your house was about to crumble wasn't the most persuasive incentive for evacuation.

It was pleasantly cool inside, despite the range being alight all the time. I guessed there was some kind of temperature-control ward, and it was a welcome break from the furnace outdoors. The aroma of old parchment, metal and herbs met us, and light spilled through the open lattice windows, casting diamonds across weapons on their wall mountings.

Gabe sat at the round table in the centre of the room. "Hey, Camille, Lucas," he called. "Or should I say, Andos." Roux's training, no doubt.

Lucas grinned. "No need between friends, unless you haven't seen them for a long time."

"Waiting for Roux?" I asked.

"Yeah, he said to meet him here." Gabe turned something over in his fingers.

"There's no point starting without him," Lucas said. "I'll make coffee while we wait." He headed into the kitchen.

"Hey, I thought I better mention"—Gabe stilled his fingers—"I saw a shiny monkey-like ugly thing in the wisteria growing up the boulangerie opposite."

"Sounds like a charognard," I said. Another one.

"It was just sitting there," he added, "staring across at the Keepers' door."

"Curious," Lucas called from the kitchen as he filled the kettle. "There have been a few sightings around town. It's not their natural environment."

"Thanks for letting us know," I said as I undid my scabbard and hung it on the back of my chair. Gabe gawked at it —at me—with wonder as he usually did, but I didn't feel so wonderful right at this moment. I sat down, leant on the table and rubbed my eyes. I'd damned well lost my folklore research project, and the week was shot to pieces. I could only hope no one had been harmed.

A spear of anger pierced my chest. I should be having a

nice, quiet week geeking out with them all. Fae were going to be the end of me. But, all that aside, we had to help. If only Roux would get his ass here.

The object in Gabe's fingers sparkled in the sunlight. It was the amethyst twenty-faceted D&D die that had helped him overcome his possession by a hantaumo. I swallowed. That night had been something else. We'd all been through hell. It wasn't unusual for me to wake in the night sweat-drenched and terrified, but Gabe was sixteen years old. He should've been dealing with girls, not ghouls. No, wait, he did deal with Nora. He revealed the hidden world to her, tied her up in a basement and threatened her with a knife. Nope... not dealing with girls, then. But at least playing D&D with the guys.

"Hey," I said softly as Lucas clattered in the kitchen. "You're not playing D&D anymore. What's up with you and Félix... and the rest of the gang?"

"Nothing, really." He rested his arms on the table and passed the die from hand to hand.

"Doesn't look like nothing to me."

He shot me a lightning-quick glance, then studied the die intently, his jaw clenched. "The game, the D&D quests," he murmured. "None of it's anything compared to what I've seen. The guys wouldn't understand—how could they?" His usually gentle eyes hardened as he tapped the die against the table. "They don't have a clue."

A feeling I knew all too well. I took a deep breath and sighed. "Alice. We've been friends since the beginning. Our mothers used to get us together as babies. I can't tell her about any of this. She's dating a goblin and she doesn't know it, plus she doesn't understand why I'm keeping certain company." I glanced at Lucas, who was pouring hot water into the coffee pot. His gaze met mine. It was as though he was always aware of me.

"I noticed the goblin," Gabe said. "Raphaël seems like an okay guy, but is it ethical? I mean, he *can't* tell her, but it just isn't right, her not knowing."

"My thoughts exactly. That's my problem, and I miss sharing everything with her. We used to be so open."

Gabe met my gaze. "Same."

I forced a smile, then we stared into nothing for a moment until a thought occurred. "There's Nora."

Gabe winced, his bottom lip wobbling. "What I did to her..." he muttered. "I... I... I shouldn't have..."

I sat up and faced him. "Would you have abducted her, tied her up and held her at knife point without being possessed by a hantaumo?"

"I... I mean, she was such a bitch. She was the bitch queen from hell. She was the psycho bitch queen, empress of the legions of darkness. I really wanted to."

A stifled chuckle came from the kitchen. I shot Lucas a glare. It wasn't possible to have a private conversation with him around.

"But would you really?" I said. "We all have... impulses—it's whether we act on them that's important."

"Of course I wouldn't have," Gabe replied.

"Exactly." My shoulders dropped. Finally, we'd gotten there. "She knows you were possessed and that you wouldn't have acted that way toward her with free will, and she chose to keep her awareness of fae. She knows what you know."

"She thinks I'm a freak... I am a freak—I let that thing..."

"No," I said firmly. "It used you. And to hell with what anyone thinks. You did the right thing in the end. We wouldn't have defeated the hantaumo without you. You're made of solid stuff, Gabe."

For a second, there was a twitch of a lip as he almost grinned.

"You could talk to her," I ventured as Lucas brought the coffee things over on an ancient wooden tray.

Gabe's face fell. "That's never going to—"

The door swung open. Finally, Roux was here and we could get on with sorting this mess out. But it wasn't a ragged cloak that stepped in, but a chequered shirt and a snowy-white beard. Grampi.

I stiffened. He was incongruous here. Completely out of place. But this had been his headquarters for years, and although I knew he'd been here regularly since he could communicate again, I hadn't. I'd been focussing on the project. Once again, I was having to join the dots between worlds. And by the glint in Grampi's eye, he wasn't happy.

"What's going on?" He swung his gaze between Lucas and me as Lucas transferred the coffee things to the table. "Everyone's gold is missing."

"That's not the only thing missing right now," I replied.

Grampi studied my face intently. "Camille, you look terribly pale." No doubt my encounter with the black ward. But he wasn't only concerned—annoyance was clear in the narrowing of his eyes. "What happened?" He glared at Lucas as though he was the root of all my problems.

The door opened and Roux stumbled in, his beard tangled, his face red, though for once, he didn't have his staff. He itched his sides through his cloak. "Damn scraples. Got them eventually by bringing in a whole lot of sarramaucas from Fae. They love eating the critters." He pulled up his sleeves to reveal long scratches. "Half the job was getting the sarramaucas back into their cat baskets. Couldn't exactly leave them around to suffocate everyone." He drew out a chair and flopped into it. "Right, what's going on?"

Lucas slid us all coffees then sat down. Roux and Gabe took theirs with appreciative nods. Grampi ignored Lucas. He took a stool from the kitchen and sat on it by the wall, his stiff posture and jutting jaw radiating aggression. His glare was fixed on Lucas as he fiddled with the strap of a crossbow that hung from its wall mounting, teasing the leather between his fingers. Way to be a team player, Grampi. I was so not used to him being like this, and it crushed me.

Gabe eyed him warily.

I attempted to ignore Grampi. "The members of my research project have been kidnapped by a dwarf. He's holding them in Rancie mine." Boy, I hoped they were alright. "The dwarf is also hoarding gold, so that might explain the thefts."

Grampi shook his head.

"So that's where the gold's going," Roux muttered, picking up his cup. "How is he stealing it?"

"No idea. Although charognards could be involved." Lucas sipped his coffee. "The dwarf has a black ward."

Grampi and Roux turned to him, eyes wide.

"You have to be joking?" Grampi glanced at me. "That's why you look so terrible?"

"Thanks for the compliment." I clamped my tongue to prevent me from saying more.

"But that would mean a massive amount of power." Roux's wild eyebrows rose. "Whoever is involved would have to be one of the singular fae or deific. And to go to so much trouble, they must be up to something serious."

"A dwarf deity?" Gabe's gaze flickered between us.

"There's plenty to choose from," Roux replied. "Although there could be another being behind the dwarf."

"The name... Ras. Is it anything to go on?" I asked.

"It's just a typical dwarf name," Lucas said. "Probably a pseudonym."

I sat back. "What does he want with the project? Though I suppose they could have been in the wrong place at the wrong time. And there's still the unexplained behaviour of the ore serpents, and the question of why normal folk can see golden-horned sheep."

Gabe fiddled with his cloak and shot a look at Roux, who was shifting in his chair, focussing solely on his coffee cup. There was definitely something going on, and by the way Lucas's eyes were narrowed, studying them intently, he thought the same thing. It had started when I'd mentioned Bécut's sheep...

But then, Roux was completely unsteady on his feet.

Could it be...? "Bécut said he saw two hooded figures when his sheep disappeared. One of them wobbling all over the place. I thought it had been that Gidditch goblin, but..." I glared at Roux.

Lucas's lips twitched as he turned to the mage. "What did you do?" There was a dangerous edge to his voice.

Roux looked this way and that. "Well, well, well... I mean, it was just one of those things."

"It wasn't his fault," Gabe blurted. We all turned to him, and he shrank into the collar of his cloak.

"Now, now, boy," Roux said. "No need to explain."

"Oh, I think an explanation is more than necessary," Lucas growled. Gabe's eyes almost popped out. Grampi's eyes merely rolled, unimpressed with Lucas's inner drac coming to the fore.

"It was just the revealing potion we were working on," Gabe said, his voice high, his words hurried. "We thought Bécut's sheep would make good test subjects. He keeps them so far away from anyone, and most of the time they're in Fae anyway. I used my Nerf guns to sprinkle them with potion and they got a bit excited. Charged off." Gabe's hands were trembling, largely due to the death gaze Lucas was boring into his skull.

"A little miscalculation," Roux blustered. "The flock's reaction was a small point we hadn't considered. The potion did seem to rile them somewhat."

I tried to hold back a smile. I could see this was serious, but all the same... Grampi wasn't being so subtle, glaring at Lucas as his laughter barked out. He wasn't amused at Roux and Gabe, he was ridiculing Lucas's annoyance. Irritation rose up in me. This really was too much. But then it must be hard... or at least weird for Grampi. Lucas had replaced him as one of the Keepers. Perhaps he was struggling to accept that things were moving on.

"A small point?" Lucas said, glowering. "Everyone in town has seen the sheep. If we're not careful, we're going to draw the sort of attention that wouldn't be good for any of us."

"Yes, well..." Roux squirmed. "The whole affair was highly regrettable. Lessons learnt and all that."

"But if the two goblins and the troll hadn't started the sheep thing," I said, "then how are they involved?" Perhaps they *had* just found the horn.

Grampi continued to laugh. Lucas's glower transferred to him, his lips peeled back. If he had hackles, they would've been raised. I guessed he wouldn't spring on an old-timer, but I wasn't going to take the chance. Time for a change of subject. "So how much gold has been stolen?"

Relieved by the distraction, Roux dropped his shoulders. "Half of fae Tarascon has reported a theft."

"What? Not the human side of town?" I asked.

"Human gold doesn't hold the same degree of power as fae gold," Lucas replied. "Fae tend to avoid it."

"And I have a dwarf informant," Roux added, "who told me that in their court alone, they've had ten tons of gold stolen. And that's just one court. There are hundreds of others." He glanced between us.

Lucas's and Grampi's mouths dropped in unison.

"It's not actually that much gold in volume," Gabe said, tapping his phone. "Melted down, a ton of gold would make a cube with sides of about sixteen inches, and would be worth around sixty-eight million euros."

My turn for a jaw drop.

Lucas gulped down his coffee then placed his cup on the table. "The dwarves control Fae's mineral resources, and as gold is one of our forms of currency, it makes them powerful."

"The dwarves must be livid," Roux said.

"But what does Ras want all that gold for?" I asked. It wasn't as if Fae had a consumer society.

"Why, there's only one reason, of course," Roux said, sitting up.

"Magic," Gabe squeaked.

Everyone nodded.

"Ummm, forgive me if I'm wrong," I said. "But if they have tons of gold, isn't that going to be one hell of a spell... collude?"

Roux pursed his lips. "One hell of a collude, indeed."

CHAPTER 21

A COLLUDE WAS A COLLABORATION BETWEEN THE WILL of a person and the force within a substance such as a herb. For more oomph, various minerals were used. Most potent of all was gold. That much I'd picked up during the hantaumo affair. Gold meant power, and Ras definitely had that if the black ward was anything to go by, but what else was he going to use the gold for? I poured cream into my coffee and took a sip, gazing around at the others at the table and Grampi near the kitchen.

"The time of year has to be significant." Lucas slid his chair back and crossed an ankle over his leg.

"You don't say," Grampi snapped.

Grinding came from Lucas's jaw.

I glared at Grampi. Would he just cut it out so we could get on with finding the project?

"Most definitely," Roux said. "Midsummer and the sun

are associated with gold, and the metal is most potent at this time of year, with the sun at its annual zenith."

"So could Ras be planning something with the gold on midsummer's day?" I asked.

"For maximum power, midsummer's at midday would be ideal." Roux frowned. "But the sun has masses of strength a week either side. There's really not much difference."

"So there's a chance he could use the gold at any time," Lucas added. "But bearing in mind it's midsummer's eve tomorrow, we need to get this sorted now."

Roux tapped his fingers on the table. "Of course, the metal has an affinity with Abellion, the sun god, ruler of the Pyrenean pantheon."

"He wouldn't be behind this, would he?" I asked.

Grampi shook his head. "Not his style. Doesn't often get involved with the human realm, and he's so powerful, he wouldn't need the gold."

"And the bounds at the dolmen of Sem this morning?" Lucas asked Roux.

"The bounds are fine." Roux straightened his cloak. "But the cracks are a little worse again. The small patch we saw when we were up there before the hantaumo attack is now a couple of feet wide and extending toward the dolmen. The locals are instinctively keeping away from the place."

I could understand why. The atmosphere around the cracks in the cave on Monsieur Pons's farm hadn't been pleasant.

Lucas sat back and dragged his hand over his mouth. "I don't like it. The bounds run through Rancie. We checked them when we visited the mine and didn't see anything, but Ras had a potent glamour in operation. It fried our phones."

"What would he want with the bounds?" Gabe asked, his eyebrows knotted.

Lucas drew in a breath through his nose. "I don't know."

I placed my cup down. "So we need to figure out what Ras has planned for the gold, then we need to get into Rancie and rescue the project."

Grampi sprang up and paced about.

"To get through a black ward," Roux said, "it would take a Collude of Exceptional Infiltration. But a number of its ingredients are extremely rare. We don't have them in stock, although we might be able to gather them in, say... twelve hours at a push."

"Bécut could probably break through the ward," Lucas said.

"Good luck with getting him to do that," Grampi scoffed as he paced from the front door to the kitchen and back again. His restlessness was unsettling. "If the dwarf was worried about Bécut being a threat to his plans, he never would've used Rancie."

"Slaughter," Lucas called.

"Yes, gov." The Man's head popped up from under the table.

"How many of Bécut's sheep have you managed to recover?"

"Only that original one. We're still out looking."

"Oh?"

"The Men have scoured everywhere for them. No idea where they've gone."

Lucas gestured Slaughter's dismissal. The little guy disappeared behind Roux's chair.

"We may be able to use that to our advantage," Lucas said. "If Ras has the sheep, Bécut might be persuaded to get them back. But anyway, it would be too dangerous to break through the ward without knowing what Ras is up to."

"We need to figure that out," Roux said.

Lucas nodded. "And we need to prepare for all eventualities. Roux and Gabe, strengthen the wards on the Keepers' post. We don't want our gold going missing, too. Then prepare the Collude of Exceptional Infiltration in case we need it. Camille and I will visit Bécut again and see if we can persuade him to break the ward."

Grampi, amidst pacing, opened his mouth to speak, but Lucas continued. "The dwarf king, Morion Auberon, has a network of spies. He always knows what's going on, although he keeps everything close to his chest. If anyone can give us information about Ras and what he's up to, it's him. Camille, after we've seen Bécut, you and I will take the fastest route to the dwarf high court."

Grampi spun around. "No way."

We turned to him. His face was flushed, his fists balled.

"Now, now, Izac," Roux said. "It sounds like a sensible plan."

It sounded sensible to me too, if it would help the project. Not to mention, I wasn't going to turn down a trip to meet the dwarf king.

"She doesn't even know what the journey entails," Grampi bellowed at Lucas.

Presumably "she" was me, rather than the cat's mother. Anger clenched my sinews tight. Why couldn't he speak directly to me? I wished he'd go on home and let us deal with everything, because right now, I wasn't anyone's concern. Who the hell knew what was happening to the project?

Lucas rose, his chair sliding back, his gaze furious. He leant toward Grampi, palms on the table, body rigid. "That's because you haven't given me a chance," he roared.

The volume of it alone should've bowled Grampi over, but he stood his ground, his glower deepening. "It's too dangerous for Camille." His voice was soft and slow and absolutely lethal. I don't think I'd ever heard him speak like that. A part of me wanted him to stop this madness. I wanted him to be the Grampi I'd always known and loved. But most of me was seriously pissed off at how difficult he was making everything when lives were at stake.

Lucas stepped around the table to face him. "Camille needs the experience." He met Grampi's tone. "It's not safe for her, having so little knowledge, especially with everyone aware of her Keeper invite. She needs to train, and you're putting her in danger if you don't allow her that."

Grampi fumed. "How dare you tell me I'm putting my own granddaughter in danger. You've already subjected her to a black ward today."

Lucas winced.

"What she really needs"—Grampi's voice rose—"is to have nothing to do with you... you despicable, evil, abominable..." Before I knew what was happening, Grampi grabbed a crossbow and arrow from the wall, and in one unbelievably swift movement, loaded it and aimed it at the centre of Lucas's forehead.

Scraping filled the room as Roux and Gabe eased their chairs back. All I could think of was that this old man who stood before me was the Keeper I'd never known. But Lucas... Grampi wouldn't shoot him, surely...

Lucas's eyes darkened, assessing the situation. He was unarmed, his scabbard and blade resting in the kitchen, not that he would have had the opportunity to defend himself. He raised his hands in surrender, and with it, cold fury cut through me—fury sharper than the arrow tip pointing at Lucas's skull.

Every part of me seethed at this conversation spoken about me. How could either of them have my best interests at heart without even consulting me? "This is too much," I bawled, lasering one and then the other with my gaze. "Grampi telling me what not to do, Lucas insisting I train, not to mention Papa muscling in. I'm done with your crap. Completely and totally done. This is my decision. Whether I go with Lucas today, whether I become a Keeper, whether I train, it's my choice. Not either of yours." My body trembled with indignation.

"You shouldn't be involved in any of it," Grampi said, his voice shaking. "Not with this... not with the hantaumo, as a child or as an adult."

"But I am involved." Outrage stiffened my words. "And

it's my project that's been kidnapped. I'm not going to sit here and let who knows what happen to them."

"Camille," Grampi pleaded.

"No," I cried. He just wouldn't listen. "I'm a grown woman. I make my own decisions, and if you don't like it, get the hell out."

He stared at me, stunned, then he lowered the crossbow, disarmed it, threw it across the room and stormed into the street.

CHAPTER 22

LUCAS EMERGED FROM THE KEEPERS' POST LIBRARY with an armful of scrolls. I'd cleared away the coffee things and rehung the crossbow, but my hands still shook. Dismay flooded through me, my argument with Grampi ringing in my ears. I'd never spoken to him like that. I'd never needed to.

"Right." Lucas unrolled the scrolls on the table. "We have to plan our journey. Travelling to the dwarf high court isn't simple, and we need to move as quickly as possible. There's a chance that Morion Auberon won't know anything, although that's improbable. If so, we'll have to think again. Roux's collude will hopefully be ready by then—that's if we can't get Bécut to help."

Roux and Gabe were rummaging in the kitchen apothecary drawers for ingredients, Roux muttering instructions, Gabe hanging on every word.

"No chance for Bécut," Roux called.

I studied the scroll closest to me—a map delineating continents and seas. "Where is this?" I needed a distraction from the image of Grampi's stunned face.

"Fae," Lucas said, running his gaze across the parchment. "All of it. The equivalent of a human world map."

Each of the continents was divided into smaller lands with tiny, scrawly writing I couldn't read.

"Though it doesn't work like human cartography," he added. "Fae isn't exactly round—it just is. The borders of many lands aren't consistent with one another. Some have more distance, and some lands, while they look tiny on here, are actually massive, and vice versa. This map was the best general impression of the place anyone could come up with, using the most stable lands and borders."

"And this?" I pointed to a black line skirting the rim of the map.

"The bounds. And that"—he jabbed his finger at a dot in one of the larger lands partly surrounded by sea—"is where the assembly holds court, in the main elf stronghold. It's one of the most secure places in Fae." He slid his finger to a point almost as far from the bounds as was possible. "This is where the dwarf high court is situated."

"I guess we're not walking directly." I gripped the edge of the table, forcing my fingers still.

"Nope. We'll take a series of ways. Normally, if we wanted to travel there, it would take three days." He gestured from point to point across a series of lands. "We'll have to take the faster route, but it leads us through Les Profondeurs, which is what had Izac so riled."

I tensed at Grampi's name.

Lucas placed his hand on mine and tilted his head, his touch solid, his warmth grounding. His eyes met mine. "I don't know what you could have said to him."

"Maybe he's right," I replied. "Maybe I shouldn't be doing this. After all, I'm about as prepared for it as the next random stranger you could pull off the street." And that was the truth. I waited for him to jibe me again about needing to train.

"I think," he said softly, "that you are still Izac's little girl in his eyes, and he's more than qualified to know the dangers you'll face as a Keeper. He doesn't want you to come to harm."

I studied Lucas's inscrutable face, my eyes narrowed. Compassion wasn't his typical state. Yes, I'd heard plenty of reports that he was an empathetic doctor, but... well, I hadn't expected it, and his touch was so damned reassuring. But even that couldn't shift what was creeping under the surface. "How ready am I for any of it? I mean, as a folklorist, give me an invite to Fae and I'm all yours..."

He quirked an eyebrow. "Literally."

I shook my head and resisted the urge to kick him. "But being a Keeper is another matter entirely. It's aggressive, it's violent, it's..." I thought back to the charognards and the brawl in the Peppered Parsnip. It was, I don't know... It made me feel alive. But that wasn't what I'd been getting at. I stared down at the map. Shit, this was messing with my head so much.

His mouth curved up a little. "You're right for this role,

and it's not just me who thinks so. The assembly does too, and they have methods of appointing Keepers—partnering them with the right person. Besides, you passed the interview and met the minimum requirements." He pursed his lips.

"Interview? I haven't had an interview."

He drew his hand away and studied the map intently. "That series of nightmares you had earlier in the year when Inès was ill."

"How do you know about that?" He only arrived in Tarascon a few weeks ago.

Images that had drifted away flooded back. Monsters. My masked tormentor... "It was you," I growled. He'd pitted me against the worst horrors from my nightmares.

"Yep." He nonchalantly pulled a map out from under the pile.

"You completely devious, rotten..." I didn't have the words.

He shrugged. "The interview is a prerequisite for a Keeper. I conducted it because... well... I didn't want anyone else doing it."

Ghastly dream sequences swam before my eyes. I had no idea what to make of them. "I'm going to process this... and when I'm done, I'll find a way to kick your ass so damned hard."

He grinned, but it wasn't funny. He'd screwed with me. But we didn't have time for that now. I took a deep breath. "Les Profondeurs—the depths. What do I have to be concerned about?"

"It's an underground river with a tendency to reveal your darkest fears. We have to wade through it."

"Sounds like fun. And you think I'll be okay going through this thing?"

He raised his brow. "If you're psychologically sound, you should be okay."

That was up for debate, but if he could do it, so could I.

I glanced at the map Lucas had placed on the top of the pile. It was similar to the first, but dotted with points and marked by hundreds of lines criss-crossing Fae like flight paths. "What's this?"

"The ways—the most important ones. It's not possible to include all the connections at this scale. We have other maps that detail them within individual lands and human countries. With so many combinations of pathways, it's possible to reach most places in Fae via only a few way markers."

He pulled out a map of Tarascon and the surrounding area, and placed it to the side of the original. "Here's the way not far from Bécut's spoulga, and the one above your farm. And here's the one in fae Tarascon."

That was news to me. It appeared to be up on Cousterous, the foothill behind the café.

"The ways from Bécut and fae Tarascon lead to Summer," he continued, "which has one of the most important way markers in Fae. It's also possible to travel in the usual way across land borders, but with horses being the typical mode of transport, it's not the fastest option."

He rattled off more place names that went over my head. But it was clear this trip wasn't going to be as easy as my visits to Wayland's and Dame Blanche's. As he slid out yet another map, this one of a sprawling cave system, my phone rang. My mother flashed up on the screen. If this was a dinner invite, I was going to pass.

I picked up. "Hey, Maman." Lucas headed into the kitchen. Dodging Roux and Gabe, he piled things into a bag.

"Hello, sweetie. I'm just calling to see if you've heard from your father."

"Why, what's up?"

"It's only that he was going to meet Stephan Sissoko for lunch. I'm in a taxi on the way to see Yvonne, and I noticed his car is still in the café car park. He's not picking up, and he was going to get back to me about our plans for tonight."

Shit. No way. I'd forgotten Papa was having lunch with Sissoko. He wouldn't hang around the café for no reason, ignoring my mother's calls. The project had gone to Rancie, working through lunch. They must have invited Papa along, which meant he was in trouble too.

A small part of me insisted that he shouldn't have messed with my life, my special week. And yet there was that confusing parental love... My throat tightened. He was in serious danger with the rest of them.

And now Maman would worry and probably call the police. There was no way we were going to explain all this, and if the police investigated Rancie, they weren't going to come away from the black ward as healthy as I had. There had to be something I could say to take her mind off Papa and give us time to sort things out.

"Uh, yes," I managed. "I've just spoken to him at the café.

He's had a change of plan and he's going to tag along with the project." The lie stuck in my throat, but I forced myself on. "His phone has run out of battery, but he wanted me to let you know that we're all going into the mountains where reception is terrible. He's going to stay the night with us at... uh... a mountain refuge up there, so don't worry if he doesn't text."

"Oh, I'm so sorry," she said. "He's muscling in terribly. I'll have a word with him about it later, but can I speak with him now briefly before he goes out of range?"

No, no, no. "He's just left in Sissoko's car." She had to buy it—she was so laissez-faire most of the time—she really had to buy it.

"Alright, sweetie. Tell him I'll be out late tonight, and then I'll be leaving first thing in the morning to visit Colette."

My hand tensed around the phone. She definitely wasn't attempting to spend time with Grampi, but she was falling for my story. That was the main thing. Sometimes I hated how easy-going she was, but definitely not right now.

"Sure," I replied. "I'll pass on the message."

CHAPTER 23

Bécut's spoulga rose before us as we hiked closer, its sturdy walls a defence against the world. We were all set to head to the dwarf high court, but the cyclops was our first stop.

Lucas had strapped a pack over his scabbard containing food and supplies—I'd grabbed leftovers from the café when I'd told Guy I was off into the mountains with the project. Hopefully, the excuse was enough to prevent anyone being concerned. We'd be back in twelve hours or so, according to Lucas, so fingers crossed my alibi would hold.

I couldn't help worrying about the project. About Papa. He was such a fathead, but he hadn't always been that way. Or was it that I'd not noticed as a child?

I had all these lovely memories. The summer he'd taught me to swim, he'd been encouraging and supportive, not controlling like now. I used to wait on the stairs for him to come home from work, which wasn't all that often, then he'd tuck me up in bed at night and read stories doing the voices. He felt so safe.

I don't know when his interfering had started. It had crept in, getting worse as I grew older, maybe because he felt he was losing control of me. Ugh. I had no idea where love ended and hate began. They were mishmashed into a complete mess.

We reached the base of the spoulga. "Do you want the honours, or shall I?" Lucas asked.

"Be my guest."

"Bécut," Lucas yelled.

There was no answer.

Lucas shouted again.

"Go away," Bécut rumbled. A plaintive bleat came from inside.

"We've found your sheep," Lucas replied.

"My flock!" Bécut's voice wavered. There was silence for a moment, and then, "Go away."

"There's a dwarf at Rancie hoarding a load of gold," Lucas called. "We think he has your sheep for the horns."

Bécut's growl shook the ground. Then nothing.

"What's it going to take to shift his butt?" I said softly, rolling a rock under my foot. "We haven't got time for this. Maybe he'd be more amenable face to face. We should go in there."

"Into his spoulga?" Lucas stared at me as though I was insane. "It's instant death to enter a cyclops's home without an invite."

"Let's not, then," I muttered.

"Your sheep are inside a black ward," Lucas shouted. "If you'll help us break it, we can rescue them."

Nothing.

"The dwarf is cutting off the sheep's horns," he added. It was a guess, but what else would Ras be doing with them? "They need your help."

Bécut growled again, my legs trembling with the vibration. More bleating came from inside.

"I feel it," Bécut said. "I feel them, my flock, I feel their horns being removed, but I'm not going anywhere. Nowhere. Just here. Leave me alone."

"We need your help," I tried. "It's not only the sheep—the dwarf has captured a group of people." Including Papa. The thought did nothing to ease my impatience. "And we have no idea what he'll do with your flock in the end."

There was no reply.

"If his sheep aren't going to make him shift, nothing will," Lucas said, glaring at the fortification. "It looks as though Roux is right."

I couldn't stand here any longer. "We have to get going. Which direction is it?"

He inclined his head along the pass.

We picked our way over boulders, scree and patches of snow as the pass rose ever upward. The breeze built, blustering around, its chill soothing my sun-baked skin before condensing to form gauzy air-born figures with streaming hair and eerie, diaphanous faces. There was a wildness about the sylphs, unlike those at Naïs's spring. I don't think they meant any harm, although they made the going much harder, rushing against us, pushing us this way and that.

A small menhir came into sight, set amidst a plateau of cleared ground.

"Andos," Lucas said as we neared. I followed suit.

Two ways opened before us, one shadowy and inscrutable, one bright. We took the bright option and the gale stilled, the landscape transforming into lush, undulating meadows. A path led us through knee-high grass, red clover, milkwort and buttercups. The sky was somehow softer than in the mountains, and the sun shone down with a delicious warmth that lacked the baking heat of the human realm. The place felt peaceful—joyful, even.

"Is this Summer?" I asked.

"Yep. The major way marker I mentioned is a few miles away—it's a useful one to know about. Are you happy to pick up the pace?"

"Sure." Running would help me deal with my concerns for Papa and the project.

We pounded through fields and forest faster than I was accustomed to. Most of the time the path was clear, although not much wider than an animal track. The inclines were shallow and the air fresh. I attempted to ignore Lucas's physique, his stride steady and long, his supple leathers playing over his muscles as they contracted and released.

As we continued on, creatures made of ivy disappeared amidst the undergrowth, and vertes velles flitted here and there, the small fae only distinguishable from flowers and grasses by their movements. Unlike the drawings of Belle Époque flower fairies, these fae were a part of the plant life, their faces formed of leaves and petals, their features angled and organic.

As we entered a thick forest, hazel, willow, oak and beech dryads merged with their trees. Wrens darted around, and ceps clustered everywhere, their white stems almost as fat as their brown caps. The path had been carved into the soft forest floor by countless footfalls, and I couldn't help but wonder who had passed this way.

It was all utterly fascinating. I felt as though I was absorbing the place through my skin. I wanted to know more, so much more, but at the same time, being here completely fried my brain. My whole worldview had been torn to shreds, the plans I'd made for my future fracturing. I'd wanted to be part of the folklore community for so long—the normal, human realm kind of folklore—and I still wanted that. I'd worked so hard with my research. A part of me wanted acknowledgement and acceptance that everything I'd achieved had been a decent contribution to the field. But here, it was all so distant, even the project.

I should be getting ready for my date with Pascale about now. Crap. I'd been looking forward to it. He was such a sweet guy, and we'd worked well together on the project's organisation. To be honest, I'd never been asked out by someone who had the same interests as me—the drunken hookup with Lucas definitely didn't count.

Surely it helped to find your partner interesting?

Although there was no way I wanted one of those in-each-other's-pockets relationships. I supposed I'd been interested in Raoul, my first longer-term boyfriend. That was until he'd revealed his fascination with taxidermy six months in. Things with extreme-sports Alex had ended pretty quickly too, when he'd announced, out of the blue, that he wanted to settle down and have kids. I'd considered it... for about a minute.

And on we ran. After a good number of miles, I was flagging, not used to the pace. Lucas showed no sign of fatigue, those muscles still catching my eye. How did he manage to fascinate me continuously? It wasn't healthy. I had to get to the bottom of the incubus thing. I needed to figure out how much of an influence he had over me. But I had to hand it to him—he *was* interesting. Too interesting.

Grampi's concerns about Lucas and our argument came back. The thing that really hurt was Grampi's lack of belief in me. I supposed his doubts fed into my own. Yes, I could handle a sword and I knew folklore, but that was it. And here I was, diving head first into Fae again. Who knew what lay around the corner? Well, Grampi did, and he thought I couldn't handle it. But no matter how cut out for this I was, we were here, and we had to help Papa and the project.

As we broke through the forest into gentle meadowland, I slowed to a stop, my hands on my thighs. "I don't have drac superpowers," I said through breaths, sweat trickling from my nose and running down my back. My appearance was undoubtably delightful. "I'm going to have to slow the pace."

He paused next to me, a sheen of the lightest perspiration on his brow, which only accentuated the attractive slope of his forehead. "The way marker isn't much further. We're making good time." He took off his pack, pulled out waterskins and passed one over. We drank our fill, then carried on at a fast walk.

"Looks like you really have managed to get me training," I said as I wiped sweat from my forehead and scraped away the loose strands that had escaped my ponytail.

"I knew you couldn't resist," he said, staring ahead and barely restraining a smile. "It was only a matter of time." Always so sure of himself.

The path broadened as it led us up a gentle slope through lupin-speckled grasslands. We walked side by side, our footfall scattering what might have been blue butterflies but could well have been fae.

Despite everything on my mind, my attention repeatedly returned to the way Lucas's hand clutched the strap of his pack, delineating the sinews along his arm, and the way his jaw shifted, the skin playing over his cheeks. It completely irked me, the constant pull I had toward him, even though I knew what lurked beneath the surface, not to mention what a complete git he could be.

"How do you do that?" I asked. "Is it some kind of fae glamour you use to look..." I wasn't going to give him the satisfaction of saying "so damned fine". "To look reasonably together all the time?"

He laughed. "Hot doctor at nine o'clock," he said, mimicking Alice's ringtone. "I don't do anything. You're just attracted to me. That's all."

I stopped in my tracks. He didn't know that. "It's well known in folklore that dracs are incubi. You use your powers to influence people." It was time I got to the bottom of this.

He paused and met my gaze, his lips parted as if for one rare moment he couldn't think what to say. Then he smiled wickedly, his eyes sparkling. "Yes, I'm an incubus. I have that power, but I don't use it—of course I don't. I don't need to."

I snorted. Had I expected anything less? "Are you telling me you've never used your influence over me?"

He stepped closer, drew his hand to my forehead and brushed a bead of sweat away, studying me as though he was bewitched. I froze at the sensation of his smooth fingers brushing my skin, at the intimacy of the gesture, at our proximity.

"There," I managed, my voice rough. "You're doing it now."

He broke into laughter and strode toward the brow of the hill. "I'm not doing anything, Camille," he called back. "I never have. I wouldn't want to have your affection in that way."

"How do I know you're telling the truth?" I followed him.

"I'm always truthful with you."

Yes, after everything, I had to admit that he'd never lied to me. He'd just put me through hell in so many other ways. But it didn't explain how drawn to him I was.

"Look," he added, his gaze solemn. "I'll show you what

it's like to be under the influence of an incubus, if you want. You need to experience the sensation. Dracs aren't the only ones with that power. There are plenty of fae that might try it on."

"What? So you have an excuse to get your hands on me?"

"I've already had my hands on you." His eyes sparkled. "But joking aside, it's part of your training. It's crucial you're not vulnerable. And, contrary to what you think, I do want you to trust me."

I scrutinised his face. To know what the whole incubus thing felt like would mean I'd be able to brush my concerns about his influence aside. But after the verity... "How can I let you do that when you spiked my drink?"

He met my gaze. "The usual way verity is administered to prospective Keepers is much worse."

I barked a laugh. "So you were doing me a favour?"

"I was trying to help."

"That's a new way of looking at it." But despite his fae trickery and his warped way of looking at the world, I couldn't deny he'd gone the extra mile for me repeatedly. I was struggling to trust him, but the thought of being manipulated by some evil fae creature turned my stomach. I needed to know how to protect myself.

"Alright, do it. But don't go too far, and don't make me do anything I'll regret."

"You have my word," he said, his expression earnest.

I let my hands trail against lupins, the breeze drying my sweat.

"It wasn't difficult to get you into the sack, anyway." Lucas smirked. "I didn't need to use incubus enticement."

My jaw clenched. Two could play at that game. "Really? I saw it from another perspective."

"Oh, did you now?"

I'd one hundred percent wanted to jump into bed with him that night. "It took about five minutes to small-talk you right into my taxi."

He roared with laughter.

"Okay," I said, "joking aside, I guess there was mutual *initial* attraction. We were very drunk and not in our right minds. Most importantly, we consented to spend the night together."

"Agreed." He brushed a butterfly from his arm. "And considering I've never attempted to charm you using untoward means, admit it, Camille, you really are attracted to me."

I shot him a dirty look. "After seeing your true, delightful inner self? You wish."

He chuckled. "Nope, you don't get away with it that easily. You said to me that I was influencing you just now, and I wasn't."

"Just testing you." But he was right. The folklore students flirting with him at the café came to mind. I wasn't the only one attracted to him. Putting all his faults aside for a moment, he was good-looking, strong, intelligent and capable, which made my reaction an instinctual alpha-male-who'd-make-a-good-protector thing. Nothing more.

We strode on in silence, my body tense against whatever incubus stunt Lucas was going to pull, but I couldn't feel anything other than his usual allure.

"Ummm, it's not working," I said as we wound our way through grassland on the other side of the hill.

CHAPTER 24

"I'm not doing it *now*." Lucas's lips quirked. "You're anticipating it. I'll do it later, when you least suspect —to give you the full incubus experience."

"I really am going to be learning all about fae today," I replied dully as we continued down the hill.

He just grinned.

But there was something else that had been on my mind ever since we'd met Wayland. He'd mentioned that Baeserte, the boar god, had kicked Lucas halfway across the Pyrenees centuries ago. Plus, Lucas had said that his uncle was Count Estruch, the originator of European vampire myths in the twelfth century. "How old are you, Lucas?"

He raised an eyebrow.

I adjusted my scabbard, which was sticking to my back. "I mean, it's not a pleasant thought that I may have slept with someone older than my grandfather." I could never understand the thing in fantasy novels where the heroine ended up with the elf guy who was five hundred years old. It didn't make sense. I mean, surely they would have varying mindsets.

"Ageing in Fae doesn't work like ageing in the human realm," he said. "Fae often talk about time in terms of human years because the human realm has consistent and measurable chronology, but here in the various lands, it's all over the place. Most fae are immortal. We age in mindset, not in years, and that's reflected in our appearance."

This was getting interesting. "Just wind that back. Firstly, 'immortal'. You'll live forever?" That was kind of inconceivable.

"I'll live forever unless I'm killed by a weapon or a disease."

The path disappeared and we waded through knee-high grass, a throng of vertes velles diving for cover. "So if your appearance reflects your mindset—and I'd say you look about thirty or so—that means you have the mindset of a thirty-year-old?"

"Pretty much. Thirty-one on my ID. I've been around for a while though, in human terms. When I was in my early twenties—going by my appearance—I fought with Charlemagne."

I gaped. Charlemagne, member of the Carolingian dynasty who lived in the ninth century. "Holy fuck. The actual Charlemagne? I don't believe it."

He smiled. "Right by his side. We needed to create a unified Europe after the fall of the Roman Empire."

I studied the light playing in his ebony irises. It was just too much. "Then you're old. Umm, *very* old."

"No, I'm this age." He pointed to himself. "Fae don't develop as easily as humans. Some never progress and always look youthful. I spent a regrettably long time in adolescence. That wasn't much fun, I can tell you." The grass thinned and we picked up the path again, the ground levelling. In the distance stood a menhir.

"It also depends where you spend your days," he continued. "There are some lands where time, measured by human standards, slows down or speeds by. Years can pass in a flash. I completely missed out on the fifth century, and a few others. Plus, it can work the other way. Fae brought up in the human realm, unaware of their heritage and convinced they're human, age accordingly. It's a sort of reverse-verity effect."

"Curious." And that was the understatement of the year.

"Humans age much more slowly in Fae, too."

"Like those kids who wandered into Fae on the Pons farm and came out years later not much older?"

"Exactly."

That might have explained something. "When I was younger, I always thought Grampi looked incredible for his age, but then the goat thing happened and he seemed to gain years overnight."

"That would be the effects of the curse."

The standing stone loomed above us as we drew close, spirals carved into its surface. We both acknowledged it with an "Andos", and I let out a long breath. The way marker meant we were making progress toward helping the project and Papa.

As we stepped onto the dry earth around the stone, the air distorted. I caught flickers of light and dark, rock and sand, ice and sea. There were so many lands beyond this point, but I struggled to focus on any one of them.

Lucas gestured to an impression of deep green forest, umber earth and grey limestone, and we headed through onto an incline above a narrow valley, a stream gushing in its midst. All about us stood pine, the trees thinning nearer the water, the opposite slope scarred by rocky outcrops and dark cave entrances.

"Come on," he said.

We jogged down to the stream, jumped across boulders that lay in its rushing waters, then hiked up the far side of the valley, following a ridge that skirted the occasional gaping cavern. I wanted to ask Lucas more about Fae, about his life, about everything, but I was still trying to process what he'd said, so we continued on in silence until Lucas led the way into a cave.

"This is us." He paused in the shadows and rummaged in his pack, producing a small herb bag. He poured dried green leaves into his hand and focussed on them. A soft glow emerged from his fingers then floated upward, lighting the tunnel with exceptional clarity. "A lumière. An easy collude as long as you have moonwort."

Watching Lucas perform a collude blended with the

massive fae overwhelm I was experiencing right now. The idea of doing something like that was amazing, but it also meant taking one step further from everything I'd known. I tried to breathe away my bewilderment as I followed Lucas into a narrow tunnel.

Once we'd taken the first bend, all sense of the outside vanished. The lumière shone brighter than a torch, the light hovering above us when it could, glimmering with iridescence, illuminating the dusky limestone walls smoothed by water thousands of years ago—if geology worked that way in Fae. The air was cool and chalky, and everything except our footfall was utterly silent.

We ducked under ridges, wiggled through the occasional low squeeze and clambered down rock faces, all the time descending. When our route forked, Lucas chose his path with confidence, as though he'd been here before.

We entered a large chamber the size of a cinema with five exits leading off. Above, on the arched, rocky ceiling, rugged horses galloped, delineated in charcoal and ochre, their expressions mischievous and so alive. As Lucas strode from one passage to another, I gaped in awe at the artwork. "It's utterly stunning."

"I want to be certain of our route," he muttered, examining rust-coloured lines and dots on the wall beside an exit. He headed to a rock face painted with sweeping lines that, with the undulations in the stone, formed a group of cave bears. "I remember this... but..."

I stepped to the side to see one of the bears, but Lucas was blocking the view. In the strange light of the lumière, his face appeared as old as the cave and, at the same time, young and full of life. I followed the line of his cheek that curved to his broad mouth. His lips played in thought, the dip under his jaw deeply shadowed. He turned to examine a different part of the rock face, and all I could see was his back, his pack and scabbard doing little to hide sturdy shoulders that framed his strong yet lithe body. He shifted his arm, the play of his triceps engrossing.

It was that lure again, that attraction I couldn't pin down. I stepped closer, needing to know more, wanting to understand who and what he was. He must have heard my foot fall as I approached, but he continued his examination.

I paused behind him, catching his scent. Rosemary and cedar mingled with earth. I placed my hand on his arm, and he tensed at my touch, the sensation electric.

He turned, studying me, his brow narrowed. "Camille." He shook his head gently, wistfulness widening his eyes. "We have to get to the dwarf court."

"Of course," I murmured, shifting closer until only a breath lay between us.

He swallowed, then encircled me in his arms, drawing me to him. A recollection surfaced of the two of us together like this in his bedroom that night. Then the image was gone, but his arms remained.

His heart pounded against my chest, the stiffness between his legs hardening. I needed to be closer still. I slid my hand to his neck and ran my fingers over his pulse. His breath hitched. Wanting so much more, I planted a kiss under his jaw, his stubble rough. His grip tightened, blazing fire through me.

I drew back and met his gaze, his dark eyes unfathomable. His lips parted, and I couldn't resist. I took his lower lip between my teeth and tugged.

CHAPTER 25

CLOSING HIS EYES, LUCAS LET OUT A DEEP AND THROATY moan. As I released his lip, he pulled away, stepped to the other side of the exit and examined more rock art.

I stood stock still. Why had he walked off? But more to the point, what the hell had I been doing?

He glanced back. "And that was an incubus at work."

My jaw dropped. "Bastard. Fucking bastard."

But he'd offered to show me, and I'd agreed. Even so, it left me reeling. The attraction I'd felt moments ago was still there as it pretty much always was, but the compulsion to act was gone, leaving my chest open and raw.

He cocked an eyebrow as he ran his fingers over the rock face. "What's the matter, Camille? Enjoying yourself a little too much?"

He'd been the one with the swelling in his pants. "But... I... What I did... it was all so natural." It hadn't felt like I was being coerced. It hadn't even felt odd that I'd wanted to be close to him then and there.

He leant against the rock. "An incubus's power lies in influencing you subtly. The worst you might think is that you had a lapse of judgement in a moment of lust. There are plenty of freaks out there who'd use their power over you, given the chance, and you wouldn't know it. Not even afterward. It's the worst kind of abuse."

I slid down the smooth limestone, my scabbard tightening as my blade angled. Clutching my knees to my chest, I shook my head. It had been me, but it hadn't. I felt... used. Everything about fae was so confusing. Lucas was so confusing. The irritatingly sweet taste of him was still on my lips.

He strode over and offered me a hand.

I glared at him, ignoring it. He just couldn't help the amusement playing on his lips, but he took a breath and met my gaze, gravity in his eyes. "Camille," he said in a low, steady voice. "I didn't want to do that to you, and I'll never do it again."

I sprang up. "You damned as hell better not. If you so much as try, your long fae existence will come to an untimely and gruesome end. Now, which way are we going?"

He nodded, and for a second his face flickered with something that might have been relief, then he headed down the tunnel to our side. "This way."

The passage opened out to form a broad corridor of rock, the walls sweeping up into a stunning peak above. And on we continued, ever downward. My vulnerability from Lucas's stunt chafed like grit under my skin. I supposed the experience had been invaluable, and if it happened again, I'd attempt to put a stop to it. All the same. I just felt pissed.

"I guess that was one more example of your drac weirdness, seducing women with freaky fae powers." I couldn't resist snapping, I was so utterly riled.

"Not just women, men too," he said nonchalantly, "and creatures of an ungendered nature."

I glowered, unable to shift my irritation. Thinking of his weirdness brought back the memory of him crushing the table in the events room. Now *that* was curious. I'd been worked up at the time, thinking he'd sabotaged the project, so I hadn't given it much thought. He'd almost seemed jealous, but why would he be? Although Pascale *had* been asking me out right when it happened. Lucas would've been listening in, as always.

I could try something...

"I can't believe the project has been kidnapped," I said lamely with exaggerated sorrow in my voice. "Especially when I should be out with Pascale right now." I was a terrible actress.

Lucas didn't answer.

I glanced across at him. Colour had risen in his cheeks.

Oh. My. God. I had him. Payback time. "Hmmm. I'm not sure how Pascale and I would've ended the night... I expect we would've gone back to my loft..."

Actually, I did know how we would've left things. We would've geeked out on folklore, and that would've been beyond amazing. And despite Pascale being hot, and a lovely person, no matter his intentions, we would've gone our separate ways. I wasn't going to risk a one-night stand with a colleague, especially one that might become my tutor if I made it to university. If there was something more between us, we would be taking it very slowly.

Lucas's jaw was mousetrap tight, his neck ridged. Small veins throbbed at his temple.

"We would've kissed in the doorway," I continued, "then hurried up the stairs..."

His teeth scraped, his mouth twisting, his gaze boring into the darkness along the tunnel. I had him so damned bad.

"And," I continued, "he would have unbuttoned my—"

Lucas hurtled into me, slamming my back against the rock, the impact jarring my bones. His hands gripped my arms to my sides, his face almost touching mine, his eyes wide with fury. "Don't speak," he growled in his drac voice. "Don't say one more word."

His warm breath tickled my lips. I stared at him, my mind empty of everything but his body pressed against me. Flames burned low in my middle. This couldn't be more of his incubus thing. I didn't feel compelled to act on my desire, although part of me wanted to.

Common sense doused the flames, and my blood grew cold. Lucas was pinning me to the wall, for heaven's sake. Perhaps I really was in danger.

I pulled away, feeling annoyingly empty without him next to me. Striding on, I cast a backward glance. Lucas still stood there, his chest heaving, his gaze heavy as though he'd somehow developed a neanderthal ridge.

Delight trickled through me. I'd riled him. I'd gotten him

back, not just for the incubus thing, which I'd consented to, but for his teasing about my attraction to him.

"Jealous." I spat the word.

He shook himself and sprang into a run, catching up with me at drac speed. "We need to get to the dwarf court," he rumbled. "No more distractions."

We picked up our pace. I was happy to do that, but let it go after earlier? No way. "What was that? Some creepy, possessive drac behaviour?"

He looked as though he would boil.

"Otherwise," I continued, "for you to have such a strong reaction, you must have proper feelings for me." I laughed at the absurdity of the notion.

There was only silence. Our footfall and the distant trickle of water didn't begin to fill the void.

"You don't say," he replied flatly, staring ahead.

With that, I couldn't think of another remark. And actually, this whole conversation was pointless. Yes, I guessed in the short time we'd known each other we'd developed feelings—I don't know what kind of feelings, I hadn't managed to figure that out on account of the positive stuff being mingled with the hell he'd put me through at first. But there was a sort of friendship born out of having been through so much together—from having risked our lives for each other—which was the reason I found Grampi's warning so difficult to take. But that was all. There was absolutely nothing more between us.

Chapter 26

Our stony silence was palpable as we continued onward, the lumière lighting the passage. I pushed my confusion of emotions away. We were here for the project, here to find Morion Auberon, the dwarf king, to figure out what Ras was up to.

We entered a cavern filled with stalagmites and stalactites, some forming glittering, larva-like masses, some in strange shapes—a mushroom, a hunched old man. In other places, the floor rippled like a frozen ocean, and calcite hung from the ceiling, droplets in suspended animation. We trod carefully through, not wanting to disturb the pristine beauty, then we took a series of turnings before the passageway opened out, a river rushing past at the end.

I glanced at Lucas.

He nodded. "Les Profondeurs."

We paused where the limestone dipped to form a small shore. The river was about as wide as a two-lane road, the cave ceiling about six feet above the gushing inky water that looked cold and deep. The torrent disappeared into darkness beyond the range of the lumière.

I shivered. My instinct was to retreat, but we'd gotten this far.

Lucas tightened the straps on his pack so it sat higher on his back. "Don't stare into the waters." His voice was still stiff. "You'll want to. As we wade through, the river will pull out your fears. Don't think about them too much. Let them flow over you, and you'll be fine."

"It looks deep."

"It's an optical illusion. It's fairly shallow all the way, certainly not more than waist height. Don't let it fool you into panicking."

Part of me wanted to ask what happened if I panicked. Probably best I didn't know. I adjusted my scabbard. "How far is it to the other shore?"

"Maybe two hundred yards."

I followed Lucas into the water, the lumière accompanying us. The cold was numbing, the rocks and pebbles underfoot unsteady and slippery. The bank sloped gradually. By the time I was up to my knees, water rushed against me. We trod upstream, side by side.

I was purposely not looking at the water, but I couldn't help notice in my periphery that at one moment it was blacker than black, the next it shone with otherworldly blue, a blue that held unfathomable depths.

Maman, Papa and I had once gone to Lac du Serre-Ponçon on a sailing holiday. On seeing the size of the dam holding the waters at bay, knowing how deep it was, I'd not been able to take the dinghy out. I'd had the strangest sensation that I'd wanted to walk into those depths, to drown in them, and yet it was the thing that petrified me most of all. It was like that now.

My chest tightened as the water deepened. It was almost up to my waist and it dragged hard. Each step was a struggle. If we lost our footing, we'd be whisked away into darkness. There was no escape from an underground river.

And with the rushing of the water, fear rushed through my mind. At the forefront, unsurprisingly, was the thought of Papa, Pascale, Meera and the rest of the project being in danger. But other worries came too. Alice being hurt by that lying rat of a goblin boyfriend. The croquembouche—the ogre Alice and I had been terrified of as kids—with its teeth around me, readying itself to feast. The black ward at Rancie submerging me. I let the fears flow away as Lucas had said, and attempted to breathe deeply so the bands of apprehension gripping my chest would ease.

Lucas glanced over. "You okay?"

"All good." I wondered what thoughts were trawling through his mind. What did a predator like him have to fear?

The river deepened, encircling my waist with icy fingers. Rocks jutted from above, and Lucas had to duck to get through.

"It's a little deeper than the last time I passed this way," he muttered.

More fears came as we continued. Fae interfering with the project, messing everything up and preventing me from gaining recognition for my paper. My mother out with friends... all the time. The hantaumo queen, her teeth piercing my neck. Grampi unwilling to speak to me because of how I'd shouted at him.

The thoughts wouldn't let up... Me not being cut out for Fae, just as Grampi had said. Me leaving Fae, somehow never able to return. Lucas devouring me. That was an interesting one. Was I really scared of his drac form?

As I took the next step, my boot struck a rock, then slid on unsteady stones, my footing slipping away from me.

Lucas caught my arm. "Steady there."

I murmured my thanks. I needed focus on what I was doing.

The rock above us lowered, and we were both forced to stoop. My leathers clung to me, thick and cloying, the cold biting. I made myself take long and steady breaths, ignoring the sense of claustrophobia at only having a few feet of breathing space. If the river was to surge...

Nope. Not going there.

The ceiling lowered again. We had to dip down into the water and struggle against the flow. The image of Papa came to mind. His opinions about my lack of career, his interference in my life. Hell, I was cold, my body shaking.

Ahead of us, the ceiling slid right into the water.

"This is the lowest point," Lucas said. "Though I've never been through here with the water so high. There was a reasonable gap before." His brow knitted and I caught a glint of fear in his eyes. He blinked it away. He was fighting demons too.

"How far does it extend like this?" I asked.

"It's just a spur, maybe three feet across, then the roof raises straight up, and it's not much further to the far shore."

"So we have to go under." I shivered some more. "Best get it done with as quickly as we can."

"I don't think we have any choice," he replied. "Let's make it brief and with complete focus. Shut every fear out."

"You don't have to tell me twice."

He held out his hand. I grasped it, his warmth a relief against the chill.

"On three," he said.

"One, two, three," we chanted in unison, then hauled deep breaths and plunged forward. The lumière sank with us, unaffected by the water.

The current was strong. We released each other to half swim, half clamber against it. I forced my encroaching fear back as I took stroke after stroke, working furiously against the river. In the light of the lumière, Lucas's distorted form was doing the same. I had to think of nothing but getting through, of making it under the spur, otherwise I would drown in the deep, dark underground.

I had to have made it past the spur by now. I raised my hand, but all I could feel was rock. I swam harder and tried again, but still rock. My heart thrashed as I pushed on, fear pressing in, my chest burning. I needed air.

An image of my father shimmered before me, back when he'd ripped apart my history paper to help me in the future. The vision shifted to when he'd arranged my extra gym lessons, even though I'd gotten onto the team, then to when he'd explained all too clearly why being a waitress at a café was no better than being a piece of shit.

I didn't want to see anymore. I needed to push it all away. I needed air, but I could only see Papa's unsatisfied face. I wasn't enough—not enough to get into university, not enough to have my paper published. I was never enough for him.

The water was so cold. I couldn't keep fighting it, my chest hurt so much. I couldn't stop myself taking a breath. Water poured into my lungs, and the strength left my limbs. The river swept me away and darkness encroached, but all I could feel was the utter cold terror of not being enough.

Spikes drove into my middle, and I was pulled against the current by my waist until something hauled me from the water, gripping me in its bony arms. Even in my befuddled state, I had the sense that whatever held me was dangerous, its touch nauseating.

It dropped me onto hard rock. I retched, threw up, then lay there coughing and spluttering, dragging small gasps of air through my raw throat into my aching chest.

The lumière bobbed above, its light glinting on a slumped mass of black hide and sinew half in the water, its hideous skin desiccated against bone, its face hardly more than a hollowed skull. It was a creature from my nightmares. But that thing... that creature... was slipping little by little into the river.

The dark waters took hold of it and swept it downstream.

Lucas.

CHAPTER 27

LUCAS HAD SHIFTED INTO HIS DRAC FORM. IT HAD BEEN his claws I'd felt around me, and he'd pulled me out of Les Profondeurs. Now he was being carried away by the river. If he was swept under the spur, I wouldn't have the strength to dive beneath and rescue him, but if I could make it to him before...

I sprang up, dove into the water and thrashed stroke after stroke toward him, keeping my head above the flow. Papa's eyes bored into me—I wasn't enough. Not enough to do this, not enough to do anything. But going with the current, I sped forward and reached Lucas just before he hit the spur. I locked my arm around his neck, rammed my feet against stones on the riverbed and dragged him backward toward the shore. With more strength than I knew I possessed, I hauled him up onto the rock, then fell to my knees with cold and exhaustion.

For a moment he just lay there, and through the fog of

fatigue, urgency prickled that I had to do CPR or something, then his chest heaved. He released a stream of water from his revolting saw-tooth mouth, then his whole chest arched as he wheezed and gasped.

He rested on his side for a second, then stretched, his chest, limbs, skull, all of him filling out, until the sculpted form of everyday Lucas lay before me, naked and pale.

"Argh. I don't ever want to go through there again," he muttered.

Relief flooded through my body, but all I could do was draw in shallow breaths. He'd saved me. He'd had to risk himself because I wasn't skilled enough, strong enough, knowledgeable enough to be a Keeper. Shaking consumed me, my teeth chattering.

He grasped my hand. "You're freezing. We need to get moving."

He rose, searching for something. I followed his gaze to his pack. It had caught on a rock in the shallows with what looked like his trousers. His shoes lay on the edge of the shore with his blade, scabbard and tunic.

"The way marker isn't far," he said as he gathered his things. "It will take us straight to the high court. Hopefully we'll have the opportunity to warm up there." He pulled on his trousers and shoes then crouched down by me. "You okay?"

I realised I'd not spoken. My ineptitude, my stupidity at even thinking I should go along on this trip, had stolen my words. Grampi had been right. And the thought that we had to return through Les Profondeurs was too much to bear. But

Lucas would think I was ill if I didn't speak. I was cold as hell, but that was all. "Yeah," I managed. "I'm fine."

He nodded and rose, then attempted to put on his tunic, but it was ripped across the middle. He stuffed it in his pack. "My drac form doesn't like clothes."

"Why did you change?" I asked.

"I... uh... wasn't doing so well in the river. When you lost your footing, shifting was my only chance to grab you." Of course, dracs were in their element in water. He had to be an excellent swimmer, but Les Profondeurs had taken him all the same.

Something stung my waist. I rolled up my top to see incisions from Lucas's claws.

He caught sight of the wounds and his gaze lit with fury. "Thick-skinned and insensitive." He shook his head, closed his eyes for a moment, then opened them. "I'm sorry."

I released a sharp laugh. "For saving my life?"

His lips parted. "No. For hurting you."

"Small price to pay." I got to my feet. My head swam for a few seconds, then everything steadied. I still shook with cold, the memory of Lucas's drac touch sending shivers down my spine, and not in a good way. There had been something so dark and detestable about him.

Lucas hauled on his pack and scabbard. We followed a dark tunnel that led off from the back of the cave, just big enough for us to walk through without stooping. In seconds, it opened out into a circular chamber. A squat menhir stood in the centre.

"Andos," we pronounced.

"The way leads right into the heart of the dwarf high court," Lucas said. "Despite Les Profondeurs being a massive deterrent from entering here, I expect it to be heavily guarded."

He stepped forward. I followed him, and the cave morphed into a cavern, the rock darker, the light of the lumière draining away in the larger chamber.

Armour clinked behind us.

We swung around to face a troop of dwarves advancing from the other side of the menhir with axes, spears and hammers raised. They sported massive beards, helmets that covered their jowls, and a battle-ready amount of chain-mail and armour.

I made to draw my blade, but something rammed into my legs, bringing me to my knees. My back was struck, propelling me forward into the grit, pain spreading through my ribs and spine. What I guessed was a foot dug into my back as my arms were tied together behind me. I really didn't need this after Les Profondeurs. Couldn't the dwarves have greeted us with a nice "Hello"? I forced my head around to see Lucas in the same predicament.

"We're going to have to go along with this," Lucas managed as a dwarf shoved his cheek into the dirt. "Think of it as a nice warm welcome."

"Well, well, well," a gravelly voice proclaimed. "What have we here? Lucas Rouseau. Currently number four on the dwarves' most-wanted list. After your father, your mother and your brother, that is."

That was news to me.

"He's exaggerating," Lucas murmured. "Nothing to worry about."

We were hauled to our feet before the troop, a stocky dwarf with a wild gaze at the fore. "I'm sure the king will be pleased to hear that we have such an honoured visitor." He roared with laughter. "Can't see you getting out alive." The whole troop joined with his guffaws.

"And look at that," he continued. "You've brought a moonwort collude—a *plant*—into the realm of mineral and fire." The dwarf swung his axe back, then threw it at us.

I flinched, but the weapon soared above our heads and cleaved the lumière in two. The light vanished and the axe clattered to the ground. Luminescence from the rock walls lit the cave dimly.

"Let's get you to the king," the dwarf said.

We were directed along a broad tunnel, the air growing warmer the further we went. I stopped shivering, although I couldn't shift the icy remnants of Les Profondeurs. What was I even doing in Fae? I was completely not cut out for this. Lucas would have managed far better in the river alone, not having to rescue me. And now what? Lucas had been so sure he could get information about Ras from Morion Auberon, but we hadn't exactly had the warmest of welcomes.

Eventually, we emerged into an immense space. It had to be a cavern, although I couldn't see the far walls. To our side, a huge medieval fortress rose up in the blackness with impenetrable square towers built for strength rather than beauty. Dropping away before us was a massive stone city with countless buildings either hewn from rocky promontories or wedged next to one another in a spiral of streets.

Life bustled beneath innumerable lanterns. I strained to see the dwarves properly, but we were too high. A glowing river of lava cut through one side of the metropolis, and far, far above, from what might have been the cavern roof, pinpricks of light glittered, forming subtle arrays like nebulae.

"Crystals," Lucas said. "Way up in the roof. Quartz, amethyst, garnets. They catch the light of the city."

We were led to the castle, marched under the central portcullis and directed through courtyard after courtyard brimming with everyday castle life, the ring and hammer of smiths filling the air. It seemed so strange to live here, deep in the Earth, rarely seeing the sun.

At the central keep, we were ushered down a corridor. The walls glimmered with dwarf courtly scenes depicted in carved rock and inlaid metals. Finally, we were ushered into a massive throne room, grey stone arches rising high above. At the far end, Morion Auberon sat in a metal throne upon a broad, stepped dais. Guards and advisers stood on either side.

Morion's armour and helmet were an exquisite mix of copper and silver metals worked into spirals and sigils. His beard was tied in three plaits that stood out at angles, and above a hook nose shone two glinting eyes, assessing us as we approached.

We were thrown to our knees before the steps.

"Get up," Morion roared. Our hands still tightly bound, we struggled to our feet. The king strode toward us.

Morion's gaze locked onto Lucas, his dark eyes flashing. "You conniving, devious, despicable drac. How dare you enter my kingdom? The Massacre of the Underlands will never be forgotten."

The king drew a dagger from his armour and thrust it under Lucas's ribs. I flinched as blood streamed along Lucas's V-cut and onto his trousers. It looked like Morion was another of his fans.

Lucas mustered about as much concern as if he was sitting in the café drinking a noisette. He merely raised an eyebrow. "How dare I enter your kingdom? That's the question, isn't it? You haven't killed me because you know I wouldn't come to your delightful court without reason."

"You're a Rouseau—the epitome of evil." Morion sneered. "What justifiable reason would you have to come here?"

"I'm not my family," Lucas replied. "You have no right to judge me by their standards."

"I'll judge you as I see fit," the king bellowed.

Lucas raised his chin, his gaze like steel. "I'm a Keeper, elected by the assembly, and I'm here on that business alone."

"Krotite," Morion called.

An ancient dwarf with a snowy beard as long as his white robes shuffled forward. "Yes, sire," he croaked.

"Surely you were at the assembly when this was decided?"

"Sire, he was indeed elected by the assembly. He is a Keeper at Tarascon. Camille Amiel"—he nodded to me—"was elected as his partner. It was she who defeated the hantaumo queen."

There were mutterings from the advisers. It seemed my reputation preceded me.

"Sire," I said, hoping I was on safe ground with the address used by Krotite.

The king's gaze swung to mine.

Strength of command radiated from him, and I forced myself not to look away. "If it hadn't been for Lucas, I wouldn't have managed to take the queen's life. We worked together to bring her down." It was the truth, although I couldn't help note that Morion's opinion of Lucas was pretty much in line with Grampi's.

Morion stepped back, drawing the bloody point of the dagger from Lucas's abdomen with a twist. The only sign of Lucas's pain was the stiffening of his jaw.

"Camille Amiel," Morion said. "There isn't a single fae that hasn't welcomed the queen's death. But to be partnered with this drac..." His laughter echoed from the arches, his advisers accompanying him. "What a terrible twist of fate."

He stepped back to Krotite. "But why would the assembly appoint Lucas Rouseau to be a Keeper?" he asked the old dwarf. They conversed quietly. Morion's face hardened, then he nodded.

He turned to us, his hands on his hips, his legs spread wide. "Tell me, Lucas Rouseau, what the hell do you want?"

This was an improvement on "Why don't I kill you

now?". I wondered what Krotite had said. No doubt Lucas had heard.

"I know where your gold is," Lucas replied, the corners of his mouth flickering up.

The advisers around the dais exchanged glances.

For a split second, Morion's eyes grew wide, then his face hardened once again. "Of course you know where my gold is," he cried, raising a hand. "The largest hoard of gold in all of Fae is not without repute. Everyone knows it's stored in my vaults."

Lucas's gaze narrowed. "No, it's not. It was stolen. Just a little at first, then more and more. And"—he cast his eyes haughtily over Morion—"you're not wearing your renowned golden-scaled armour because it's been stolen too, as well as a whole lot of other gold from various races."

What was visible of the king's skin grew bright red. He took a breath and pulled himself up to his full height of about five feet. "You know nothing," he roared.

"The whole of Fae knows how closely you guard your secrets, Morion," Lucas replied. "Stop playing with us. Let's work together to get the gold back."

Morion looked as though he was about to erupt.

"We will tell you what we know if you give us information in return," I said. We needed to stop quarrelling and help everyone trapped in the mine.

"You are in no position to bargain with me, Amiel," the king roared, then said more softly, "But, agreed. Although if I find out this is a drac trick"—he glowered at Lucas—"you will both die."

Lucas nodded his acceptance. "I wouldn't expect anything less."

"Then what do you know?" Morion's eyes bored into me.

"A dwarf has been hoarding gold in Rancie mine on the bounds near Tarascon," I replied. "We're concerned about his motives. He's raised a black ward."

The king stared at us for a moment, then he turned back to his throne and sat down, his hands resting on the arms. "If the dwarf has raised a black ward, then he is deific."

Krotite stepped over, nodding. "It is as we thought."

The king glanced between Lucas and me. "We have strong reason to believe that the dwarf in question is Anthras."

My mouth fell open. Ras was short for Anthras, one of Abellion's servants. The myth was well known in the region, or at least it had been. Not many folk took interest in that kind of thing these days. "Anthras was a dwarf prince who crafted gold on Canigou, the mountain of the gods. Working with divine gold, he grew powerful, able to wield great magic. But he became jealous of Abellion, the greatest of all the gods and ruler of the Pyrenean pantheon."

Morion nodded. "Anthras attempted to steal Abellion's circlet to gain the god's power for himself, but Abellion caught him red-handed and condemned him to dig for gold in Coume dels Gours until he became truly remorseful for his crime." Morion ran his fingers down his central beard plait. "The crotchety old beggar isn't capable of remorse. His hate for Abellion grew like a disease."

"Then what's he up to now?" Lucas asked.

"He escaped Coume dels Gours just over a year ago." Morion jutted his jaw. "He gave us the slip."

"But if he's behind this, sire," Krotite said, "if he's hoarding the missing gold, we can only presume one thing."

The king nodded. "He wants to take down Abellion."

CHAPTER 28

MY FEET THUDDED AGAINST CREAKING, RICKETY BOARDS as I pounded down the Keepers' post stairs, scabbard and blade in hand. The sky, visible from the lattice window above the walled garden, held an early-morning glow. At least I hadn't slept late.

I'd bedded down in one of the spare rooms last night amidst dusty sheets, and Roux's voice had woken me. When we'd called him with an update on the way home, he'd confirmed that he wouldn't have the collude ingredients to break the black ward until morning. Morion Auberon had offered us the better part of his army to assist in defeating Anthras once the ward was down. Boy, did Morion want his gold back. But at least a plan was beginning to take shape.

The return journey from the dwarf court hadn't been quite so traumatic. The dwarves had control of Les Profondeurs's flow via a series of syphon caves. They ran the river at full volume most of the time to protect their border, but for us, they reduced the torrent to a trickle. We'd waded back through, the water stirring at our calves, and our fears stirring in our minds, but nothing more.

Back at the Keepers' post, I'd fallen into bed. My worries and everything I'd experienced in Les Profondeurs were too much for my exhausted state, and oblivion had taken me. I shivered, thinking of those dark waters, my inadequacy for the task at hand all too clear. University was beginning to seem like the most sensible option.

"What I need right now is breakfast." Roux was rummaging in the pantry as I strode into the kitchen.

"Good. You're back." I propped my blade in the corner. "Did you manage to get the ingredients for the collude?"

"Everything except the metals, which we have here." He pulled out a box and rummaged in it. One side of his straggly hair stuck up, and his face was mottled with red. "I'll add a little gold, palladium and copper. But yes, I have the alioth root, the scaldrake toenail, the tincture of black henbane prepared by a tranga, and the quail's egg laid on a full moon."

"How—" I'd been going to ask how he'd known when the egg was laid, but it really wasn't important. "Great." I massaged my bleary eyes.

"And I've worked up a healthy appetite." He pressed a hand into his cloak. There was something of a pot belly under there. I supposed I was hungry too. We'd had gloopy porridge at the dwarf court. It couldn't have been Morion's finest fare, but our baguettes had been ruined in Les Profondeurs.

"There's no food in," Lucas called from the meeting

room as he stropped a sword, one of a number lying alongside his chair. He looked fresh. His wounds had healed thanks to one of his potions last night, as had my cuts and bruises. He'd cleaned up, too, and donned fresh Keeper gear, which was more than I'd managed with my quick wash and yesterday's clothes.

I poured myself a glass of water and downed it as Gabe pushed through the door.

"Morning," he called as he headed into the kitchen. No doubt he'd gone home to sleep—I couldn't imagine his father allowing him out all night with Roux—but he looked terrible, his eyes bloodshot, a scattering of pimples on his chin.

Lucas placed his sword down and joined us. He took a bottle from the shelf and poured honey-coloured liquid into four cups. "A little something herbal. It's not as strong as the wake-up potion, but it's more sustaining. Good for the long haul."

He met my gaze as he handed me my cup. "Better this morning?"

"Considering I was half drowned, assaulted by dwarves and..." I'd been going to say manipulated then pinned against a wall by an incubus, but the memory of his body sent shivers through me, my pulse rushing.

"And...?" A glimmer lit his eyes, his freshly shaven jaw flexing. He knew exactly what I was thinking, damn him.

"And, I'm good," I said stiffly. "It looks like we're ready to break the black ward. Let's get on with it."

His gaze lingered for a moment, then he regarded the others. "We know that Anthras is planning to take out Abellion using the gold he's stolen, and we know he's likely to do this any time now, considering it's midsummer's tomorrow. But before we rush in to Rancie, I'm concerned we still don't know exactly how he's planning to do it."

"It doesn't make sense," Roux said. "There's no way Anthras could destroy Abellion." Having not found breakfast, he glanced longingly at the goblin bakers across the street. He couldn't be serious. Their food was terrible.

Lucas propped himself up against the worktop. "Trying to take out the god of gods would be like blasting a cannon at the sun."

"Agreed." Roux took a sip of potion.

"Couldn't we petition Abellion?" Gabe asked, peering at his drink with interest. "Let him know what's happening. After all, Anthras is his escapee." Presumably, Roux had updated Gabe.

"He's difficult to reach this time of year," Roux replied. "He's so powerful right now, he barely exists in his corporeal form, more like the sun itself than a god. But we could do a brief evocation to cover all bases."

My phone rang. I tapped accept, although I didn't recognise the number.

"Is that Camille Amiel?" a male voice asked.

"Yes, who's speaking?"

"It's the manager at Hôtel Teranostra. I have you down as the contact person for the Toulouse University folklore project. We've had a few concerned calls from relatives. They've not been able to contact their kin. On investigation, we don't believe the party returned to the hotel last night."

My stomach hitched. How was I going to explain this one? Lucas, who no doubt heard, raised his brow as if to say, "Can I help?" I shook my head.

"I'm sure it's a misunderstanding of some kind," the manager added. "But with the concerned relatives, I wanted to make certain."

"Uhhh." Time to make up some serious crap. Or rather, expand upon the crap I'd already told Maman. "Yes, I'm so sorry you weren't informed. The project decided to stay overnight at a mountain refuge"—being vague was probably sensible—"and the reception is particularly bad there. I'm sure they'll be in touch later. If not, I'll send an update."

"Good," he snapped in a way that implied anything but. "And I'd appreciate it if they'd let me and their relatives know in the future."

"Definitely," I replied, but the call had ended.

I pocketed my phone. "We need to get this sorted right now. Apart from the fact that it's midsummer's tomorrow, someone is going to realise the project is missing and call the police, which I'm guessing will complicate matters.

"The last thing we need is them searching Rancie." Lucas chugged his potion.

"We have to perform the collude," I said. "What are we waiting for?"

"Camille, we need to discuss this thoroughly." Roux looked down his nose at me. "There are lives at stake. It's also essential that we refuel, so we have our wits about us." He swirled his cup. "This is helping, but I need some food."

"Really? All you can think about is breakfast?" But he

did have a point. Who knew what would happen once the wards were down, and we needed our strength. I took a sip of potion, immediately feeling refreshed.

"Getting back to Anthras," Roux said, "he's notoriously clever. What if he's attempting some kind of short circuit—channelling Abellion's power against the god himself."

"Is that even possible?" I asked.

Lucas and Roux exchanged a glance.

Roux placed his cup down. "The rite of L'Or du Sang... blood gold."

"That could be it," Lucas muttered.

"Would someone care to explain," I asked.

Gabe's eyes shone. "The rite of L'Or du Sang involves combining gold with fae or human sacrifices to alter the way magic works. In a nutshell, thirteen captives are placed at equal distance around a golden circle. Their blood is released to drain onto the metal, which starts a chain reaction, igniting a gold fire in the centre. It burns outward to consume the victims."

Roux nodded. "Well done, boy."

Gabe attempted to restrain his smile, dimples forming in his cheeks.

I rubbed my forehead, not liking the sound of this.

"Though the mage is supposedly protected during this process," Roux added, "the resultant output of power is thought to be of a degree that will influence the cosmos."

Gabe's fingers tightened around his cup, excitement radiating from him. "The only record of the rite being carried out was in Prague in 1543 by a movement known as Annihilation Alchemy. The practitioners managed to wipe themselves off the face of the Earth, but they might not have performed the ritual correctly. Most mages consider it to be theoretical."

"So part of me wants to ask about the influence of the cosmos bit," I said, "but most of me is caught up on the fae or human sacrifice. I mean, are the project and my father going to be sacrificed in some ritual?" I couldn't help raising my voice.

Lucas and Roux glanced at each other.

"If that's what Anthras is doing," Lucas said, a frown knitting his brow, "then I suppose so. Although we can't be sure until we get in there."

Great. Just great.

"There's something else." Lucas's frown deepened. "The type of magic involved would cause the gold to fulminate, which might be the biggest problem of all."

"Seeing as I failed chemistry, an explanation wouldn't go amiss." I'd been awful at the subject, a part of me enjoying rejecting Papa's pet topic.

"A fulmination is an explosion," Roux said. "Gold is extremely volatile when mixed with certain substances such as ammonia or chlorine, but even more so when mixed with blood and magic. In the rite of L'Or du Sang, the gold particles agitate until, boom!" He flicked out his fingers.

Gabe tapped at his phone. "Even a little gold would cause a sizeable explosion with just one victim, but with thirteen... It's difficult to calculate, not knowing exactly how much gold Anthras has... but working on an estimate, and taking into account the dwarf's deific power..." His face fell. With trembling fingers, he passed the phone to Roux.

Roux studied the screen and nodded, his lips thinning. "The resulting discharge will take out everything from Toulouse to Barcelona, and probably a similar-sized chunk of Fae too."

My mouth fell open.

Lucas chewed his cheek, staring into the wall.

"The magic raised from the rite would be unprecedented." Roux passed Gabe's phone back. "It's quite possible that Anthras would do serious damage to Abellion."

"Not to mention," Lucas added, "Rancie is close to one of the most important points on the bounds—the dolmen of Sem. I can't even begin to imagine the consequences of a fulmination there. Worst-case scenario, the explosion rips the realms apart."

The room swam a little. Things were going from bad to worse. I needed to focus on what was in front of us before I completely lost it. "So we have to stop Anthras. Got that, loud and clear. But we still don't have much of a plan. Once we get through the wards, what are we going to do? He'll be souped up with magic, right?"

"He'll have masses of power," Lucas said. "But if he's trying to perform the rite of L'Or du Sang, which is highly complex with lengthy preparation, he'll be occupied with it. It's likely he'll have his defences arranged beforehand. That might be to our advantage."

"If there wasn't so much gold, I'd say remove it to remove his power source," Roux murmured half to himself. "But it's not an option. And having said that, I must add the metals to the collude ingredients. We won't be able to break the ward without them." He pulled open one of the drawers in the apothecary unit, then slid it shut with a snap. He tugged open another, and Gabe went over to help him.

"So," I said to Lucas, "we have to get in there and attempt to kill Anthras?"

He grinned. "Yep. And we have the dwarf army. They should be in position already, holding back a few miles into Fae for risk of provoking Anthras. But they'll have their scouts around the mine ready to give the word as soon as the ward is down. And in the meantime, there's always the Men."

I swallowed, images from Les Profondeurs reminding me yet again that I wasn't cut out to deal with this.

Roux and Gabe pulled out more drawers, then Roux turned to us. "We have another problem. The gold is gone."

Chapter 29

Lucas shoved between Roux and Gabe and searched the apothecary cabinets. "The gold can't be gone. It's impossible. We've got gold coin, gold ore, gold ingot, gold powder..."

"Why is the gold with the other herbs and minerals?" I asked. "Shouldn't it be locked away or something?"

Lucas glanced back. "The place is warded. Only those permitted can enter. The gold should've been safe." He slammed a drawer shut with his fist. "But it's all gone, even the horn we took off the goblin."

Roux paced about, his cloak swirling. "The ward was down for a moment when I removed it to apply a stronger defence. I was in the library. We were exposed for seconds at most."

"That charognard was in the vines across the street," Gabe said.

Lucas glowered. "Anthras is using the charognards to gather the gold. It was waiting."

"What are we going to do now?" I asked. "Presumably, without the gold, we're stuffed."

"I have a small amount at my place," Lucas replied. "Maybe a half ounce, max. I can go get it, but it will delay us."

Roux tugged his beard. "Everyone's gold is gone, so yours probably is too. You could check, but it will waste valuable time."

The mandragore in the jar above the espresso machine came to mind. Damn it. I'd completely forgotten about the creature with everything that had happened. But it had produced a sizeable gold nugget.

"I know where there's some fae gold, and I can get my hands on it in a few minutes." Unless Guy had spotted it, of course. Though, I would have heard something if he had.

"Good." Curiosity glimmered in Lucas's eyes. "So the plan is, Camille gets the gold. Roux and Gabe, you—"

"Wait a minute." I angled my chin. "We're not going to drag Gabe into this, are we?" He was sixteen, for heaven's sake, and he'd been through so much with the hantaumo.

Gabe's lips parted and he blinked slowly. "I... I need to help. I have to help."

"Absolutely." Roux's tone was pompous. "He's my apprentice, and he needs the experience."

Gabe grinned.

"Besides," Roux added, "the collude is complicated and I

can't perform it without him. After we've broken the ward, he can keep out of harm's way."

I couldn't argue with that. "Alright. Then Gabe, come with me. I might need help. We'll pick up some food while we're at it."

Gabe shrugged a shoulder. "Sure."

"Roux, do a brief collude to petition Abellion," Lucas said. "I doubt he'll answer, but it's worth a try. I'll stock up with herbs and weapons. We'll meet at my car in the café car park in fifteen, then head straight down to Rancie. Anthras will have defences around the place, so we'll have to perform the collude quickly and quietly. The Men can scout for us."

"Let's get on with it, then," I said, scouring the labels on the apothecary cabinets. Mugwort... mullein... There it was, mandragore. I pulled open the drawer and took out one of a few fist-sized brown roots. It was similar enough to Guy's, although definitely not alive, and it didn't have leaves. Lucas and Roux eyed me quizzically. Ignoring them, I grabbed my blade and headed to the door, Gabe following.

Outside, it was already too hot, even though the sun hadn't yet risen above the mountains.

"So tell me, Gabe," I said as we strode down the leafy street. "You've been home, right? Only you look wrecked." Although he did appear to be a little brighter than before, thanks to Lucas's potion.

"Yeah, of course." He glanced at me from the corner of his eye. "I climbed in the window just before my alarm, so Papa wouldn't worry. He's too busy with the rebuild of our boulangerie to notice anything suspicious. Then I headed back out."

I gnawed at my lip. "It's a school day, so now you're going to pull a sicky?"

"Come on." His eyes widened with faux desperation. "I heard you and Alice laughing about the times you skipped school to go skinny-dipping in Font Romèu."

Really? He'd overheard? "Well, that wasn't for your ears." We passed the Peppered Parsnip and headed into the café car park.

"Skiving at Font Romèu isn't as worthy a cause as saving the folklorists and"—he swallowed stiffly—"the whole area."

He had a point. "Just don't get in trouble."

"I won't," he said with a wonky grin. "And anyway, that stuff Doctor Rouseau... Lucas gave us was better than coffee."

We pushed through the doors into the café.

"If Guy is about," I said, "I need you to distract him. Just chat to him or something."

He nodded. "Sure."

I drew in the aroma of coffee and freshly baked bread. It soothed me as it did every time I arrived for work, but today, I needed it badly. Anthras and his plans loomed, but knowing the café was here with the townsfolk was such a comfort.

The place buzzed with the pre-work crowd—regulars plus a handful of strangers. The D&D gang stood around a table sorting takeout drinks. Gabe eyed them warily as we headed to the counter. Guy was behind the till. Damn, I'd hoped he'd be in the kitchen finishing the baking.

"Woo-hoo! Camille!" Guy's hair flopped into place as he struck a full-body pose of astonishment. "Thought you'd be off with the project in the mountains. Or is everyone back?"

I pressed my nails into my palms. An alibi had been the last thing on my mind. "Uh, no, they're still out there. I came back early to... uh... make some preps for their return."

I glanced at the shelf above the espresso machine. The mandragore was still there. Fingers crossed, it was alright. I just needed a moment without anyone looking...

Guy was the only one behind the counter. The sweet warble of Dame Blanche singing came from the kitchen. The others were probably doing something out there too, or they were in the office. Voices rose above the general chatter in the café. I ignored them to focus on the task at hand.

"Just let us know when you need refreshments," Guy added, "and we'll be on it. Oh, and we had eight more acid attacks last night. The police think the crims are pouring the stuff out on our fields, fly-tipping it or something. But why the hell would they do that? Why not just dump the containers? And Alice is going to be stoked to see you." His grin extended from ear to ear.

"Oh?"

"I'll let her tell you—" His attention tracked away to the seating area. "Hey, you guys!"

I followed his gaze. Gabe stood with the D&D gang, Félix right up in his face.

"You're such a creep, dressing up like an elf every day," Félix snarled. "What a weirdo."

My lips parted. Gabe and Félix had been best friends for

years. Even with their recent problems, I couldn't believe Félix was speaking like that. But then, Gabe was providing a distraction. Perhaps he'd provoked Félix on purpose. Guy marched around the counter, his sights locked on the boys. I had my chance.

"You can talk," Gabe growled at Félix as I pulled the jar from the shelf. "All you do is sit around playing a game all day."

The poor mandragore. It was lying on its back looking rather grizzled, its eyes closed, its mouth turned down, its wrinkles deep. But there was the gold ingot—no, two ingots—tucked underneath it. I pulled the creature out and stuffed it in my glamoured pouch with the gold, then placed the dried root in the jar. I hated that I was denying Guy his riches. If there was anyone who needed them, it was him, but lives were at stake.

"You and the others," Gabe continued as I screwed on the lid. "You never do anything but play D&D. You're such babies."

Heat rose in Félix's cheeks, his face stiffening with hurt and rage. The rest of the café was watching with curiosity.

"Right, you two," Guy said, pushing between them. "Time to take a break. I'm sure I can find a few choquettes for everyone."

As I placed the jar on the shelf, Félix sprang around Guy and shoved Gabe in the shoulders. "Freak!"

Gabe stumbled back, his lip curling, his eyes flashing. "You're such an asshole, Félix."

Shit. Surely Gabe hadn't intended it to go this far?

Guy attempted to get between the two again, but they sidestepped him. Time for an intervention. As I strode over, Félix swung his fist at Gabe, catching him on the jaw. Gabe released a yowl of fury and returned the favour, driving a blow into Félix's stomach.

Guy grabbed Gabe's arm, but Gabe twisted away and pounced on Félix. The two of them fell to the ground, toppling the table, takeout cups flying. They wrestled with hands clawing and knees driving into stomachs.

The D&D gang chanted, "Félix, Félix, Félix, Félix."

I seized Félix's T-shirt, and Guy grabbed Gabe's cloak. We tried to pull them apart, but they clung to each other like rowdy mutts.

"If you want to continue playing D&D in here," I yelled, "that's enough!"

The D&D gang fell silent. Félix released Gabe and jumped up, shooting daggers at him.

Gabe clambered to his feet. "Idiot," he muttered.

Félix stepped toward him, his fists clenched. "You dumped us," he said softly. "You left us... I was your best friend, and you just left me."

Gabe's mouth fell open.

Félix shook his head, his hair and shirt in disarray, his chin held high. With a glance at the gang, he marched out, the others following.

The show over, everyone returned to their drinks. Guy tidied up, muttering at the mess. Nora was standing in the washroom doorway staring at Gabe, her eyes wide.

"Right, Gabe. Over here." I yanked him behind the counter. "Some distraction," I hissed.

"It wasn't a distraction." Gabe was still bristling. His cloak was ripped, the dark flush of a bruise was blossoming on his jaw, and his ear tips were missing, revealing his actual elf ears. "That geek has been at me ever since the hantaumo attack."

"Ever since you started ignoring him, it sounds like. Not to mention, you've had no sleep, and I guess you're pretty riled about the prospect of Anthras blowing us all up—because I know I am—so let it drop."

"Camille!" Alice cried, emerging from the back. "Just the person I wanted to see." Not the best timing. I glanced out the front window, but Lucas's SUV was empty. I had a moment for her.

I grabbed four goat cheese and tomato demi baguettes and shoved them at Gabe. "Take these and go wait for Lucas and Roux in the car park."

He ground his jaw, then with a glare, he strode out.

Alice came over and drew me into a hug.

"Hey, sweety," I murmured, squeezing her tight as if I could communicate through my body how much I needed her.

She pulled back, grinning. But it wasn't the usual Alice smile. It was bigger—unrestrained and toothy. Her eyes sparkled, and she just looked zingy. She wore her best Alice skirt, a gorgeous chiffon top and a punky padlock-chain necklace.

"What was that racket a moment ago?" Her warm eyes

trawled the café, her round, sweet face home to me. "I completely lost track of the profit and loss."

That was something. She got really engrossed in figures. "Félix and Gabe scrapping," I replied. "But what's going on? Guy said you have news, and you look all shiny."

"Yeah, she's got big news," Guy said as he passed with the D&D gang's crushed takeout cups.

Beaming, she took my hands in hers and squeezed. "I know it's soon... and I know that Raphaël and I haven't known each other for long... but last night, over a romantic dinner at La Ciboulette..."

Oh, hell no. Please no. Please, please, no.

The sparkle in her eyes intensified. "Raphaël proposed, and I said yes." She jumped up and down, spring-boarding off my shoulders, then she shoved her hand under my nose. A beautiful gold ring with a large lozenge diamond shone from her finger.

I stared at it. I could feel myself gaping, my breath shallow, my chest contracting. This could not be happening. I had to say something about Raphaël being a goblin, but how could I?

"I... I... I... You can't..." was all I could muster. "You... don't know him. It's been weeks. It's way too soon to get married."

In an instant, as if a portcullis had fallen over her face, all that shine and glimmer was gone. "Listen to yourself. Where's my friend? The girl who grabbed life by the horns, who ran off to Venice on a one-night stand, who always had my back, no matter what I did? You were the most supportive person I've ever known. What the hell is up with you, Camille?"

Breath left my chest. This was so unfair. I wanted to explain everything, to pull her to me, to tell her that I was here for her, that I always would be. But that rat, Raphaël. If she only knew... I had to try harder. "Two weeks, Alice, or is it three? And you want to spend the rest of your life with him?"

Her lips pressed tight, her jaw tensing. "I'm fed up with you. You've treated Raphaël like crap from the start, not speaking to him and feigning illness when he's around." Her gaze flared. "How can you be so mean?"

All I could do was haul in one shallow breath after the other as her eyes burned fire into me.

"And you're sneaking around with Lucas. You never tell me what's going on—and I sure as hell know something *is* going on." Her voice rose. "If anyone should be worried, *I* should be concerned about *you*. We used to tell each other everything. Well, I've had it, Camille. I've had enough. *Enough!*" She banged her fist on the counter.

I flinched, desperate for her to stop.

"Until you can be civil again," she added, "and respect my decisions... Until you tell me what's going on"—for a moment her mouth opened and closed as if she was trying to find the words—"then you can forget our friendship, because it's all based on shit."

Her words cut into my heart. And still, there was nothing I could say.

CHAPTER 30

"IT'S MUCH TOO QUIET," LUCAS SAID SOFTLY AS WE crouched on the mulch before the wrinkled mandragore. "I don't like it."

I glanced at Roux and Gabe, who were quietly preparing the collude. They were stationed as close as possible to the dark ward without suffering from its effects. Roux's petition to Abellion hadn't worked, unsurprisingly, and the Collude of Exceptional Infiltration was all we had.

Lucas prodded and poked the mandragore, dappled sunlight mottling his face. The creature's limbs shifted, and it grizzled, but its eyes were still closed. I rubbed my sweaty palms over my trousers. Even though we were under a canopy of chestnut, ash and birch, it was unbelievably hot.

"Anthras is either watching us and biding his time before he makes his move," Lucas muttered, "or he's so certain the black ward will hold, he's not bothered we're here."

Even though we'd snuck up here via a little-used lane

then crept through trees and undergrowth, if Anthras wanted to track us, with that much gold and thus magic at his disposal, he wouldn't have any trouble.

"All that power," I said. "Once we've broken the ward, what are we going to do against him?"

Lucas grinned. "Stakes like this make everything so much more fun."

"Really?" I scowled at him, wishing Roux and Gabe would hurry up, and hoping that Papa and everyone else was alright.

Slaughter popped out from behind a tree. "The Men are ready, gov—stationed all around. Nothing will get past them."

Lucas nodded. "Good."

Slaughter took up position a little way away, his face contorted into a battle grimace, his tiny but sturdy hands wrapped around his axe.

The place felt creepy, like last time I was here. I glanced about, but there was nothing except trees, brambles and the odd patch of ore serpent venom. The rest of the Men were extremely well hidden.

My stomach twisted, the demi baguette I'd nibbled on the drive here churning. When we'd faced the hantaumo, we'd known what we were up against. It was fight or die. Simple. This time, we didn't really have a clue.

But it wasn't just that. It was my row with Alice. We'd argued in the past. Not much, but every now and again we had a blinder. Usually because of a misunderstanding on one or both our parts. We'd always learnt from it, though, and grown closer.

But now... now there was no way we could make up because I couldn't be honest with her. I would have to fabricate a permanent lie, which wasn't healthy for either of us. I certainly couldn't tell her the truth. I balled my hands and wriggled my shoulders as if I could shake it all off, but I couldn't.

Impressions from Les Profondeurs returned once again, cloying like treacle. I wasn't enough. Not enough to sort out the mess with Alice, or get my research noticed without academic qualifications, or keep fae away from the project. The list went on. And I certainly wasn't enough to be here, traipsing around with a sword on my back like some deranged LARPer in the hope that I might be of help. But with so much at stake, I had to try. I just needed to be sure not to hinder Lucas as I had in the river.

The mandragore squirmed a little. "It really doesn't look well," I said.

"It will be fine. Its epidermis needs moisture." Lucas removed the lid of a mineral water he'd brought from the car. He poured the contents over the thing amidst coughs and gripes, its fat limbs flailing, the green leaves on its head fluttering. As the water soaked in, the creature limbered up, thrashing around. It rocked its whole plump body until it tipped onto its side and clambered up on rooty feet. Teetering about and narrowly missing a pool of ore serpent venom, it made its way into a bramble thicket.

Good, it was okay.

We got up, and I leant against a chestnut, watching Roux and Gabe, the rough bark pressing into my palms. Lucas scoured the area, listening with drac hearing, then his gaze fixed on mine. "What is it, Camille?"

"What? I'm fine." I glanced away. "Well, apart from the fact that my project and my father have been kidnapped by a psycho dwarf who's about to blow us all to smithereens."

"You're not fine. There's something dragging you down."

I had to give it to the guy. He was perceptive. I hauled in a long breath then released it. "I had an argument with Alice. A bad one."

Lucas turned back to the forest. "The goblin boyfriend?"

"He's asked her to marry him. I have no idea what to do."

"Fae and human integration." He smirked. "Can't be a bad thing."

"The integration isn't the problem. It's that she doesn't know what he is. It's not right."

"Hmmm. It does occasionally happen." He turned to scan the forest behind us. "I could break his legs. Persuade him that he might be better off living a very long way from here. Although the goblin court would have something to say about that, especially as he wouldn't have done anything wrong in their eyes. Besides, I'm not their favourite person right now."

"What with Grampi, the dwarves and everyone avoiding you like the plague in fae Tarascon, you really are very popular."

"It's my charm." He bumped his brow.

I shook my head. "No leg-breaking. And running

Raphaël out of town doesn't seem right either. What if he *is* the one for her, gross goblin and all?"

"There it is again. Goblin prejudice." His lips quirked.

"It's not prejudice, it's just the thought of sleeping with... ugh. I can't go there." For a moment, I thought Lucas winced, but it was just the mottled light playing on his face.

"There's always verity," he said.

I spun around, glaring at him. "You have to be joking? How could I do that to my friend? How could I rip everything she believes to be true from under her?"

"But it's not true, is it?" His gaze bored into the trees.

Fury shot through me. It was all too clear he didn't understand. "You did that to me. You took away my life, such as it was, by showing me the truth." Damn, this still rankled.

He glared back. "And if I hadn't, you'd be hantaumo food by now."

"But that wasn't why you did it, was it? You wanted me as your partner."

"The assembly decided upon you. We've been through this." He turned ninety degrees and surveyed another part of the forest, his jaw rigid. "But that's not all of what's troubling you, is it? There's been something up since Les Profondeurs."

Yep. Much too perceptive.

But there was no harm in saying what was on my mind, at least the part of it that concerned him. "I'm not cut out to be a Keeper," I snapped. "It's ridiculous. I'm just an ordinary person. I shouldn't even be here."

Fuck. I pressed my nails and my back into the chestnut, my blade digging into me. I was aware of how self-absorbed I was being, but facts were facts, and everything was becoming clear. Despite how intrigued I was about Fae, and how free I felt there, not to mention how amazing it had been letting rip with my blade, it made sense to go to university and qualify properly. Qualifications meant approval, a piece of paper certifying that I could do the job. I loved folklore research. It wouldn't be a hardship to become a student. Hell, it would be unbelievable, and I needed the validation so much. So why did it feel like a heavy weight on my chest?

I leant my head back against the tree, pressing my skull into the ridges as if I could press away my thoughts. We had to free Papa and the project. That was all I needed to be concerned about right now.

Roux gave us the thumbs up, ready to start the collude. If Anthras was going to make a move, it would be now. My stomach swam a little more. I glanced at Lucas, wondering if we needed to take cover, but he was already looking at me, his gaze scrutinising, those intelligent eyes seeing more than was comfortable.

He raised his chin. "Maybe it doesn't matter if we have enough skill or energy or resources to face what life throws at us. Maybe it only matters that we try."

I frowned. His words made sense. They really did. But it was as if they lay on the surface and wouldn't sink in.

He nodded to Roux and drew his blade. I followed suit. Slaughter adjusted his axe grip. Roux and Gabe began chanting in a stream of Old French, their arms outstretched in the centre of the septagram they'd formed near the black ward, alder leaves and the other collude ingredients around them. Roux hadn't wanted us involved this time. The collude required a carefully pronounced invocation that the two of them had practised repeatedly since yesterday.

Luminescence shone between them, then it flared into a blazing, crackling light that poured out toward the mine. The ward responded with a maelstrom of black fire. Light and dark vied for dominance until light blazed so intensely it filled the forest and consumed the blackness. I shielded my eyes, unable to see. The crackling grew to a roar.

Above the clamour came cries of "Arghhhh" and "Nooooo".

In an instant, the light snuffed out, leaving Roux and Gabe at the centre of a charred septagram, flames licking up their cloaks.

I was pretty sure that wasn't supposed to happen.

CHAPTER 31

ROUX AND GABE FLAPPED INEFFECTUALLY AT THEIR burning cloaks. We ran at them, scattering Men. Lucas pounced on Roux, and I dove on Gabe, knocking him down and rolling him in the bracken until the flames died. Gabe's eyes were wide, his breath ragged, his hair and eyebrows singed.

"You okay?" I asked.

"Yep." He grinned from ear to ear. "That was awesome!" I wasn't sure if he meant the collude, the fire or the rescue. Perhaps all three. He glanced at the ward, which still flickered with black fire, and his smile faltered. "But we didn't do it. We didn't break through." That realisation was sinking into me too. What the hell were we going to do now?

Roux, having received the same rolling from Lucas, lay on the ground groaning. "I don't know why the damned thing didn't work. It really should have."

Lucas scanned the forest. "Still no sign of a deterrent

from Anthras. I guess we just proved his defences are enough to keep us out."

The bracken shifted beside Lucas. He sprang up, drawing his blade. Out shot an ore serpent. We must have disturbed its hiding place. It looked as if it was going to dart off, but then it stopped and retched in Gabe's and my direction. I'd been in this position before.

I jumped up, dragging Gabe with me. The venom landed partially on a dagger that had fallen from Gabe's cloak. The blade sizzled to nothing in seconds.

I stared at the waft of vapour drifting upward. The metal had disintegrated, just like that. "Roux," I said slowly, an idea forming. "Tell me something..."

"At your service. He clambered up, stepping on the blackened rim of his cloak. The whole thing tore away, revealing spotted Y-fronts. "Abellion's breeches," he muttered.

"More like his underpants," Gabe said, attempting to restrain a grin, his own cloak not much more than scorched rags. But all I could think about was the venom. The ore serpent was retching again, but it didn't have that violent about-to-erupt look.

"If the serpent's acid can dissolve that dagger," I said. "I'm guessing it can dissolve gold just as easily?" The serpent gained control of itself and dashed off down the hillside.

"Most definitely," Roux replied. "The creatures are drawn to it. I believe it's one of their favourite forms of nourishment. The acid they produce digests—" He stared at me, his mouth opening and closing like a goldfish's, his beard bobbing. "My dear girl," he managed, "that's why the serpents are here. It has to be. They're producing excess acid and they've been drawn to the surface instinctively because of the massive stockpile of gold in Rancie."

Lucas grinned. "That's it. If we can get them to dissolve the gold, Anthras will be powerless."

"We need that serpent." I jumped up and sprinted through the trees to where it had disappeared over the brow of the hill. There it was, slithering away at high speed, its body twisting one way and then another as it headed down to the pass between the two peaks. Sunlight flashed off its metallic skin, making it easy to track, even in the undergrowth.

"Stop," I yelled. To hell with keeping quiet. The collude had already caused a racket. "I don't mean any harm, but we have to talk. Your lives depend on it... Our lives depend on it."

Lucas raced ahead and leapt at the serpent. It darted to the side. He landed on all fours, empty-handed.

A troop of Men charged for the creature, spear-throwers raised.

"Don't hurt it," I yelled.

The Men disappeared back into the undergrowth.

Lucas shot forward. Taking a wide birth around the serpent, he headed it off and pounced. The creature swerved again, and Lucas landed face first in the dirt.

Scales flashing, the serpent crossed the pass and shot up the opposite slope. Then, without reason, it slowed to a halt. Lucas joined my side and we approached at a cautious walk.

Beyond holly and scrub, an alcove of rock rose up, trapping it. It shook, terrified. The host of wild miniature warriors at our sides brandishing spears, axes and slingshots probably wasn't helping.

"Please," I said. "We don't mean you any harm. Please listen."

It dove at a crack in the rock face and elongated, forcing its head inside a crevice.

We sprang forward and grabbed its thinning tail. It squelched in our grips, reducing to metallic slime. We pulled, stepping further and further back until it elongated into nothing more than string. Another heave and it popped out of the rock.

It resumed its previous shape and lay shaking on the ground, its spines flat against its body. "Don't kill me," formed in my head.

"We won't harm you," I said hurriedly. "We know how to help you with the excess venom."

At that, it cocked its trembling head. "Help? If you can help, you must. We're dying." We released its tail.

Gabe and a puffing Roux came to a halt beside us.

"There's a large quantity of gold stored in Rancie mine," I said. "It may be what's brought you to the surface and caused you to produce too much acid. If Anthras gets chance to use the gold, it's going to explode, and everyone in the area will die, serpents and humans alike. But if you can bring your kind here to dissolve it, Anthras will be powerless."

Gabe eyed the serpent with curiosity. "If the gold is gone, won't the dwarves be pissed?"

Lucas shrugged. "An army of angry dwarves is better than the place blowing. Not much better, but better."

"Green vitriole is the thing," Roux said. "The dwarves have it in abundance—a little brewing and that gold will precipitate right back into its solid state. We just need to contain it so it doesn't run off into the water table. And once it's redistributed, the ore serpents won't be affected anymore."

The serpent tilted its head, its tongue flickering out. "Your theory makes sense, but there would have to be a lot of gold in Rancie to pull us from the depths."

"There's a lot alright," I said. "Going by reports—"

A deep rumbling filled the air, and the ground shook. The serpent looked as panicked as I felt. We all turned around, Men included, and peered through the trees to the peak that hid the mine. Nothing. Just my chest vibrating and my feet shaking. It had to be an earthquake, although they were rare in the Pyrenees.

The rumbling rose to a crescendo, and with an almighty boom, a large chunk of the mountain above the mine crumbled away.

CHAPTER 32

FROM THE HOLE IN THE MOUNTAINSIDE, A SOFT GOLDEN glow rose to meet the sun. The air around the mine shimmered with a glamour.

"It wouldn't take too much to guess," I murmured, "that whatever Anthras has planned, he's not waiting until midsummer's day."

"I think that may be an accurate assumption." Lucas turned to the serpent. "You and your kin have to help—and quickly. It's the only chance we have."

The serpent nodded. It dove at the rock, becoming slime that oozed into the fissure.

"We still don't know how we're going to get inside the black ward," I said.

Lucas scowled. "We're going to have to figure it out, and the snakes need to be ready—"

Roux cleared his throat from the side of the rocky alcove.

We turned around. Roux and Gabe stood stock still, their

faces pale, their eyes wide. Charognards emerged from the bushes behind, chattering noisily. They were big. Much bigger than those at the Pons farm. These were more like metallic goblin apes. And as if their claws weren't enough, they held knives. We drew our blades, my pulse hitching as they surrounded us.

Roux's beard quivered. "I think we found Anthras's defences."

The charognard behind him screeched, peeling its lips back to reveal sharp teeth of all sizes. Jumping up and down, it pressed the undulating knife into Roux's back.

These charognards were more intelligent than the ones in the cave, as well as larger, and it was clear what this creature meant—drop your weapons or your friends die. My heart thumped, hope draining away. Captured, our chances of stopping Anthras were zero.

I glanced at Lucas, who nodded. We cast our blades to the ground and raised our hands. More charognards scampered toward us from the undergrowth, ivy twines in their claws. They grabbed our hands and tied them behind our backs.

Doing something akin to a body search, they took our pouches. There went my mobile, along with any chance of help, although I had no idea who I'd call, and the thing was probably fried anyway. A charognard drew a pair of Nerf guns from Gabe's tattered cloak, the garish yellow-and-orange plastic standing out amidst the woodland and the fae. What good did he think those were going to do?

A couple of charognards gathered our swords from the

ground and attempted to wield them, slashing around. One sliced off the ear of a compadre, silver glitter cascading to the forest floor. The injured creature yowled furiously.

In a flash of skins and stone weapons, the Men appeared and launched a spear assault. Countless charognards emerged from the undergrowth and held them off, as the creatures behind us jabbered irately and edged closer. We took the hint, and with more screeching and a fair amount of claw-flashing, we were directed across the pass and up the hill toward the mine.

"At least if we get inside the ward," Lucas whispered at my side, "we may be able to do something from there."

"Yeah. Or we may be toast." I gazed longingly at my blade as it was carried off into the forest.

We headed upward, drawing too close to the black ward. I tensed, expecting the icy terror and mirky gauze I'd felt the first time I'd encountered it. The world flashed black for a second, and we were through without any other effects. No doubt the charognards had some kind of dispensation.

We were led into the mine entrance that Lucas and I had taken before. A storm swirled in my stomach. I had to prepare myself for the worst. Papa and the project could be injured or... Nope. I couldn't even contemplate the idea.

At first the passage was dark, then we rounded a bend, and I gasped. The main cavern gleamed. Its roof was gone, and under the blazing sun shone a massive circle of gold. Lucas gaped, and mutters of astonishment came from Roux and Gabe behind. The charognards forced us to a halt by the edge and surrounded us tightly, daggers raised.

The golden circle extended out over halfway to the rough-hewn rock walls and tunnels, and the glare was so bright, the air was hazy. Or was that from the tremendous sense of power that emanated from the metal? Either way, what with the glare, I couldn't see further than the edge, which consisted of gold bars, nuggets, goblets, horns, plates and jewellery of all kinds, jewels extracted. If Gabe's calculations were correct, the hoard had to be worth billions of euros.

To our sides, the bounds wound around the edge of the chamber, delineated by black cracks creeping outward. Above, the walls shifted. I had to be seeing things, but it wasn't the rock moving. Every inch of the place was covered in super-sized charognards. A couple of hornless sheep peered in from a side tunnel. Why they'd had to bring the sheep into the mine was beyond me.

As my eyes became accustomed to the glow, I could make out posts positioned around the dazzling circle, figures tied to them.

"For goodness' sake," one of the captives called. "This is preposterous. Let us go at once. It's utterly ridiculous being held hostage by a man dressed as a dwarf." There was no mistaking that voice. Papa.

Relief surged through me, my eyes pricking. He was alright, at least for the moment. I swallowed the emotion away. Roux had been right about the ritual. "This has to be the rite of L'Or du Sang," I whispered to Lucas.

"Hundred percent agreement." He surveyed the gold.

"But then, Papa recognised Anthras as a dwarf. He

should be seeing something else, some kind of compensatory image."

"A magical field this strong forces everyone to see the reality before them. In many cases, the effect is pretty traumatising."

My vision adapting further, I could make out Papa and the others tied to posts—Joly, Sissoko, Pascale, Meera, Simon and seven other members of the project. Thankfully, they too were alive. A huge mound of gold had been piled right in the centre of the circle between them.

Anthras wandered from one captive to another, checking restraints and muttering to himself. He was completely absorbed in what he was doing, and he looked older than before, his hunched body twisted like warped wood. No doubt he'd glamoured himself previously. As he continued, he had to clamber over the gold in places. His legs, sticking out from his light armour, were almost too spindly for the job.

"What do we do now?" I murmured.

Lucas's eyes narrowed. "I have absolutely no idea. But I'm sure we'll think of something."

Anthras cocked his head, noticing us. He picked his way across the gold toward our charognard prison.

"Well done, my metal warriors," he called.

The charognards chattered softly in response.

"Camille!" Papa cried.

All the captives glanced at us, astonishment on their faces.

The dwarf clambered off the golden circle stiffly, one leg at a time, his dark eyes peering at us from under a heavy brow. His bulbous nose dragged his face down, and wrinkles as deep as bounds cracks disappeared under his wiry beard.

"Good. Keepers," Anthras said as he hobbled over. "I had thought of inviting you to help with my plans yesterday, but your disappearance might have raised alarm bells, and I wasn't quite ready."

Charognards bunched together before us to ensure Anthras's protection.

"In fact," he continued, "Lucas Rouseau, I wasn't going to bother with you, despite my arrangement with Elivorn. But you're strong and fit. You'll make a good sacrifice."

"Elivorn?" Lucas's voice was low and deadly, his eyes blazing. "What's he got to do with it?" He lunged forward, but a host of knives and claws rose before him, the charognards jabbering their warning.

Anthras angled his head and cackled. "Why, you look so surprised. From what I've heard, you brothers have never been close. Elivorn is your father's favourite, isn't he?" He grinned, revealing grimy teeth. "But no matter. Dear Elivorn offered me rather a lot of gold to carry out my plans on the bounds, hoping my little explosion would help nudge the realms apart. I was happy to oblige. After all, this is one of the most powerful places in the world. But then he offered me even more gold to take your life, thinking that my plans might lure you here. He was right." Anthras cackled again. "I wasn't bothered about fulfilling that part of the deal, though. But as you're here..."

"That devious asswipe," Lucas rumbled, his face red with fury. And I thought I had family problems.

"Yes, yes, I gather that." Anthras smiled. "But he's been very useful. And when the bounds separate, it will be of benefit to me. Once I obtain Abellion's circlet, I'll have dominion over Fae, and none of the little beasts will be able to escape to the human realm. I'll enjoy tormenting them as I've been tormented, endlessly digging Abellion's gold."

"But you'll wipe out everything. You'll kill hundreds of thousands of people." I had to try.

He just cackled and raised a gnarled finger at Lucas. "Bring him to the circle. Throw the rest in the cell."

CHAPTER 33

THE CHAROGNARDS SCREECHED AND THRUST DAGGERS toward Lucas. He had no choice but to climb onto the circle of gold. Simon was untied and Lucas was secured in his place.

The rest of us were ushered between the bounds cracks and the gold to an old iron grille that grated off a tunnel. Light blazed into it, revealing a bend a little way back. A charognard pulled part of the grille open, and the creatures bounced and jabbered as Roux, Gabe and I were shoved inside, followed by Simon, who fell flat on the floor. The charognards slammed the grille shut and stationed themselves outside.

Simon pushed himself up with difficulty, his hands also tied, his much-too-trendy shirt filthy. Remarkably, he still wore his glasses, although they were wonky and dirty. He tried to adjust them with his shoulder, but it did no good.

"This is ridiculous. One moment tied to a post, the next

back in here. And dwarves and gold and whatever those devil-monkey things are." He was muttering hysterically to himself, not even acknowledging us. "I'm hallucinating. Although as the others are seeing the same thing, I guess we've ingested ergot or the like. It was probably in the patisserie at the café. Although what I wouldn't do for some bread right now."

"Uh, Simon?" I said.

He stepped closer, tipped his chin and peered at us through his dirty glasses. "Camille? What are *you* doing here? You obviously didn't pick up our change of plans yesterday. Absolutely typical."

"Oh, I'm catching up right now," I growled.

He assessed me with curiosity. "You're wearing a sort of medieval warrior outfit. I thought your clothes were rather basic before, but this is just weird."

"Have you noticed the maniacal dwarf outside, plus the mountain of treasure? I kind of think you're the one who's underdressed."

His eyebrows peaked in the middle. "Maybe. But those two?"

A few remaining shreds of cloak still hung from Roux's shoulders. He wriggled, trying to conceal his spotted Y-fronts with them. Gabe just shuffled.

"I never recommend judging a book by its cover." Roux straightened up, attempting dignity. "We are your rescue party."

Simon scoffed. "Now *that* I would like to see." His gaze settled on Gabe's ears. "An elf, huh. What a trip."

"One helluva elf." Gabe beamed from the recognition of his true self.

But we didn't have time for this. "We have to figure out how to get out of here." I stepped over rubble to the grille and looked out, not getting close enough to rile the charognards. The others joined me and peered over my shoulders.

I narrowed my eyes against the glare. Anthras shuffled around between his captives and the massive pile of gold in the centre of the circle. He muttered to himself, glancing up to the sun, then shifting pieces of gold here and there. It had to be almost midday, the height of the sun's power.

Lucas struggled on the opposite side of the circle, his hands bound behind the pole, his ankles tied to the front. His feet were bare for some reason. The glare had to be so bright for him and the captives. There was no way they could make us out over here.

Papa stood two poles to Lucas's side, a student between them. I could see the others too—Joly's face creased in fury, Sissoko's eyes closed, his lips moving as he intoned a silent prayer, Pascale dumbfounded, and poor Meera sobbing loudly. Pascale whispered something to her, which didn't seem to help. Anthras was happily ignoring them all, absorbed in rearranging gold.

"I have no idea what's going on." Simon's voice trembled.

This had to be hard on him. I should go easy. "They're about to be sacrificed in a ritual that will blow up the Pyrenees."

"Oh." He nodded slowly.

"I don't see how we can escape past the charognards," Gabe said. "There's too many."

"Agreed," Roux added. "It's an impossible situation."

I turned around and glared at them. "Yeah, that's really helpful. Just a little positive thinking." Though I couldn't shake off the feeling that they were right. That I was so completely not cut out for this.

I returned to scanning the cavern. A few sheep were milling about near the edge of the circle, and not too far from the grille, our weapons lay amidst the rubble with our pouches. Nearby, two charognards were playing ineffectually with Nerf guns.

"If I can just get my hands free and reach a blade..." There *were* too many charognards, but what else could I do? I wriggled against my bindings, not achieving anything.

"So not only do you mess up administration," Simon said, "and generally cause turmoil, but you wield a sword."

"Yep. Forgot to mention that when I applied to the project."

A sob echoed from along the passageway, accompanied by whispering.

"Who's that?" I asked.

"The others," Simon replied. "The dwarf only needed thirteen of us for his party."

I headed along the passageway, the others, including a slightly limping Simon, following. The bend led into relative darkness—anything was dark away from the gold's glare. The tunnel ended a little further back, and Grampi sat against the far wall with the rest of the project, his arm around a particularly distraught guy. I couldn't believe my eyes. In my mind Grampi was safely back at the farm making cheese.

"Izac, good to see you!" Roux proclaimed. "Well, of course, not good. Very terrible to see you in here, but you know what I mean."

Grampi smiled at him, avoiding my astonished glare. "I do, Roux, I do. And it's good, whilst also quite terrible, to see you, too."

"Quite," Roux muttered.

Grampi turned his attention to Gabe. "Well, young Gabriel. I hear you're an elf, and a fine one at that." Gabe beamed some more.

"What the hell are you doing here?" was all I could say. I registered Grampi's clothing. He wore a version of what Lucas and I had on, all brown leather, but looser, befitting his age. An empty scabbard was buckled about his torso.

"What's the connection?" Simon whispered to Gabe.

"He's Camille's grandfather," Gabe replied.

Simon pressed his lips together. "Explains the matching outfits."

Grampi drew a long breath through his nose, then rubbed his bushy eyebrows. "I came here yesterday, after our meeting. Thought I could investigate, help out, so you didn't have to get involved."

I folded my arms across my chest, everything from that meeting—everything from Les Profondeurs—coming back at full force once again. "And you did so well, helping out." Sharpness edged my voice. His disbelief in me cut so deep and twisted viciously, even though I was beginning to think he was right. "Aren't you a bit old for this?"

As soon as I'd said it, I wished I hadn't. I did kind of mean it in a purely practical way, but by his wince, I'd hit home. Shit "I... I didn't mean it like that."

"No. You have a right to say it... because it's the truth. With Fae's influence on my age, I might have had plenty of active years as a Keeper, but the curse took its toll. I'm not as equipped for this as I used to be."

And here I was, taking over. I didn't know how to reply.

"But," he added, "you shouldn't be here either. It's too dangerous."

"Really?" I snapped. "Really, really, really? We're here saving your butt as well as Papa's and the project's. A thank you would be much more appropriate."

"Perhaps we could continue the family reunion another time," Simon put in.

We ignored him.

"Thank you?" Grampi roared. "You haven't saved anything, you're as stuck as we are in here, and everything is about to blow."

"Yeah, well, if you just give me a second," I shouted. But there was no point arguing. I took a deep breath. "This isn't going to get us anywhere. Our weapons are outside the grille —if we can get out there somehow..."

Grampi's shoulders sank. He glanced at Roux and pointed to the corner. "There's waterskins over there, if you need a drink. The dwarf provided them, wanting us in reasonable condition for the rite."

Roux turned around, showing his tied hands. Only then did it sink in that Grampi wasn't bound, and neither were the others.

"What was I thinking?" Grampi rose to his feet, supporting himself on a boulder, an old shard of mining metal in his hand. He sawed at Roux's bounds. The twine split after a few hacks, and he did the same for Gabe and me. At least this was something. There was more potential for escape with free hands.

A croaky chanting reverberated from the cavern. We glanced at one another then rushed to the grille.

The rite had begun.

CHAPTER 34

ANTHRAS STOOD BETWEEN THE CAPTIVES AND THE PILE of gold, his arms raised in supplication. "O, sun, mighty source of life, I hail to thee. My offering of gold is colossal and worthy of your power. O, Abellion, when the sun is called, you are called too. With my benefaction of gold, hear my evocation."

The charognards screeched, the rite working them up. Even so, Anthras's words rose above the clamour, somehow amplified. The sunlight and the glow intensified. Only the sheep strode about uninterested, a couple of them pausing between the gold and the cell to nuzzle in the dirt. They were hungry.

"We have to figure out a way to stop the rite," I said, adjusting my view through the grille by stepping on a rock. Around me came the shallow breaths of Grampi, Roux, Gabe and Simon. The students had stayed at the back of the tunnel.

The haze around the gold grew thicker, power creeping over my skin like static. Lucas was still straining. It was a point in his favour that he never seemed to give up, but as he hadn't made any progress, perhaps his bindings had been magically reinforced. The other captives were watching with frightened curiosity.

Anthras drew a large golden dagger from his tunic and raised it to the sun. "The blood offering!" He stepped over to Joly.

"Let us go." Her tone was corrosive enough to dissolve the gold. "These are some of Toulouse University's finest students. Keep me if you have to, but release them." Even now, held at knifepoint by a dwarf demigod bent on the domination of Fae, she was collected, and damn, she still looked great.

The cackle that emanated from Anthras was high and creaky. He knelt before her and raised the knife above him.

"No!" Lucas and Pascale yelled, almost in unison, but to no avail. Anthras thrust the knife down, slicing into the side of Joly's calf. She cried out, blood spilling down her leg. It ran over her bare feet and pooled on the gold. The haze thrummed, invigorated.

Alarm tightened my chest.

Joly's head wobbled to the side as though she was going to faint. She forced herself still and glared at Anthras. She was a superstar.

"Blood meets gold," Roux said.

Grampi nodded. "First stage of the rite."

We watched, wincing, as Anthras repeated the procedure around the circle, the power building. He cut open trousers where necessary, ignoring the pleas of the students, Papa's rants, Meera's wailing and Pascale's cussing. Finally, he approached Lucas.

"Rouseau, you really are a prime specimen." Anthras sliced open the leather of his trousers. Then he reiterated his chant and focussed once again on his raised dagger. "The thirteenth victim," he pronounced as he slashed downward. Lucas held his chin out and glowered, not moving a muscle as the blade cut his leg open.

As his blood poured onto the gold, the haze built to an intense light that flowed from one captive to another.

Anthras shook with delight. "The first stage is complete."

The light pulsed, then a shard surged from the circle and shone into our cell—a golden laser pointing right at Roux's underpants.

We gaped at Roux. He chuckled weakly and shrugged.

"What?" Anthras howled, turning to us. "Who dares mess with the rite of L'Or du Sang?" His shaking grew. This time, it wasn't from elation.

He clambered across the circle, struggled down and shuffled toward the cell. "How dare you interrupt my rite?" he muttered over and over. The two sheep, regrettably positioned between him and the cell, gazed about in curiosity. Anthras waved his arms, but they weren't going to budge.

"Damn it," Anthras cried. "Get these sheep out of my way. When I told you to dispose of them, I didn't mean shoo them into some tunnel. I meant destroy them. It was bad enough that the violent little beasts had to come here to be dehorned in the first place."

The charognards leapt on the poor sheep. They hauled them out of the dwarf's way and ripped them apart.

I closed my eyes against the gore, then whispered to the others, "If Anthras comes in here, do what you can to distract the charognards. I'm going for my sword." I hated the thought that none of them other than Grampi knew how to fight. They were guaranteed to get hurt. But If I didn't do something, we'd all be dead.

Anthras approached, following the golden beam that infiltrated our cell. The charognards opened the grille then leapt in and slashed out with razor claws and daggers, forcing us back until we were halfway to the bend. Damn it. I needed to be as close as possible to the exit to have any hope of escape.

Some charognards climbed the walls, ready to pounce should we make a false move, though the pair with Nerf guns were more interested in sliding the pumps back and forth. Anthras hobbled in behind the charognards, but he hadn't closed the grille. That could be useful.

And still the spotlight shone on Roux's nether regions. His face red, he stepped to the side, attempting to avoid the beam's focus, but it followed him.

"Give it to me," Anthras half cackled, half croaked as he approached, his hand outstretched, his beady gaze boring into Roux. "I would kill you now for your impertinence, but it would unbalance the rite. Besides, time is of the essence."

He'd set up the ritual so the sun would be at its zenith at the crucial moment. We were managing to delay him, although I didn't have a clue how.

"Well, I... well." Roux drew his hand down over his beard as he attempted to shift out of the beam again.

"I don't think there's much choice in the matter," Grampi whispered.

Roux rummaged in his underpants, pulled out his hand and unfurled his fingers. In his palm lay a gold mandragore nugget. He'd only needed one for the collude. Next time I asked Roux for something, I was definitely going to check where he'd stored it.

Anthras snatched the nugget from him. "I can't have that amount of gold out of place, or the collude will be in disarray."

As he half shuffled, half skipped back down the tunnel and out to the golden circle, the charognards withdrew, creeping backward. This was our chance.

"Now!" I cried.

My heart pounding, I ran for the nearest charognard and kicked it into the rock. I struck another on the chin and thrust my boot into a third's middle. It shrieked and gasped, but this lot were tough. I wasn't really doing much damage. The two on the wall dropped their Nerf guns and launched into the air. I grabbed the leg of one, mid-flight, and swung it into the gut of the other.

Grampi was doing a great job taking out a number of them with a series of skilled kicks. Heads smashed on jagged rock, dark blood and glitter raining down. There was still life in Grampi yet.

Gabe, Roux and Simon were hurling stones and kicking charognards as best they could. I was surprised Simon had stuck with us. I'd expected him to hide in the back of the tunnel with the others, especially with his ankle.

Despite the charognards' numbers, we had a narrow, defensible position. As Grampi thrust his knee into a metallic chest and Gabe knocked a critter out with a rock, a gap appeared in the onslaught. I took my chance and sprinted for the grille.

Seeing their comrades in peril, a load of charognards in the cavern headed to the cell. I had to get out before they blocked my exit. I dashed forward, but a charognard sprang at me from the wall and bulldozed into my chest, thrusting me back. Hitting jagged ground, air gushed from my lungs. The charognard landed on my chest, pinned down my arms and drew its fetid, razor-toothed jaw toward me. Struggling to draw breath, I twisted and arched, but it had me.

Water sprayed its face.

"Take that, you critters!" Gabe clack-clacked a Nerf gun pump and blasted everything in sight.

Surprised to be wet, my charognard glanced at its fellows. Burbles and screeches and yowls rose in their throats. My assailant jumped off and scampered about wildly, all focus lost. The others did the same.

"It's the revealing potion," Gabe said. "It made Bécut's sheep go wild and scatter. Looks like it's having the same effect—"

I didn't wait to hear the rest. I hurtled out the grille, shoved past the worked-up newcomers, who'd also taken a dousing through the bars, and grabbed my blade.

CHAPTER 35

CHAROGNARDS SPRANG AT ME. SWEEPING MY BLADE IN an arc, I cut them down, blood and glitter covering my skin as limbs flew and guts spilled. These larger charognards were harder to finish off, but their method of attack was the same as those on the Pons farm—pounce and slash. They were predictable, at least.

I skewered one, sliced off the head of another and took out three more, wincing against the golden glare. Anthras had begun chanting again, oblivious to the scuffle, or perhaps focussing on more important matters.

Seeing the opportunity, I dove for Lucas's sword and the pile of weapons. If I could get them to the others... But the charognards continued their assault, and I could only defend myself.

Roux, Grampi, Gabe and Simon were holding the fort in the cell, hurling rocks at charognards. They'd taken out most of the original lot, thanks to the potion, and the creatures by the grille were jumping around crazily, preventing others from entering.

As I fought on, the room grew brighter, my back became hot and sweat prickled over me. Fending off charognards, I managed to turn back to the circle. The huge pile of gold in the centre was on fire. Yellow flames suffused with violet rose toward the sun, merging with its light. Lucas still strained relentlessly. The others were stiff with dread.

My muscles were already growing tired, the barrage of charognards endless. Catching a glimmer in my periphery, I swung around to defend myself. Before I could strike, a huge charognard slammed into my back, its claws piercing my shoulders and ribs as I fell flat on my face, grit filling my mouth.

I couldn't move from the weight of the thing. I glanced upward, desperate for some means of escape. The gold fire blazed, flames creeping outward toward the captives. Nope, no help there. The claws withdrew from my torso and pierced my neck, pain flashing through me. The creature's grip tightened. I screwed my eyes shut, terror wringing my gut as I waited for the end. I really hadn't been cut out for this.

The commotion around me filled my ears—my heart pounding, the battle raging, the fire roaring, Anthras chanting, the captives screaming and the charognards screeching. But as wiry fingers constricted my throat, another sound filled the air—creaking, and then a blast of thunder.

The charognard's grip eased a little, then it released me. My heart thrashing against my ribs, I turned my head to see

Anthras staring up at the sky, horror contorting his face. I craned my neck a bit more. Above the gold fire, the sky was scarred by ugly black cracks.

The ward was breaking.

Boom!

The cracks in the ward multiplied.

Anthras jumped up and down in fury. "What's this? Another interruption to my rite? Charognards, defend!"

A host of creatures bounded away. Unfortunately, not the one on top of me.

Boom!

The ward flashed black, then it crumbled into a million dark shards that rained down on us like glass. A massive head peered over the top of the cavern wall with a single huge, glaring eye.

Bécut. He'd broken through the ward.

"You killed my sheep!" he roared.

He swung himself over the edge and climbed down the cavern wall, charognards pouncing on him. With a massive hand, he batted them away.

As I struggled against the critter on my back, the rubble around the edge of the cavern shifted and swayed, glinting copper and silver. Hundreds of ore serpents swarmed in from the side tunnels. I dropped back down, unable to believe it. The serpents had pulled through. My thoughts were broken by cries of "Hack the monkeys to pieces, lads" and "Go for the ugly dwarf". The Men.

"Defend the circle!" Anthras screeched.

Masses of charognards leapt to the circle's edge, building

a living barrier. Yet still there were plenty of them to battle
the new arrivals. The serpents, releasing venom, dissolved
charognards instantly, but already fallen Men and slashed
serpents lay lifeless on the ground. This time, I couldn't feel
too bad for the Men, who after death partied and feasted in
the Cave before popping back into existence to cause more
trouble. But I felt deeply for the serpents.

Anthras chanted wildly. The fire grew to a fury, the
violet brighter, the flames creeping closer to the captives.
The haze thickened even more, pulsing with power. I
couldn't just lie here. I had to help.

With all my might, I arched myself up and dislodged the
distracted charognard on my back. Jumping up with a spin, I
took off its head, then tore into anything that came my way.
We had to reduce the charognards' numbers so the serpents
could make it through the barrier and dissolve the gold.

All around, charognards fell, pierced with spears or
corroded by acid blasts. Fragments of solidified blood glinted
in the glare. We were doing significant damage, but the
charognards were giving as good as they got, keeping us away
from the circle. They herded Men and serpents toward the
bounds cracks and shoved them in. Blood-curdling screams
and wretched hisses filled me with dread as fae tumbled into
the abyss.

Grampi, Roux, Gabe and Simon had made it to the pile
of weapons and were defending their position outside the
cell. Simon managed to cut off the foot of a charognard
dangling from a rock. He stood there gawping at the
dismembered leg. The creature shrieked, bared its teeth

and dove for him, claws outstretched. Grampi slashed its throat.

Bécut had made it down to the cavern floor. He was more than twice the height of a man, and by the looks of him, a hell of a lot stronger. His preferred method of retaliation was stamping on charognards or smashing their heads together.

As I continued my attack, a charognard caught me off guard, scampering low across the ground and biting me on the shin. It was met with an axe in the forehead.

"Looks like we got here just in time, ma'am." A blood-and-glitter-covered Slaughter retrieved his axe and drove it through the leg of another charognard. "Honestly, look at the mess Lucas has gotten himself into this time." He nodded to the circle.

"Can't tell you how good it is to see you, Slaughter," I said.

He shot me a black, toothy grin and defended my back.

As we fought, a myriad of charognards joined the existing barrier, and even though we'd killed masses of them already, there were more attacking us than before.

"There's thousands of them," I cried. "Where are they coming from?"

Slaughter's axe caught a critter in the eye. "No idea. Never seen so many in my life."

I was struggling to hold the charognards at bay, every part of me aching, not just from my wounds but from the strain of my muscles as I thumped, kicked, hacked and battered by any means possible, and still we hadn't managed to advance. Desperation filled me. Men lay about, their throats open, their bodies broken. Serpents, lacerated and lifeless, gazed up at me with unseeing eyes. The horror of the carnage was tight and raw, and panic rode on my fear.

A mass of charognards leapt from the cavern walls, some heading to the barrier, some joining the battle. That had to be the last of them, surely? But the cavern walls undulated, the rock bulging, warping, twisting.

"Are you seeing what I'm seeing?" I yelled as hundreds more charognards pulled themselves out of the rock.

"It's Anthras's magic," Slaughter said. Even his eyes were wide.

Shit. With unlimited charognards, we didn't stand a chance.

CHAPTER 36

Bécut was rallying bravely, covered in charognards, and the Men fought wildly, their enthusiasm and energy boundless, but the serpents were falling in droves.

"Slaughter..." I struck a charognard in the mouth with the hilt of my sword. As it fell back, I pierced its chest. "Make sure there's plenty of serpents in reserve to dissolve the gold. We need them alive."

He disappeared, and I battled on. Hell, it was so hot, the energy of the rite thick and cloying. More charognards were popping out of the walls. I had no idea how we were going to take down enough of them to make a difference.

"Um, Camille," an out-of-place voice said from behind. It sounded so normal, as if the owner wasn't part of the battle but was trying to get my attention in the street. For some reason, the charognards retreated. My breath heaving, I glanced over my shoulder. There stood Gidditch, Wheezle and Eggnog, the goblins and troll who'd caused me so much trouble. A guard of Men surrounded them, weapons raised.

I searched about, trying to figure out why the charognards were holding back in a circle around us. In the midst of the battle, it was completely incongruous. "What's happening? Why aren't we being attacked?"

"We want to talk to Lucas," Gidditch said, swaying a little, his large ears twitching. "He said when we were ready to tell him where we'd really gotten the golden horn from, we should let him know. But we can see he's a bit busy at the moment."

Gaping and utterly dumbfounded, I glanced over to where Lucas's eyebrows were singeing.

"We were thinking," Eggnog said, "that we've had enough of clearing up ore serpent venom." A leather sack was strapped to his rotund bulk, the contents wriggling.

"Yeah," Wheezle added, her long nose wrinkling. "We want to admit what we've done."

I just couldn't believe they stood here talking to me like this.

Eggnog rubbed his bald round head. "Coz we're fed up cleaning up acid, the sun keeps glinting and flashing in our eyes, making us squint, like the damned thing has some kind of problem with us. And it's a furnace up on Les Calbières."

Wheezle wheezed. "We didn't just find the horn."

"We sawed it off a sheep," Eggnog said. "But we thought that the sheep was wild. We didn't know it *belonged* to anyone."

I pulled myself together. "Right now, I don't care. Tell me why the charognards aren't attacking you."

Wheezle spluttered. "Oh yes, the battle. Very nasty—"

"What's going on?" I roared.

"Oh," Eggnog said. "It's on account of Madame Bovary."

My look must have shown that I didn't have a clue what he was talking about. He reached over his shoulder and opened his pack. A blacker than black and ridiculously fluffy head poked out. The sarramauca from the Peppered Parsnip gazed at me with a haughty expression, her whiskers twitching.

"Fae don't like her." Eggnog shrugged. "They keep away instinctually, on account of her annihilating her victims by sitting on them. We've gotten used to her, though."

The charognards, fighting against their instincts, cautiously shuffled toward us. One took a clawed swipe at me. I jumped to the side.

"Just another form of abuse she's subject to," Gidditch pronounced. "It's not just trolls being marginalised, but sarramaucas, too. 'Tisn't right. Not one bit."

I really needed clarification. "The charognards are keeping away because they sense that... thing?"

The sarramauca narrowed her eyes.

"Madame Bovary is not a *thing*," Wheezle replied. "She's a highly sensitive creature."

Whatever. I could use this to my advantage. A couple more charognards dove in. I skewered one and cut down the other. Gidditch, Wheezle and Eggnog eyed the gory and glittering remains.

"Give me Madame Bovary." I brandished my sword and glared at them as menacingly as I could, which given the circumstances, probably transmitted a high level of danger.

Eggnog raised his hands. "No way. I don't want her hurt. And anyway, if I give her to you, we're going to get attacked."

Another charognard swiped at us. I took it out. The rest of the critters were baring their teeth in readiness to pounce.

"You don't understand," I growled, raising my sword to Eggnog again. "You don't have a choice in the matter. And if you... she doesn't help us, we're all going to die—even you if you leave right now because there's a dwarf over there who's about to blow up everything for miles around. What do you think he's doing? Having a midsummer party?"

They glanced between each other nervously.

But I could offer them something. "Stay with me and Madame Bovary, and you might not get attacked. Though we'll be going right into the fray."

I placed the point of my sword at the thick roll of skin that was Eggnog's throat.

Wheezle and Gidditch reluctantly nodded their agreement. Eggnog met my gaze and passed the pack to me. "Look after her."

I couldn't guarantee her safety—I couldn't guarantee anything, considering we were about to be blown sky high— but I would try. I nodded and hooked the pack over my shoulders, expecting a smothering sensation, but nothing. The sack was protecting me.

I glanced about. The hazy aura of power was so intense, my vision warped a little. Anthras was chanting furiously.

Most of the captives were wailing as the fire drew near. Papa's head was pinned back to the post as though he was riding a rollercoaster. The rest of the place was thick with battle. The Men took down a group of charognards, and in the resulting gap, three large serpents made a dash for the barricade. Just what I needed.

I took a step toward the encroaching charognards. Like frightened wildcats, they scampered back, their instincts once again getting the better of them. Swallowing away a voice that said there was no point in trying, that I really wasn't cut out for this, I ran for the serpents.

Charognards scattered before me, jabbering in terror as they sensed Madame Bovary.

"Men, serpents, this way!" I yelled. I had no idea if Gidditch, Wheezle and Eggnog were following. They would have to look out for themselves.

As I reached the serpents, they swerved away, wary of my load. "Stay by me!" I shouted. "No matter what you feel, stick to my side."

For a second they continued their flight, then they saw the charognards retreating. They overcame their instinct and joined me. Together, we shot forward.

The charognards positioned on top of one another in the barrier became restless at our advance, their eyes wide with terror. We headed straight for them. They gripped each other, trembling. As we made contact, instinct prevailed, and they sprang in all directions. The gold shone before us, and the serpents released everything they had.

The acid sizzled, the top layer of the closest gold

dissolving then disappearing into the stockpile underneath. Pascale and Meera, the captives on either side, gaped in disbelief. Serpents that had followed in our wake discharged their venom, and the haze dimmed a little.

"What's happening?" Anthras screeched, hobbling toward us, his face lit with fury.

I didn't wait.

"Follow me," I bellowed. Madame Bovary wriggling on my back, I ran at the still-solid charognard barrier to my side. The creatures leapt out of my way, and I continued on around the edge of the circle. Serpents flooded in as the barrier fell. Men took down the panicked charognards with spears and arrows.

"More venom!" I yelled. "But don't spray the captives."

"Charognards, get them!" Anthras screamed, but the critters weren't listening. They were utterly spooked.

"Yes! Camille!" Lucas cried. "Go!"

Amidst the turmoil, I caught a glimpse of Grampi, Roux and Simon sprinting to the gold. They hacked at Lucas's and Joly's ties. Gabe had the other Nerf gun and was coating the charognards. And still I ran.

Lucas jumped down as I dashed past. He grabbed a blade from Roux then joined the clash. Some of the captives were screaming as they were released, the sight of the ore serpents one shock too many.

"Camille," Papa shouted from his pillar. "What on earth are you doing?"

I returned to my starting point on the circle, Gidditch,

Wheezle and Eggnog gasping behind me, Madame Bovary squirming on my back. I brandished my sword in readiness for the next charognard to come my way, but most had retreated.

On one side of the gold, they'd been forced back to the bounds by the Men and Lucas, and they were dropping into the abyss. Although on the other side, Bécut was taking a pounding, his skin torn by countless teeth as he held the critters away from the circle. Then from the tunnel closest to him, in poured dwarf after dwarf, axes and swords raised, armour shining. Backup had arrived.

A good portion of the gold was sizzling in acid, and in places it had disintegrated completely. The gold fire was now more a large bonfire than a towering inferno, the haze of power ebbing away. The last of the captives were being released, the serpents dissolving the gold where they'd stood.

Grampi, Gabe and Simon, covered in cuts and bruises, were helping the limping captives and directing them into the cell to avoid the acid. Simon sported a particularly nasty bruise to one eye. One of the students lay flat on the ground a little way off, Roux at his side. I hoped to hell it wasn't serious. There was no sign of Papa. He was probably in the cell already.

Joly gazed at me intently before joining the others. She still looked remarkably collected, leg wound, burns and all, her swept-back dark locks barely out of place.

Meera and two guys stood nearby, weeping hysterically. Pascale was trying to guide them to the cell. As they passed, he took me in, his eyes flashing with disbelief. "Camille, what are you wearing?"

Was my Keeper gear the height of his problems right now? But all of them had to be struggling with the fae revelation, though I was more concerned that I couldn't see Anthras anywhere.

CHAPTER 37

THE FIRE WAS STILL BURNING, AND I COULDN'T SEE PAST it. With Madame Bovary writhing in my pack, her claws jabbing at me, I sprinted back around the circle to the only remaining acid-free patch of gold.

Anthras was dragging a captive toward the fire with one hand. He held a dagger to his hostage's neck with the other.

I shoved closer through a throng of Men, their weapons raised.

My breath grew shallow. The hostage was Papa, his eyes screwed shut, his body trembling.

"Just one sacrifice," Anthras muttered. "That's all I need. There's still enough gold. Just one sacrifice will initiate the rite."

The Men glanced at me, unsure whether to strike and risk Papa's life. But they would have to. Even a small explosion would take out us and the surrounding villages. My pulse pounded in my ears, my heart thrashing. I was about to witness my father's death.

But before Anthras could pull Papa any further, Madame Bovary hooked her claws into my back and hauled herself out of the sack. She leapt off my shoulder and landed on Anthras's head.

Wheezing and gasping, he thrashed his body as he tried to remove her suffocating influence, and still he clung on to Papa. The dagger sliced in, blood trickling down Papa's neck. But Anthras was distracted. I had my chance.

I sprang onto the gold and kicked the dagger from Anthras's hands. Anthras released Papa and tore at his face. He staggered to the side, wobbled a little, then fell forward onto the gold, Madame Bovary jumping artfully onto his back. She shimmied and twitched her tail, then curled up. The dwarf lay there unable to move and barely able to breathe. The fire died down, then extinguished, and with it, the haze dissipated completely.

All I could do was stare at Papa, my jaw slack. There was a movement to my side. Lucas, Roux and Grampi had drawn up beside the Men.

Lucas's breath was ragged from the fight. "It's over. The charognards are down."

Legions of Men, snakes and dwarves clustered around us. A very bloody Bécut stood behind them with Wheezle and Gidditch on his shoulders and Eggnog at his side. The rest of the enormous cavern lay still, bodies everywhere, glitter eddying in the air.

Lucas grinned. "Kind of wondering where you got the sarramauca from, I have to say."

As I struggled to think of a reply, unable to take in that it really was done and dusted, the light in the cavern grew once more, the remaining gold glaring. My heart leapt into my throat. It had to be Anthras, his rite still working, but he lay there on the ground, desperate for breath. Madame Bovary hadn't shifted. And anyway, the light felt different somehow. The glow wasn't coming from the power Anthras had raised or the gold fire, it was coming from the sun.

We gazed upward, shielding our eyes from the brightness. The sun expanded, suffusing the sky with iridescent light. It should have been sweltering again, but there was only welcoming, nurturing warmth. The radiance grew, filling the cavern. All the confusion, panic and worry I'd carried since this whole thing began fell away. There was nothing but pristine, indescribable light.

As though supported by an invisible hand, Anthras, still recumbent, rose into the air. "Nooooooo!" came his muffled cry. "Anything but returning to Abellion."

I stepped back. Madame Bovary stood up, needled Anthras, then licked a paw and swept it over her much-too-fluffy face. Satisfied with her appearance, she sprang daintily to the ground and sauntered away.

"No, no, no, no," Anthras yelled as he spun gently, rising into the indescribable light. "I don't want to go back. I would rather die than return—" His words faded as he disappeared into the luminescence. The light dimmed, and above us shone the familiar disc of the sun.

"So that's how you evoke Abellion," Roux muttered. "Forget colludes and the like. Just attempt to blow him up."

Anthras and Abellion gone, the exhaustion, gore and devastation of the battle returned. I'd almost lost Papa, Lucas and everyone to the gold fire, but seeing Papa at Anthras's mercy stirred something deep within. I couldn't believe he was safe and lying before me on the gold. He was badly singed, his skin red and blistered, his salt-and-pepper hair frazzled, and of course there were the gashes on his neck and leg, but other than that, he looked okay. I bent down and flung my arms around him.

"You're alright," I repeated over and over into his neck.

He wrapped me up. "Camille, my chouchou."

I was immersed in him like those bearhugs when I'd been little. If only it would last forever. Then he pulled back and smiled. "I have no idea what's going on. Dwarves, gold, serpents, small prehistoric men. Must have been something in the baguette I had for lunch yesterday."

I could only smile. Around us, the others began to clear up.

"But I have to say," he continued, peering thoughtfully at me, "just so we can all learn from this experience. It might be worth considering how you dealt with the dwarf. You may have been able to creep up on him from the back without using that, ummm, cat. With that thing jumping on his head, he could have gone a lot further with the dagger."

"What?" An icy chill wove through my veins. I sat back, pushing Papa away from me, my head full of his words.

There was that all too familiar hardness in his gaze as he

met my eye, propped up on his elbows. A trickle of blood ran down his neck. "I think it might be useful to analyse the strategy of this little situation and break apart each move, so we can see how the folklorists and myself might have been rescued more quickly. Ideally, before we were knifed." He glanced at his leg and winced.

I couldn't believe him. "So let me get this straight. You're not saying, 'Thank you, Camille, for saving my sorry ass'. You're wanting us to go through what happened so that I can improve for the next time I save the fucking Pyrenees?"

"Language. But, absolutely." He nodded. "A perfect learning experience. When that dwarf pulled me to the ground just now, I twisted my ankle. I definitely think that could have been avoided if you—"

And then it sank in. It sank in so damned hard that I couldn't believe I'd not realised it before. "That's it, isn't it?" I rose to my feet, utterly stunned by the revelation. "I'm not enough. I never have been enough for you, have I?"

He scoffed. "Now, Camille—"

"Not after I got on the gym team, or won that history prize. I'd been so proud of those achievements and others, but each time, it wasn't enough for you." I seethed, my fury scolding. I could see it now. All these years, I'd felt like shit because of him.

"Camille," he tried again.

"But that's not the truth, is it?" I yelled. "I was enough. I did a damned good job writing a top-notch paper and getting on the team. And I—well, Madame Bovary, but that's beside

the point—we just saved your life." It was as clear as day.
"The problem isn't in me. It's in you."

His mouth hung open.

"You're the one who, for some sorry reason, can't congrat-
ulate his daughter when she does well, who needs her to
achieve more and more, who is never, ever satisfied. None of
this crap you've spouted for years is about me. It's all about
you. And I'll tell you one thing... this damned rescue was
good enough." It really had been. Despite all my doubts, I'd
kept going, and we'd managed to take Anthras down. I'd
proved my doubtful self wrong.

I drew in a deep breath, then said softly, "I. Am.
Enough."

The words were iron in my blood.

Stony incomprehension covered Papa's face, the small
lines at the side of his mouth tensing as they always did when
he justified his actions. There was no doubt he'd attempt to
reason his way out of this, but I didn't want to hear it ever
again.

I shook my head and walked away.

Behind me, Lucas was barking orders. "Clean the place
up. Identify the wounded. Deal with your dead. Men, we
need healing and forgetting potion from my house plus herbs
to glamour the fae activity in the mine. Dwarves, get the gold
out of here. Return it to its rightful owners."

The grille at the cell's entrance had been pulled down,
and the project huddled inside, talking amongst themselves. I
stepped over and entered the tunnel feeling lighter than I
had for a long, long time.

CHAPTER 38

SITTING AT MY DESK IN THE EVENTS ROOM, I FAST-
forwarded through the footage on a camcorder that had
miraculously made it back from the mine. Apparently, fae
didn't record well, if at all. Even so, I wanted to check there
was nothing incriminating.

I shifted, easing my limbs and running a hand over my
neck where the charognard had almost choked me. My
wounds had healed thanks to several doses of high-potency
potion, and Lucas's fortifying tonic had given me a much-
needed boost. But I was still processing the grim events in the
cavern, and I was a little stiff, the sensation not aided by the
grime that covered my glamoured Keeper gear.

That aside, the windows and doors were open, the
golden sun lowering behind Cousterous. A cool, early-
evening breeze brushed my skin, the first let-up in the heat
for days.

The events room had been elected by the police as a base

for processing everyone. And considering it was full with almost every human who'd been at Rancie, plus a handful of police officers and paramedics, the place was much too quiet.

The project had readily drunk hefty amounts of healing and forgetting potions at the mine. Who wouldn't take something prescribed by a doctor? Their wounds and burns had just about healed by the time the police and paramedics arrived, everyone convinced of the story we'd concocted that they'd been trapped by the rockfall when exploring. But they were dazed, confused and kind of broken. I didn't like it, especially after my experiences with verity, although I couldn't see an alternative. It all felt rather *Men in Black.*

We'd been here for hours, now. Most of us had given our statements and had been checked over properly by Lucas and the paramedics. Having devoured the refreshments that Alice had provided, the students talked quietly while they waited for next of kin to pick them up.

Sissoko was on the phone, explaining what had happened to someone high up at the university. Roux chatted animatedly to one of the students about thermonuclear dynamics. At least *Roux* was animated—the student just looked startled. Gabe had disappeared to get himself a hot chocolate, having taken the whole thing in his stride. Meera was still upset, and Pascale was chatting to her, their clothes a charred mess, blankets around their shoulders.

Thank heavens, Maman had picked up Papa and Grampi a few minutes ago, because I wouldn't have been able to take more of my father's stony silence. He hadn't spoken to me since the argument, and I had no idea how much of it he remembered.

And Joly… She was sitting at her desk, her torn and filthy clothes still somehow stylish. Even now, she was calm, collected and in control. And… *Recent Experiences of Ancient Folkloric Phenomena* was in her hands, the coffee stain distinguishing it from her other paperwork. She'd been reading it for the past ten minutes. I couldn't help but glance over constantly, my stomach churning, though what I really should have been worried about was the false statement I'd just given the police.

The video came to an end, the camcorder clear. I placed it in its case as a shadow crept across my desk.

"Uh." Simon's lips were parted, his scratched glasses now permanently askew.

"Yes?" As he'd had the forgetting potion, I supposed we were back to square one.

He stared at me, as though trying to grasp a memory. "I was going to say put the camcorder away carefully… but I have the strangest notion you can handle things just fine."

I'd take that as a win, and he'd proved in the cavern that there was metal underneath his airs. All I could say was, "Thank you, Simon."

He wondered off, limping a little and looking rather befuddled.

I tucked the camcorder in its case and went over to check the refreshments, almost bumping into a policewoman as I glanced in Joly's direction yet again. She was still reading.

There were plenty of filled baguettes stacked on the

table, but we needed more milk. I grabbed the jug and headed to the door as Dame Blanche came in wheeling a trolley full of brioche goûter.

"We thought you might need a top-up," she said cheerily.

"Umm, not more damnation, I hope?"

She smiled, and instantly I felt warm and cosy and just... alright, I guess. There had been a lot on my mind since the argument with Papa, as well as everything else.

"Not this time, dear." Her bright eyes twinkled. "I'd say the folklorists have had enough damnation for now. I've baked a little comfort into this batch, though. Thought it wouldn't go amiss."

If Meera was anything to go by, it was a good call. "I guess not."

I slipped past the trolley and headed across the café with the milk jug, the place as busy as usual with the after-work rush. Gabe sat in one of the comfy armchairs. His face was flushed, his smile a bit too broad as he talked to someone hidden by the wingback.

As I passed Gabe's table, I caught a glimpse of a perfectly groomed shoulder-length bob. Nora. The rigidity she'd held since the hantaumo attack was gone, and she was laughing with Gabe. That was a turn-up for the books.

Félix was with the D&D guys in their nook, eyeing them with curiosity rather than malice.

As I headed behind the counter, the entrance doors were flung open. "Whooooaaaa!" Guy cried as he darted in and sprinted to the mandragore above the cappuccino machine.

Every head turned toward him.

He unscrewed the jar, pulled out the root, raised it over his head and whooped again. "Yessssss! We're rich! Everyone, look at this!" He opened his other hand to reveal a nugget of gold. "Papa found it on the doorstep just now with a massive gold bar and a pile of gold bracelets. It's the mandragore root. Find a mandragore at midsummer and get totally rich!"

I'd asked a couple of Men to take a little gold to the Pons farm. It only seemed fair after the acid damage, and as I'd stolen his mandragore droppings.

Alice emerged from the office. "Woo-hoo! Go Guy!" she cried, her face beaming. "But where the hell did that come from?"

"I haven't got a clue, but... the farm is saved!" Guy pronounced theatrically. A huge cheer rose up.

Alice pumped her fist, then caught sight of me. Her smile disappeared instantly, and she glared for a moment before stalking back to the office.

My elation at Guy's happiness drained away. The situation with Alice was a complete mess. But I would have to do something about it, and soon. There was no way I'd lose her friendship.

I drew a fresh jug of milk from the fridge, returned to the events room and placed it with the drinks. Pascale was staring at me, peering up from under his brow as though he was attempting to put his finger on something. Meera, next to him, looked terrible. Her eyes were rimmed with red, and she trembled. I grabbed two plates of brioche goûter and carried them over. Lucas, who was talking to a paramedic, tracked me.

"Apparently, this is a special batch of brioche. I'm betting it's worth a try." I placed the plates in front of them, then drew my arm around Meera and squeezed her gently.

"Bet you didn't expect to have to rescue us all when you signed up for the job," she said softly.

"High maintenance." Pascale ran a hand through his currently dirty blond hair. "That's us." But there wasn't any humour in his eyes. More like hardness and confusion.

"You wouldn't believe how high." I forced a laugh.

Meera peered into the middle distance as if chasing thoughts. She tore off a corner of brioche and nibbled it half-heartedly, then her shoulders fell, the tension in her temples and jaw dissipating. Her lips flickered into a wan smile. "Some research week. I'll give you two space." She pushed her chair back and headed over to chat to Sissoko, brioche in hand.

I took her seat. This was the chance I needed.

Pascale tried to smile, but his lips just pursed then sagged, a frown creasing his forehead. "We missed our date."

"We sure did."

"Well, the project's over. We're all going home." He studied my face nervously. "We'll be back, of course. But..."

There it was, the "but". He was trying to say what I wanted to express. "But the last couple of days have been a shock. We both need a chance to digest everything and recuperate." There was no point going out on a date, anyway. We couldn't have a normal relationship, me always hiding the truth. It raised the question of how I was ever going to have a regular relationship with anyone who didn't know about the hidden world, but that was something I was going to think about on a less stressful day.

Pascale smiled. "My thoughts exactly."

Lucas's dark eyes flashed, the corner of his mouth turning up. Damned drac hearing. He finished his conversation, grabbed his medical bag and headed out.

I drew my attention back to Pascale. "But I'm glad we met. We almost got to geek out about folklore. Maybe we'll get the chance one day."

"Yeah," he said. "We'll be returning to finish the project at some point, and you—"

"Camille," Joly called. "Could I have a word?"

Blood drained from my face and the room swayed.

"What's up?" Pascale asked. "You've gone white."

"She's read my paper," I whispered.

He grinned. "You have nothing to worry about. Go get 'em."

CHAPTER 39

JOLY PULLED OUT A CHAIR AND NODDED encouragingly. She wasn't exactly smiling, but it wasn't a look of contempt either, though that astute gaze was the same.

"Sit down, Camille," she said.

"Uh, thanks." I obliged, perching on the edge of my seat.

"I've read your paper." She glanced at *Recent Experiences*, now lying on the desk at her side. "And I have to say, I'm impressed."

My heart thumped furiously.

"Your reasoning is extremely thorough, your arguments sound and based on a remarkably wide range of research indicative of a broad knowledge of the field. And your conclusions that modern-day folkloric phenomena are related to recent cultural contexts are solid. I believe your theories will be of benefit to those working in the area. I'll recommend the paper for publication, although I can't guarantee anything."

The room swayed a little more. Joly had just given her approval of *my* paper. "I... I..." Words wouldn't come. But I had to pull myself together. "Thank you for reading it. I really appreciate you taking the time." Neutral, yes. But I didn't have a clue what else to say. If I wasn't careful, I'd start fawning at her feet, and despite everything, I still wanted to be professional.

She nodded. "Furthermore, due to the outstanding research that I would have welcomed from one of my PhD students, in addition to your diligent work on this project, I would like to offer you an expiated place on our pioneering folklore studies degree."

My jaw dropped.

"With your knowledge base you could easily go straight into the master's, but you have a significant gap in education and no prior study at degree level, so I wouldn't have a strong argument with my colleagues. However, I think you could take the most important modules in a year, then move on."

She raised her chin. "And despite the setbacks the project has faced, it will be rescheduled to the summer vacation. Once again, I'll be needing an assistant."

I couldn't believe it. I just couldn't believe it.

It was everything I'd ever wanted. At least, it had been... before the verity. But I also didn't get it. She'd said my "diligent work on this project", but I'd been the scapegoat for everything that had gone wrong, even for Simon falling down the slope.

"Well?" She drummed her fingers on the table. "What do you think?"

I pushed my confusion aside. What really mattered was that she'd offered me an expiated university place. What did I think...?

So much had become clear during my argument with Papa, and I'd been digesting the fallout ever since. My whole life had been built around the idea that I wasn't enough. It meant that even though I'd gone my own way toward folklore studies rather than the hard sciences that Papa prized, under the surface, I'd been led by an incessant drive to have my paper published, to have recognition, to prove that I was someone. But all of that had come from those raw childhood feelings.

A part of me wanted to go to university for that piece of paper, that title that proved my worth. Of course, I wanted to study folklore, too. It was my life. But there would always be the divide of me knowing what others couldn't possibly imagine.

With my awareness of Fae, I'd been given access to so much more than reading and research and study could ever give me. What academia offered *was* truly fascinating—it was the examination of how people perceived the world through folklore. What Fae offered was direct experience.

Yes, I was scared. To be honest, after everything that had happened with Anthras and the hantaumo, I was shit-scared. My feelings of not being enough, plus Grampi's doubts, fed right into that, making university the safer option. But I was also intrigued and excited about Fae. Besides, I couldn't ignore the buzz I'd felt using my blade and scuffling at the Peppered Parsnip. And now, without a shadow of a doubt, I knew what I wanted to do.

I'd been staring at my paper on Joly's desk. She studied me, waiting for my answer.

I met her gaze and placed the flat of my palm on my chest. "Thank you for your generous offer. I appreciate it more than I can say." And that was the truth. "But now isn't the right time for me to attend university."

I couldn't believe myself. Was I really saying this? But Fae lay out there... "And as for the project"—I glanced over at Simon, who was suggesting that a student move their trip-hazard bag—"I think there's someone else who would like the job very much."

My shoulders, my arms, my fingers, every part of me tensed. This was Professor Margot Joly I was turning down, and I couldn't imagine my rejection would be appreciated.

She smiled stiffly, her jaw tight, then she released a bell-like laugh as she shook her head. "Camille, I owe you an apology."

I hadn't expected that.

"For a lot of things." She inhaled deeply, her chin touching her chest before rising again. "I saw the osencame at Madame Mazet's, and I saw you save her photograph."

"What?" I couldn't have heard right.

She nodded slowly. "And I saw the goblins and troll interfering at Chalet de Larcat, as well as the goblin at the window the morning we arrived."

But she couldn't have. My breath caught in my throat.

"And," she continued, "I remember everything that happened in the mine. The dwarves, the Men of Bédeilhac, the serpents, the cyclops... you."

This couldn't be right. Maybe she hadn't drunk the forgetting potion, or she hadn't had enough of it. Yet she was so calm.

She swallowed. "When I was about your age, I had to make a choice between safe normality and delving deeper into the fascinating and terrifying world I'd always been able to perceive." She bent down, rummaged in her handbag and drew out a bottle of pills. "I chose the former."

I couldn't believe my ears. But Lucas had said some people could naturally perceive fae.

She unscrewed the lid and tipped a pill into her hand, then knocked it back with a sip of water.

"As I progressed through my career, I began to make a name for myself. Approval is alluring indeed." She raised a perfectly arched eyebrow, and even though she'd cleaned up, a black smudge lay beneath. "I've had to accept my choice, and the pills help me to not see, although they're not always effective. There have been many times I wondered what would have happened if things had been different."

I just stared at her, my mouth open, my eyes wide. We'd had similar choices.

"When I realised you could see what the other project members couldn't, it was easy to blame you for the fae's interference. You were a threat to the normality I'd so carefully crafted, that had to be maintained for the success of the project. The two worlds don't easily combine."

Anger flared through me as it sank in. "You knew and yet you blamed me?"

She drew back her shoulders and met my gaze. "Yes, and that's where my apology comes in. I'm sorry for my actions. You didn't deserve to be used in that way."

Heat rose to my face. "Too right, I didn't." But as quickly as my fury had grown, it dissolved. Joly's reaction was knee-jerk against a reality she'd attempted to hold back for years. From my experience after taking the verity, I could understand something of that.

Joly put the lid on the pill bottle. "For what it's worth, I think you made a sensible choice."

Chapter 40

Wrapped in Maman's embrace, I shut out the farmyard, the goats and my parents' car packed and ready to go. Her palmarosa scent made me five years old again. Despite everything, despite all the niggles I had with her—and the ton I had with Papa—I loved that I could be transported back to that safe, cosy time.

"To think that your father needed rescuing from a mine." She pulled away and beamed. "The whole ordeal will teach him not to interfere, though I'm glad he's safe." She squeezed my arms. "And good job you for figuring out where he was."

"All in a day's work," I said. And the day's work was well and truly done. Everyone had been picked up not long after my conversation with Joly, and I'd headed on home, the windows of my truck wide open, the air balmy, the sun still bright and effervescent. I'd had the best shower of my life, then changed into shorts and a strappy top. I felt like a new person.

"Although, next time," Maman added, "if you suspect he's gone missing, I want to know." She batted my arm.

"Yeah, sorry about that." I hated that I'd lied.

She squeezed me again. "And I'm sorry we're leaving so soon."

Papa emerged from the farmhouse and walked over stiffly. "After that little ordeal, I need my own bed." His voice was gruff, his eyes hard. It was the first thing he'd said to me since Rancie.

"Completely understandable," I said. I didn't have a clue where we stood. He'd definitely forgotten about the fae, but the argument...

"Camille..." He pulled me into a bearhug. "Chouchou. Harsh words back there in the mine."

I drew in a sharp breath. Lucas had said that with the dosage of forgetting potion he'd given the project, there was a chance Papa might recall the row, though he'd reposition it in his mind to blank out all fae involvement. But it was good he'd remembered. It meant we didn't have to go through the whole thing again.

"I have no regrets helping out with the gym team, the history paper and everything else," he said, stepping back. "I'll always want what's best for you."

I tensed inside. Those things hurt so much, and they'd laid the foundation for all I'd had to battle with. But I hadn't expected anything less. Papa couldn't see how he'd undermined my confidence, and that was just how he was. And anyway, it was me who needed to deal with the consequences. I didn't need an apology for that.

"I'm sure you do," I replied neutrally, and left it at that.

Grampi came over from the barn, his steps slow and laboured—completely understandable after the last couple of days, I had to remind myself.

Papa didn't take his eyes off me. He just smiled faintly. "Right then, let's be off. I've had enough of this place."

Maman hugged and kissed me again. "Love you, sweetheart. Keep in touch, won't you?"

"Sure will. Have a good journey," I said to them both.

Grampi embraced my parents, then they climbed into their estate, Maman driving.

"Bon voyage," I called as they pulled away.

And just like that, they'd gone, the project was over, and weirdly, it was as if the last few days had never happened. Except... everything had changed.

Grampi wrapped his arm around my shoulder, his grip strong. "Cherie."

I closed my eyes at the sound of his voice. He was my rock, which made his disbelief in my abilities all the more difficult to bear.

He pulled me a little closer. "What I witnessed in Rancie proved me completely wrong. You're as competent as any newly appointed Keeper, if not more so. You were brave, resourceful and rather kickass, if I do say so myself."

A smile blossomed on my face, and I tried to swallow the lump in my throat. This was the old, supportive Grampi.

"I still don't want you to take on the role," he added lightly, "because I'm a selfish, doddery git who wants to keep you all to myself. But you would never thrive like that. You have too much of me in you to be content with a comfortable life. I may not like it, but if you decide to become a Keeper, I'll respect your decision."

My smile grew wider, and I kissed him on his bristly cheek. "Thank you. That means the world to me... You mean the world to me."

"I'm still not happy about that drac, though, Camille." His mouth tensed, then released, then tensed again, his moustache shifting.

I turned to face him. "This is a lovely moment. It would be nice if you didn't spoil it."

He frowned. "I can't imagine I'll ever be alright with him. I have no idea what the assembly was doing placing you two together, but I'm open to being proved wrong. Just do me a favour and use your head around him."

I imagined Grampi's expression if I mentioned I'd slept with Lucas. Nope. He really didn't need to know that. "I will," I said.

He gripped my shoulders. "Now, I'm going for a bath and bed before I fall down on this very spot. The charognards were more of a workout than I've had in years, and I still have glitter in my hair. You?"

"I... don't know." I glanced about, taking in the balmy sky and the verdant trees. Perhaps it was because of everything that had happened in the mine, but there seemed to be something about the evening. The air sort of shimmered. After all, it was midsummer's eve.

Folklore stated that on this night, as well as at other turning points of the year, the veils between the realms were thinnest. And the shimmer was just like when I crossed the bounds into Fae. It had been a long, exhausting day, and I'd not had much sleep the night before, but I felt so alive.

"I'm not ready for bed yet." And anyway, I wanted to speak to Lucas, although I wasn't going to mention that.

Grampi kissed my head then crossed the yard to the house. I stood there, taking in the delicious air, happy being in the moment.

My phone vibrated.

I pulled it from my pocket. Lucas. *I'm taking you out.*

Just the person, though his audacity irked.

Presumptuous, not waiting to see if I want to go out with you, I replied.

His SUV pulled up at the gate, the window down. "Completely presumptuous," he said. "Let's go."

"Unbelievable." I cocked my head. "A little more information before I go anywhere with you. You have a reputation for trouble."

Light glinted in his dark irises. "It's midsummer's eve and..." He grinned. "It's a surprise."

I was open to that. "It better be good." I climbed in.

Lucas's grin deepened as he reversed and pulled away. He drove in silence, which suited me fine. I breathed the rich, honey air, trying not to notice how good he looked in shorts and a T-shirt, his biceps tightening against the cotton. I also tried not to notice the play of light along his perfect nose and jaw. After everything, he still damned well intrigued me. But by the time he'd pulled into the café car park, the place shut up for the night, the events in Rancie were on my mind. We hadn't had chance to talk since everything wrapped up.

"Here?" I asked.

"Come on." He jumped out.

We walked side by side through fae Tarascon, the place remarkably quiet. Even the Peppered Parsnip was peaceful for once.

I broke the hush. "The bounds cracks are getting worse. What's going on?"

"I truly have no idea." His broad mouth levelled.

"But your brother arranged for you to be part of Anthras's sacrifice..."

Lucas's jaw tightened. "Elivorn has been trying to take my life since we were knee high to a grasshopper. Hasn't managed it yet, though."

I barked a laugh. Not because it was funny, but because it was all so bizarre.

Lucas shot me a side glance. "I'm glad my family problems amuse you."

We passed the Keepers' post then turned off into a lane hugged by smaller dwellings.

"No, I didn't mean it like that. It's just..."

"Just?"

"Oh, for fuck's sake. Your family *is* worse than mine."

"I don't know." The corner of his mouth turned up. "Your papa really was something in Rancie. And Izac... well, he had a crossbow aimed at my head yesterday."

I laughed properly this time, and he joined in.

But the bounds were still bothering me. "Anthras said your brother wants to split the realms apart."

Lucas nodded, serious once again. "If that is the case, he may have something to do with the bounds cracks. I'll have to go back home very soon to find out what's going on." He hauled in a long breath. "Soon... but not yet." The reticence in his voice was clear, but then his lips quirked. "You know, you were pretty hot back there in the cavern."

A curious double entendre, plus he'd changed the subject. "Hot being the perfect word. You were literally roasting."

He stopped under a climbing hydrangea, and I turned to face him, scuffing a cobble under my foot.

"You saved us," he said softly, his expression earnest.

I frowned. "Everyone did their bit, especially Madame Bovary. But, hey, look how much training I had in the end."

He raised his chin. "And it only took a mad dwarf wanting to blow us all sky high."

I rammed my shoulder into his arm, and we carried on walking.

"The ore serpents send their gratitude," he said. "They're already in better shape and returning to the depths."

"That's good to hear." And it really was. They'd been in agony.

The lane ended right under Cousterous. Broad steps were hewn into the almost vertical face of the mountain. They must have been glamoured, or I would've definitely noticed them before.

"After you," Lucas said.

I wasn't averse to traditional manners. I took the lead, taking step after step.

"I bet Morion Auberon was happy to get his gold back." My legs were feeling the climb. I'd already had one workout today.

"Ecstatic, so I heard. And even more ecstatic that he'll be getting a cut for precipitating and redistributing it."

As we ascended, the luminous flush of evening deepened, and streaks of orange spanned the sky. The lights of Tarascon shone below, and a fiery glow flickered on each of the surrounding peaks.

I turned back to Lucas. "Midsummer fires?" I'd not seen them before, so presumably they were also glamoured.

"Fae have been upholding the tradition since the dawn of time."

We continued on. After three hundred feet of steps, my chest was heaving, and the curve of the summit was a relief. The air shimmered as we stepped into Fae. A menhir stood on the level ground at the top. We acknowledged it, then strode past. The rugged terrain of Cousterous transformed into a gently sloping grassland, constellations of buttercups just visible in the dusk.

"Summer?" I asked. Though it wasn't one of the areas we'd been through earlier. I caught the sound of music.

"Got it in one." Lucas held out his hand, his lips curved.

I stared at his long, elegant fingers. This was new, and I wasn't sure what to make of it. Hand-holding meant a degree of intimacy, and that wasn't us. The memory of his body pressed against mine returned, but that had been a blip, nothing more. And yet there was something about the night, something in the air. It pulsed around us... between us.

"I'm not going to bite, Camille," he said with a smirk. "No, actually, knowing me, I might. But you'll have to take the risk."

I snorted and took his hand. To hell with it. He pulled me up to the brow of the hill, and the vista opened before us, vigorous music filling the air.

A large field lay just below, surrounded by woodland. In the centre stood a huge bonfire, flickering with thankfully normal flames. Around it were goblins, elves, dryads, nymphs, trolls and plenty of creatures I couldn't place. Some played violins, drums, accordions or pipes, and the rest danced with abandon. All of them wore crowns of blossom. The scent of roses, chamomile and woodsmoke filled the air.

I stared, my jaw slack. I'd never seen this many fae in one place, and everything was so utterly alive. It just... thrummed.

Lucas grinned and pulled me to the edge of the gathering. We passed caskets streaming with wine and delicious-smelling caldrons bubbling over smaller fires.

A familiar figure emerged from the other side of the bonfire. Bécut, standing at least twice as high as anyone else, roared with laughter. He caught sight of us and strode over through the revellers, Wheezle and Gidditch at his side.

"Lucas, Camille!" he bellowed.

"Good to see you, Bécut," I called above the music, trying not to stare at his eye whilst also attempting eye contact.

Tricky. But he was looking well. The bucket of healing potion he'd taken had sorted his numerous wounds.

"Got five of my sheep back. I was too late for the rest." His grin fell.

Wheezle climbed up onto Bécut's shoulder and patted his back, her long snout wrinkling. "Going to start breeding some more, though, aren't you."

"You know, Camille," Gidditch put in, his ears quivering, "we had a hell of a job getting Bécut out again. Hadn't been away from his mountain for two hundred years. Got sketched by an antiquarian back in the eighteen hundreds and put in an almanac that went through all the villages."

Bécut nodded. "Yep."

Gidditch folded his arms. "The caption under his picture said, 'The hideous colossus waiting in the mountains.' No wonder he was offended."

"Honestly," Wheezle said. "The least humans can do is ask our permission before using our likenesses." She lowered her voice to a whisper. "Bécut didn't want to look for his sheep because of that, what with the whole one-eye thing."

A holler rose from across the field. Eggnog held up tankards.

"Ale calls," Bécut said with a grin. "We'll be seeing you."

As they headed away, fae whirled around us, easing us into the festivities. Laughter bubbled up from my middle. Laughter for the wildness of Fae and for the hell of a day having ended. With it, the last shreds of tension eased from my limbs. And still I couldn't believe the raw life pulsating around us.

A goblin twirled past placing crowns of honeysuckle upon our heads. He blanched as he recognised Lucas, then continued on. The music took hold of me, the melody ancient and familiar, wild and fresh. I was unable to stop myself swaying then twirling. Lucas broke into laughter and joined me.

I don't know how long we danced, partnering each other, then losing ourselves in the throng, only to join back together again. Eventually the melody took a more relaxed tempo and we slowed to a sway. I was grinning so broadly my face ached. But there was a reason I'd wanted to see Lucas tonight.

"I have something to tell you," I said as we swayed some more.

He took my hand and twirled me under his arm. "Oh?"

I drew a deep breath and released it slowly. The past few days had been a whirlwind. Not just outside of me, but inside, too. Now the turmoil had stilled and my path lay clear, I just needed to let Lucas know. "It's been a hellishly, freakishly crazy experience getting to know you, fae and the whole hidden world."

His eyes gleamed. "I knew you were intrigued."

"Absolutely fascinated. But more than that, all of it just feels right, and..." I met his recondite gaze. "I've decided to accept your invitation to become a Keeper of the Bounds. Your partner."

I still had some doubts, but now everything was in perspective, I wanted the challenge. Using my blade had freed something in me, and I wanted more. Plus, being a

Keeper was the perfect way to get to know Fae. One thing was for sure, I now knew I had enough in me to give it my very best shot.

Lucas paused and scoured my face, his body much too still amidst the sway. His jaw shifted a little, then he pulled me to him and wrapped his arms around me. I stiffened against him. This was a little too close. But against my will, my body melded to his.

He laughed softly into my hair. "Words I've been longing to hear. Camille, I'm so glad."

His arms, secure around me, bore the same strength he'd supported me with through the hantaumo attack and Anthras's schemes. Lucas wasn't perfect... He wasn't perfect at all. He was an arrogant, mischievous trickster that I barely understood. Not to mention, I'd never forgive him for the verity—and we still had to unpick all of that. Grampi's concerns were an important consideration, too. But ultimately, I had to go with my gut. When it came to what mattered, Lucas had pulled through every time. I was sure of one thing. He had my back.

Together, we swayed gently to the music, the melody speaking of wild plains, rushing rivers and deep forest. Of adventure and things beyond my wildest dreams. I laid my head against Lucas's chest, and something stirred within me... a feeling I'd never felt before. It wasn't because of Lucas, exactly, but because of my decision, because of Fae, because of the unbridled festivities around me. For the first time in my life, I felt like myself.

Find out how Lucas stole Fickleturn's breeches
and more...

Get Folkloric Fae,
the Folkloric prequel novella, free at:
www.karenzagrant.com

Perfect for reading at any point during the series.

Leaving a review…

Wheezle, Gidditch and Eggnog would be very grateful if you could leave a star rating or review on Amazon. This will help their plight for the accurate representation of fae in the media to reach a wider audience.

Signed…

Gidditch
Wheezle,
EGGNOG

Thank you very much!

FOLKLORIC RUSE

BOOK THREE OF THE FOLKLORIC SERIES

KARENZA GRANT

CHAPTER 1

WHAT I WANTED MOST OF ALL WAS TO LOSE MYSELF FOR the night, then all my problems would disappear.

Yes, it was a temporary solution. Actually, it wasn't a solution at all, but it would mean I could forget the raw emotion surging deep within me, just for a little while.

My plan was working. Eliot, who stood only inches away in the crowded medieval-style bar, made the perfect distraction. The combination of intense gaze, swept-back dark waves and pensive, sensuous lips was so damned hot.

As we exchanged small talk, our electric eye contact was enough to ease away eighties night at Castle Rock and Vanessa Paradis blaring out. It was almost enough to make me forget Alice standing at the far end of the bar beyond the tables, chatting with Raphaël and some of our old school friends. Thinking of her submerged me under a fresh wave of despair. She couldn't understand why I was against her engagement to Raphaël, and we'd fallen out about it. Majorly.

"I have to admit, I'm intrigued, Camille," Eliot drawled, his voice low and melodious. "The folklore you've studied in the region is curious, and it ties in with my field of history. I'd love to hear more."

He was saying all the right things. But we both knew we weren't here for folklore. Every part of his fit body under his black V-neck T-shirt was attuned to mine. And dang, his scent. Honestly, it reminded me of old churches—myrrh, perhaps—though churches really shouldn't be a turn-on, and there was nothing holy about this guy. Whatever. I wanted more.

"I'd like to tell you about it," I said, my voice slow and suggestive. "Where to start?" I tipped back the last of my awful non-alcoholic wine, my shoulders stiff from the constant bouts of Keeper training over the last couple of weeks since midsummer.

Eliot's lips blossomed into a smile. Oh my god, that smile. Playful, a little mischievous, utterly delicious. "Hold that thought." He took my glass. "What will it be?"

"Uh, mineral water would be great."

With a scorching backward glance, Eliot eased through the crowd to the bar.

Boy, did I need something stronger than water to alle-viate the turmoil, but I'd already drunk one glass of wine, and I had hand-to-hand combat with Grampi in the morning. He was lethal, despite his age, and I was taking training seri-ously. It was the least I could do to ease his worries about me being a Keeper. Plus, the instruction was top notch. I was also sparring with Lucas every evening after work. The sessions were gruelling, but I was improving quickly.

All that aside, ever since the drunken night when I'd slept with Lucas, I was being a good girl. Well, not too good— my sights were set on Eliot—but I wasn't going to make any more drunken mistakes. Sober mistakes, on the other hand, were perfectly acceptable.

I leant against a pillar as I waited, the track changing to something I didn't recognise. Unbidden, my gaze drifted to the other side of the bar. Alice. All my frustration and anguish rushed back. Not knowing what to do with myself, I folded my arms across my chiffon top as I looked around for someone nearby that I knew. No one, damn it. I'd join Eliot at the bar if it didn't look so packed.

My gaze returned to Alice. Her arms were wrapped around Raphaël's neck, a suit of armour on the wall to one side of them, a shield to the other. I missed her so much. She was my confidante, my stalwart supporter. We just sort of fitted together, and life was so much better that way. She was more than a friend—she was everything to me. She leant toward Raphaël and drew him into a deep kiss.

Ugh. If only she could see his grey leathery skin, his pot belly, his wrinkles and those jagged goblin teeth. He was a complete and utter fraudster. I narrowed my eyes so I could see the glamour he was projecting. With brown curls, long eyelashes and strong shoulders, he was dishy. If only she knew. But Alice had no idea about the hidden world, and she'd think I was mad if I told her.

They were already talking about a date for their wedding. Alice, never one for tradition, was opting for tying the knot as soon as possible at the town hall. I picked up all the details, working with her at the café.

I'd tried to justify them being together so many times. Perhaps Raphaël really did love her. It definitely looked as though he did. Maybe he would make a good husband. But how could they have a relationship based on lies? I drew in a shaky breath, the air sticking in my throat.

Alice's gaze flicked to mine, and in an instant she turned away.

Fine cracks split my heart. Shit. I didn't need this right now. I scanned the room. Where was Eliot? I couldn't see him through the crowd, but I needed to get out of here. I shouldn't even be in the same room as Alice at the moment, but Guy had dragged me to Foix, our county town, pleading that he'd needed someone to go with him to eighties night. He'd purposefully not told me that Alice was going to be here. A sweet but naïve plan to get us back together, Castle Rock being our favourite bar. If only Guy knew half of what was really going on.

Eliot pushed back through the throng and passed my mineral water. Sweetly, he'd opted for the same. "Where were we?"

His gaze locked on mine, his eyes dark—possibly more impenetrable than Lucas's, which was saying something, but I really didn't need to think of him right now. "History, was it? Or folklore. And before that, you were saying that you've just moved into the area."

"Yeah, I can't get enough of the town. Foix is stunning. I've explored the chateau repeatedly. Troubadours, chivalry, honourable gentry who cared for their people. The place is amazing."

Caught by the intensity in his gaze, I shifted closer. Even if Eliot hadn't been so fine, he would've had all my attention with those sentiments. I'd worked in the Chateau de Foix on and off as a volunteer in my late teens and loved the place. What was this man doing to me? He was certainly distracting me from Alice. All the same, I wanted to leave. I couldn't take much more of her ignoring me.

He took a lock of my hair and wrapped it around his finger. I'd worn it loose for a change. It was so often tied up whilst training or working at the café. My lips parted as I watched him. "Maybe history could wait for another time," I murmured close to his cheek.

"I really would like to know more." His breath tickled my skin.

"We could talk a little... at your place." Like that was going to happen. I vaguely noticed "You Give Love a Bad Name" by Bon Jovi coming on.

Eliot's mouth quirked. "I'd like that very much."

That was it. I couldn't resist any longer. We moved closer, his warmth intoxicating. Tilting my head, I drew my lips to his. As my eyelids fell in expectation, I caught a commotion in the crowd—people jumping aside as a figure charged through.

Before I could make sense of what was going on, the figure slammed into Eliot, our drinks flying. The two of them hurtled through the throng and hit the bar. The figure pinned Eliot against the top and drove his fist into the side of his head again and again.

Panic streaked through me. I could only see the attacker's back, but the dishevelled hair and sturdy physique were unmistakable.

Lucas.

Afterword

It's been such a wild experience writing the Folkloric series—the series has given me so many laughs already, and I'm eager to venture into more antics.

I'm guessing some of you, if you're anything like me, like to embark on armchair voyages, googling locations, or perhaps you like to geek out on folklore. So here are a few notes on the setting and local mythology. After all, Camille would never forgive me if I didn't give you the lowdown.

Most of the series locations in the human realm exist. Tarascon (its full name is Tarascon-sur-Ariège) is a stunning town in the South of France, nestled in the Ariège valley in the foothills of the Pyrenees mountains. Despite its beauty, it's no tourist town. It's situated on one of the major routes through the mountains between France and Spain, and it's an industrial centre with quite a history.

I fell in love with the area at first sight. Forest-clad mountains shelter the valley, castles perch high on remote crags, and caves descend far into the depths of the earth. The poetry and artistry of the troubadours that blossomed here in the 12th century laid the foundation for the novel as we know it, and way back in prehistoric times, the first modern humans (the Aurignacians) emerged here—the region is known as the cradle of civilisation. It's also a place associated with Arab invasion and Charlemagne, not to mention rebellion, heretic religions and the grail. As you can see, there is plenty of fuel for urban fantasy.

Above all, though, it bears a wildness and a mysterious otherness. It's not difficult to imagine other realms nearby—that an entrance might lie behind an old gnarled box tree or within a stalagmite-filled cavern. And it doesn't take much to envisage a fae town under the slopes of Coustarous.

As to the folklore, I try to draw as much as possible from the actual mythology of the region, and many of the creatures in the Folkloric series are noted in local lore. As in other places, it has its fair share of fae, goblins, trolls, dragons and giants. However, the specifics get very interesting. Think of dracs, the fae of Bédeilhac (known in Folkloric as the Men), Dame Blanche, the croquembouche, the hantaumo, Count Estruch, and many other examples—too many to mention here. Curiously, Count Estruch was a real count and the origin of the earliest European vampire myth. If you want to google what he got up to, be warned, it isn't pleasant.

The Pyrenees mountain range also has its own pantheon of gods, ruled over by Abellion, a sun god akin to Apollo. Baeserte and Aherbelste are other examples. What very little is known about them has been obtained from roman excavations. Roman gods gradually replaced the old pantheon, and more recently, Christian saints supplanted the Roman deities. In spite of that, the traits of the old gods live on in more recent personifications, so there is something to be gleaned.

Having said all this, there's not a whole load of lore to go on for the purpose of creating characters. A couple of paragraphs on how dracs shift into gold cups, luring people to their watery graves, isn't much to shape into a wily doctor with rather mischievous tendencies. I have two words for you: artistic licence. Yet when I can stick to the lore, I do so.

If you want to find out more, there's not much published in English, although Martin Locker's *The Tears of Pyrene* is superb. If you read French, try one of Olivier de Marliave's excellent tomes on the subject, for example, *Trésor de la Mythology Pyrénéenne*.

Before I finish, there are a few people I'd like to mention who have been instrumental in getting this series off the ground. Octavia Denning, my gratitude to you is unending. Dorine Maine, thank you for everything from the bottom of my heart. A special shout-out goes to my writing group: Viktoria Dahill, Katie Mouallek, Rachel Cooper and Abhivyakti Singh, for always being honest and saying what needs to be said. You keep me on my toes and striving to do my best. Jack Barrow and P.M. Gilbert, it's been great working with you. Many thanks to Toby Selwyn, my super editor, and to Deranged Doctor Designs for the top-notch covers despite my terrible cover specs. I'm indebted to my superb ARC and Street Team. You guys rock. Massive thanks goes to L.A. McBride for answering question after question with angelic patience. Rillian Grant and Minerva Grant, you make it all worthwhile. And last of all, thanks to you, the intrepid reader, for daring to delve into this utterly crazy world.

About the Author

Karenza Grant writes fun and feisty urban fantasy with plenty of humour and a little sweet romance.

Her early years in Cornwall were largely the source of her fascination with all things mysterious. She lived below a hill reputed to be the Cornish residence of the Unseelie Court, and the local myths got their claws in. Now she's inspired by a broad range of creators from Jim Henson, Arthur Rackham, and Olivier de Marliave, to a whole host of amazing authors on the urban fantasy scene. Currently, she's enjoying weaving her love of France into page-turning stories.

She has three black cats known as The Three Guardians, and a crazy lab x spaniel who is just about the only thing that can extract Karenza from her writing desk—if the pooch isn't walked, the legions of hell will be released.

CONNECT

There's nothing better than hearing from readers. Drop me a line or join me on social media. I hang around on Facebook on a daily basis and would love to see you there.

You can find all the links on my website:
www.karenzagrant.com

Printed in Great Britain
by Amazon